A marriage...

It was a wild scheme, but it just might work, Aaron decided.

But who? He needed a woman who was good with infants. Someone strongly maternal—but able to step out of little Tommy's life after just a few months.

Aaron considered dozens of women he knew, but as minutes ticked by into hours, his mind kept coming up blank, bringing him no closer to a solution.

He took a deep breath. Damn. He was right back at square one...and the only woman he wanted for the position.

The woman he'd been resolutely pushing out of his mind and heart.

The only woman he knew who was so unselfish, so sweet, so innocent that she actually seemed to have an angel watching over her!

Mariah...

Dear Reader,

The holiday season is upon us—and we're in the midst of celebrating the arrival of our 1000th Special Edition! It is truly a season of cheer for all of us at Silhouette Special Edition.

We hope that you enjoy *The Pride of Jared MacKade* by *New York Times* bestselling author Nora Roberts. This is the second title of her bestselling THE MACKADE BROTHERS series, and the book is warm, wonderful—and not only Book 1000, but Nora's eightieth Silhouette novel! Thank you, Nora!

The celebration continues with the uplifting story of *Morgan's Rescue,* by Lindsay McKenna. This action-packed tale is the third installment of Lindsay's newest series, MORGAN'S MERCENARIES: LOVE AND DANGER. I know you won't want to miss a minute!

This month's HOLIDAY ELOPEMENTS title is a poignant, stirring story of the enduring power of love from Phyllis Halldorson—*The Bride and the Baby*.

Holidays are for children, and this month features many little ones with shining eyes and delighted laughter. In fact, we have a fun little element running through some of the books of unexpecting "dads" delivering babies! We hope you enjoy this unexpected bonus! Don't miss *Baby's First Christmas,* by Marie Ferrarella—the launch title of her marvelous cross-line series, THE BABY OF THE MONTH CLUB. Or Sherryl Woods's newest offering—*A Christmas Blessing*— the start of her Special Edition series, AND BABY MAKES THREE. Last, but not least, is the winsome *Mr. Angel* by Beth Henderson—a book full of warmth and cheer to warm wintry nights with love.

We hope that you enjoy this month of celebration. It's all due to you, our loyal readers. Happy holidays, and many thanks for your continued support from all of us at Silhouette Books!

Sincerely,

Tara Gavin
Senior Editor

Please address questions and book requests to:
Silhouette Reader Service
U.S.: 3010 Walden Ave., P.O. Box 1325, Buffalo, NY 14269
Canadian: P.O. Box 609, Fort Erie, Ont. L2A 5X3

PHYLLIS HALLDORSON
THE BRIDE AND THE BABY

Published by Silhouette Books
America's Publisher of Contemporary Romance

In loving memory of Jean Z. Owen Giovannoni, who was
always so generous in sharing her vast writing expertise
with me. It's been invaluable, but even more important was
her warm friendship. A gift beyond price.

 SILHOUETTE BOOKS

ISBN 0-373-23999-8

THE BRIDE AND THE BABY

Copyright © 1995 by Phyllis Halldorson

Books by Phyllis Halldorson

PHYLLIS HALLDORSON

at age sixteen met her real-life Prince Charming. She married him a year later, and they settled down to raise a family. A compulsive reader, Phyllis dreamed of someday finding the time to write stories of her own. That time came when her two youngest children reached adolescence. When she was introduced to romance novels, she knew she had found her long-delayed vocation. After all, how could she write anything else after living all those years with her very own Silhouette hero?

Dear Reader,

In 1979 I was a professional writer of short stories and doing very well at it. But my ambition was to be a novelist, and have more space in which to tell my stories and develop my characters. One day I read in a writers' magazine that a new line of romance novels was to be introduced. It would be called Silhouette Romance, and the publisher was soliciting manuscripts. I sent in a proposal and it was *accepted for publication!* That day ranks just below my wedding day and the birthdays of our children and grandchildren as one of the most memorable days of my life.

Now, sixteen years later, Silhouette has expanded to six lines, and I have written twenty-nine novels and one novelette for them. It's been every bit as joyful and fulfilling a career as I dreamed it would be so many years ago.

Last year Silhouette Romance published its one thousandth title, and this year the Special Edition series is celebrating its one thousandth edition. That's a lot of books!

I'm proud to have been a part of the endeavor from the beginning, but it is you, the reader, who has made that possible. It is your continuing approval and support that has made writing romance novels so much a part of my life. Thank you for your loyalty!

Sincerely,

Phyllis Halldorson

Chapter One

Mariah Bentley leaned forward to peer through the car windshield in hopes of getting a better view of the narrow winding mountain road. The darkness was so totally encompassing that all she could see was the illumination of her own headlights in front of her. The moon and stars were eclipsed by tall trees and thick clouds that, according to the weather forecaster on the radio, contained the first snowstorm of the season.

Lord knows it's cold enough to snow, Mariah thought as she slowly continued the uphill climb to her hometown in the Adirondack mountains. The temperature in New York had been falling all afternoon, and now, at seven-fifteen, it was thirty-five degrees, again according to the radio, and still plunging.

She shivered and cursed herself for not having the car heater inspected when she first realized it wasn't giving out enough heat. That had been in September, right after she learned she was a casualty in the latest round of staff cuts at the state office in Albany.

Mariah still found it hard to believe she'd been terminated, but the recession had hit hard, and employees with more seniority than she had been let go. Not only had she lost her job, but the employment agencies were overflowing with college graduates, vying for any position available. Why should an employer hire someone like her with a business school certificate when they could get a B.A. or even an M.B.A.?

Now it was November. She'd been forced to accept the fact that she could no longer compete in the tight job market of the city. So after giving up the apartment she shared with a roommate, she was now heading back to the small mountain community of Apple Junction. Her parents had offered her the cottage at the back of their acreage to live in while she looked for work in some of the small towns in the area.

Mariah's mind was focused too much on her troubles and not enough on the short visibility of the road when she almost missed a sharp turn. Quickly she jerked the steering wheel to the left.

Then she saw it!

There, in the middle of the lane, was a figure. A woman dressed in shimmering white and bathed in the lights of the car. She stood facing Mariah, her right hand raised above her head and forward in the classic Stop signal. Her left arm pointed to the side of the road where Mariah knew there was a steep drop.

Mariah slammed her foot on the brake, but it was too late. The car whirled out of control into the space where the woman stood and, with a screech of tires, made a rocking U-turn into the other lane.

It was all happening too quickly. Mariah could do nothing but hang on to the steering wheel and hope the car wouldn't roll. Miraculously it didn't, but came to a jolting stop pointing in the wrong direction.

Heart pounding, Mariah's blood ran cold. She hadn't felt a bump or seen a body flying through the air, but she couldn't have missed the woman. She hadn't been going fast, but she hadn't seen the figure until she was almost on it. By then it was too late to dodge it.

Mariah's whole body was shaking, and it took all her willpower to pry her fingers loose from the wheel. Oh, dear God, what had she done! Where had the woman come from? Why was she standing in the middle of the road gesturing? Mariah felt too weak to move, but she knew she had to get out of the car and go to the aid of her victim.

Opening the door, she swung her feet to the pavement and stood, then quickly sat down again when her head spun and her knees gave way. She was weak and trembling from shock, but she had to go to the woman.

Carefully Mariah stood up again, then clung to the open car door until she got her balance. As soon as her head stopped spinning she stumbled back up the dark road to the spot where the woman had been, but there was nothing in the road. It was too dark to see more than a foot or two ahead.

Dear God, had the body been thrown over the side? Terror clutched at her chest and throat, making it difficult to breathe. She had to get help. She couldn't just drive off and leave an injured, maybe dying, person lying somewhere in the darkness!

Running back to her car, she grabbed her cellular phone. Her parents had given it to her last Christmas and insisted she carry it in the car at all times in case of emergency.

* * *

In Apple Junction, Sheriff Clifford Bentley and his wife Jessica were sitting in their living room watching the news on cable television while waiting for their daughter Mariah to arrive. The aroma of meat loaf and scalloped potatoes wafted in from the kitchen, and Cliff's stomach rumbled. All he'd had to eat for lunch was a hamburger on the run and now it was seven-thirty. Mariah was late, and he was hungry.

But he also was eager to see his daughter. Not that he and Jess didn't have enough kids to keep from getting lonely. Six in all, two boys and four girls, and three of them, Rob, Sissy and Betty Jean, still lived at home.

Right now, though, Mariah was the one who worried him. She'd been out of work for a week. She'd known for two months that she was being terminated, but still she hadn't been able to find another job. The lousy economy was taking a toll on everybody. It had a domino effect. When people were unemployed they didn't have money to spend, which put other people out of work who didn't have money to spend, which put more people out of work....

The peal of the telephone startled him, and he jumped up to answer it. As sheriff in the county, most of the calls that came in on his off-hours were for him. Someone's cat probably got stuck in a tree, or maybe the Maynard girl ran off again. That kid bounced around law-enforcement services like a rubber ball.

He picked up the phone. "Sheriff Bentley."

"Daddy!"

"Mariah." Surprise echoed in his voice. "I expected you to be ringing the doorbell, not the telephone. Did that old car of yours break down again—"

"Daddy, please, I need help!"

For the first time Cliff recognized the hysteria in his daughter's tone, and his years of police training took over. "What's wrong and where are you?" he snapped.

"I'm at Suicide Bend," she said, using the name the locals had given the sharp curve on the highway about five miles out of town. "I... I think I just hit a woman, but I can't find her. Oh, Daddy, I didn't see her until it was too late!"

Cliff froze with shock and horror, but his years of discipline in such situations took over and kept him functioning.

"Are you hurt?"

"N-no, I don't th-think so," she stammered, her voice quivering with shock. "It only just happened. I stamped my foot on the brakes and the ca-car spun around—"

"Mariah, is the woman lying in the road?"

"No, at least not where I hit her," Mariah cried in a keening tone. "I got out to look for her, but it's pitch-black out here. My car is sitting with the headlights pointing in the other direction and I'm afraid of running over her if I move the car."

"No, don't move it. Is there any traffic on the road?"

"No, none."

"All right. Now, listen to me carefully. Stay right where you are, but turn on your blinkers and leave your headlights on. Don't get out of the car, and if another car approaches honk your horn in short, loud beeps and pray that it stops. I'll be there in five minutes."

He broke the connection, then dialed the sheriff's station. "This is Sheriff Bentley. I need an ambulance and a police car out to Suicide Bend. On the double!"

Mariah dropped the phone into its cradle and turned on her blinkers. She was still fighting to control the panic that threatened to overwhelm her. Suddenly she remembered the flashlight she kept in the glove compartment.

She retrieved it and flicked it on. Thankful the battery still worked, she was dismayed at how small an area it illuminated in the vast darkness.

Her father had said to stay in the car, but she couldn't just leave that woman lying somewhere bleeding, maybe conscious and suffering. Mariah had to find her!

Again she got out of the car and headed back up the road to where she'd seen the figure.

As she walked, she flashed the light back and forth across both lanes of the highway, but there was nothing there. *Maybe it had happened a little farther on.* It was hard to tell exactly where she was in the darkness. She walked several more paces, waving her light, but still, nothing.

Could the woman have been tossed across the opposite lane and into the trees on the other side? Mariah's bare hands were cold but she was sweating under her quilted jacket and blue jeans. She knew she was overwrought rather than overheated. The breeze against her face was icy, and her terror escalated. If the woman hadn't been killed in the collision she'd certainly die of the cold if she wasn't found quickly!

Mariah was frantically waving the light beam through the trees along the roadway when she heard a siren. *Thank God, it's Daddy! He'll know what to do!* Within seconds the sheriff's official car screeched to a halt, and her father's voice called her name. Running forward in the blinding headlights, she threw herself into his strong, comforting arms.

"Daddy! Oh, Daddy, I can't find her!" she sobbed as he held her in a protective embrace.

"I told you to stay in the car," he scolded even as his arms tightened around her and another siren and headlights split the darkness.

The second car screeched to a halt and two uniformed deputies got out and hurried over to them. Mariah was so relieved to have someone taking charge of the situation that she slumped against her father and blotted out the voices around her.

Minutes later a third siren wailed its way to the scene. This time it was an ambulance, and, over her protests, the sheriff picked her up and carried her to the vehicle. Climbing inside, he laid her down on the stretcher.

"No, Dad, I'm all right," Mariah insisted. "Just badly shaken up. I don't need to go to the hospital."

"Maybe not," he said, "but the paramedic is going to examine you while the rest of us look for this woman you saw. The highway patrol is sending some officers and equipment, too. Is everything the same as when you called me? Did you move the car or anything?"

She shook her head. "No. The only thing I moved was the flashlight I carry in my glove compartment. I had to try to find her...."

He patted her shoulder. "I know, honey, but we've got experts working on it now. You just lie here and try to remember exactly what happened. We'll have to question you later when you feel up to it."

She managed a feeble smile. "Sure. I'll try to sort it out in my mind, but it was the strangest thing...."

The sheriff climbed out of the ambulance, and let the paramedic examine her. He found no injuries, but advised her to see her own physician later.

Meanwhile another car with a siren had arrived, and more voices joined to the ones outside. Why was it taking so long to find the poor woman? How far could she have been thrown? Shouldn't the impact have thrown the woman up onto the hood of the car rather than sending her flying through the air?

Mariah sat in the ambulance and talked with the paramedic and the driver for nearly an hour before the sheriff came back. "How are you feeling?" he asked her when he opened the door and looked in.

A blast of cold air swept through the interior. Before that, when the doors had been closed and the heater on, it had been quite comfortable. "I'm fine," she told him, "but why is this taking so long? I couldn't have missed that woman, but even if I had, she was out here all alone. There was no one else, and no other cars around, so where is she?"

This whole thing was beginning to get spooky as well as frightening, and Mariah shivered.

"I don't know," Cliff admitted. "We've searched in three directions for as far as she could possibly have been thrown, and there's no body."

"Maybe because it's so dark . . ." Mariah ventured.

"That complicates things, of course, but we have big, battery-powered spotlights and can see in all directions. The only place left to look is down the steep incline on the right side of the road. We've shined the lights down there, but we can't really search thoroughly unless we take them and go down. That's what we're going to do now."

The very thought was horrifying. If she'd been thrown over the edge on that side it was a long drop down. "How . . . how are you going to get down there?" Mariah asked.

"There's a turnoff road about a mile back down the hill that will put us in the area. We're through looking around here, and I've moved your car to the side of the road. If you feel up to it, why don't you take it and go on home. Your mother's upset and still waiting to hear if you're all right and what happened.''

Mariah shook her head. ''I can't do that, Dad. I've got to stay until I find out what happened to that woman. I'll call Mom, though, and tell her what's going on.''

Her dad looked as if he were going to argue, but apparently decided it would be a waste of time and nodded instead. ''Okay, but I want you to stay here in the ambulance where it's reasonably warm. I'll bring you the phone.''

Mariah called her mother and told her what had happened. It was an emotional conversation, and they were both in tears by the time it was over.

It was another hour before the sheriff radioed the paramedic.

''There's still no sign of the woman in white,'' Cliff said, ''but we did find a wrecked car. It apparently missed the curve up there and went over the side. The driver, a young woman, is dead, but there's a small child, probably less than a year old, who's still alive, although just barely. Turn up the heater in the ambulance as far as possible and warm some blankets. I don't know how long the kid's been exposed to this weather, but it's suffering from hypothermia as well as possible injuries.''

Mariah's sense of urgency and confusion intensified. A car wreck? Could that be where the woman in the road had come from? But she hadn't looked like she'd been in an accident, although Mariah's glimpse of her had been so fleeting that it had been more an impression than an actual image.

''Drive the ambulance down the highway to the first turnoff,'' Cliff continued, ''and hang a left. Follow the road to the bottom of the hill. We'll meet you there. Be careful, the trail is steep and full of potholes.''

The sheriff was waiting when they arrived at the floor of the valley. "Bring the stretcher," he commanded, his voice tight with urgency. "It's a hell of a hike to the wreckage through this thick underbrush and heavy stand of trees."

The driver and paramedic scrambled to unload the stretcher and medical supplies.

Cliff turned to Mariah. "You stay here in the ambulance." It wasn't a suggestion, it was a nonnegotiable order.

The next thirty-five minutes seemed to drag by as Mariah huddled in the front seat surrounded by the silent, total darkness that was even blacker down in the narrow valley than it had been on the road. Not only was her visibility zero, but there was nothing to distract her from her own scary thoughts. What had happened here tonight? Did she really see a woman in the road? It had all happened in seconds—the sharp curve, the figure in the headlights, and the car careening out of control in the darkness.

And now a totally unrelated car accident. When had that happened? Was it minutes, hours, or days before? And who were the passengers? A dead woman and a nearly dead child. Was it someone she or her family knew? A friend from Apple Junction?

By the time Mariah saw the lights and heard the sounds of the returning rescuers, she had worked herself up into a bundle of screaming nerves. But all was forgotten when the stretcher containing the tiny, silent, blanket-wrapped bundle was loaded into the ambulance.

"I'm going to ride along with them," she said to her dad as she climbed into the back with the baby and the paramedic.

"Okay. I'll have one of the deputies drive your car to the house." He closed the door then stepped back. The driver started the motor and maneuvered the ambulance up the hill.

"Is it badly hurt?" Mariah asked, as the ambulance jostled over the road.

"I don't know yet," the paramedic answered tersely.

"Is it a boy or a girl?" Mariah bent over the stretcher, but could see only a child totally wrapped except for its nose and mouth area.

"I don't even know that," the paramedic said. "I examined it just enough to determine that there were no obviously broken bones before we unstrapped it from the car seat and transferred it to the stretcher. It's the hypothermia I'm most concerned about. The child needs treatment in a hospital, *stat!*" He hunkered down on the other side of the stretcher and immediately began monitoring the child.

When they got back to the highway the driver turned on the siren and sped up the road to the small hospital that served the Apple Junction area.

At the hospital they were met by an emergency crew who took charge of the child, trailed by the paramedic. One of the nurses showed Mariah to a small waiting room.

"Are you a relative?" she asked.

"No," Mariah said, then explained who she was. "My dad will be along soon, but I'd like to stay here if I may. At least until the child's relatives are found. It just seems so awful for the poor little kid not to have anyone here to care about it."

The nurse smiled and nodded. "Yes, I know what you mean. We'll work with the sheriff in attempting to find out if there are relatives in the area, but by all means stay. I'll let you know as soon as I hear anything."

Mariah thanked her, then spotted a phone on a small table. She used it to call her mother and bring her up-to-date on what was happening.

"How awful," Jessica Bentley said. "I wonder if it's someone from here."

Apple Junction was a tiny community of about three thousand and they all knew one another, if not intimately at least by name. "I don't know, Mom, Dad didn't say. No one was thinking about anything but getting the baby to the hospital."

About forty-five minutes later Mariah heard her dad's distinctive voice in the hall. She went to the door and saw him standing at the nurses' station talking to the nurse on duty.

"...trying to contact someone, but so far nobody answers the phone at that number," he was saying. "Is the baby going to need surgery? We can get a court order—"

"We don't know yet," the nurse interrupted. "He doesn't have any external injuries, but there might be some internal ones. They're still trying to get the hypothermia under control. It seems to be the most life-threatening problem."

Mariah walked across and stood beside her father. "Anything new yet?"

He turned and looked at her. "We found a purse at the scene containing a driver's license that identified the woman in the car as Eileen Kerr, age twenty-one, unmarried, and an address in Salt Lake City, Utah. We're trying to contact that address now."

Aaron Kerr unlocked the door and let himself into his large old house on a hill overlooking Salt Lake City. Shrugging his six-foot frame out of a gray overcoat, he brushed flakes of snow off the shoulders before hanging it in the closet.

He'd been later than usual getting away from the accounting firm where he was a partner, so he'd arranged to meet Karen at the restaurant instead of picking her up at her home. After they'd finished eating, they'd hurried to catch a movie. Now it was after midnight and he hadn't been home since seven o'clock that morning.

It was snowing outside, and cold. He turned up the thermostat and went into the kitchen to fix himself a scotch on the rocks. It had been a hectic day, and he needed to relax before going to bed.

Picking up the glass, he climbed the stairs to the bedroom, removed his suit coat and tie and unbuttoned his shirt. *Ahhh, that felt better.*

He enjoyed the solitude of his bachelor life-style. He and Eileen were the only ones left of their family. Now that she wasn't likely to be living here with him anymore he thought about selling the big old barn of a house where he'd been born and raised. He knew Eileen wouldn't object. God knows, his sister could use her share of the money. With his share, he wanted to buy a bright new condo. It would be strictly his. He'd decorate and furnish it the way *he* wanted and not have to consider anyone else's taste.

Most of the men he knew were either married or living with someone, but the idea of a wife and children held no appeal for Aaron. Not that he didn't have all the normal male urges. He did, and he indulged them when he found a willing partner, but only with those women who were independent and more interested in getting ahead in their careers than in marriage.

The ring of the telephone on the bedside table startled him, and he reached for it, noticing that the red button on his answering machine was blinking. *Damn,* he was forever forgetting to check the machine when he came home. Who could be calling at this hour of the night?

He said hello, and the man at the other end said, "Is this Eileen Kerr's residence?"

Aaron didn't recognize the voice. "No, Eileen no longer lives here. Who's this?"

"This is Sheriff Clifford Bentley calling from Apple Junction, New York. Are you a relative of Eileen Kerr?"

"Yes, she's my sister. I'm Aaron Kerr." Why would a sheriff be calling him about Eileen?

There was a pause. "Oh. I have some bad news for you," said the man, his tone laced with compassion. "I'm sorry to inform you that your sister, Eileen, is dead."

"Dead!" The word was like a blow to the solar plexus, and Aaron sat down on the side of the bed. "But that can't be. I just talked to her a few days ago. Besides, she's only twenty-one, and in excellent health."

There had to be some mistake. Beautiful young women like Eileen might get into trouble, but they didn't die so young!

"She was killed in an automobile accident, Mr. Kerr. Her car went off the road and down a steep ravine. We don't yet know when it happened. We've only just found the wreckage."

The sheriff had to be mistaken!

"Are you sure it's Eileen? Maybe someone else was driving her car."

"Is your sister about five-three, one-hundred-twenty-five pounds, with red shoulder-length hair and green eyes?"

Aaron felt sick. That was Eileen, all right. She was known for her red hair and green eyes.

"Yes," he murmured. "Oh, God..."

"We have her purse with her driver's license, and the picture and description on that matches the body in the car. I'm really sorry, but we need someone close to her to identify the body and take charge of the child—"

"Child!" If Aaron hadn't been sitting, his legs would have given way. "Dear Lord, was Tommy with her? Is he— Is he—"

"No, he's not dead," the sheriff hurried to say. "But he's suffering from a severe case of hypothermia. Do you know how we can contact the baby's father? We need someone to take charge of him and give permission for the medical care he needs."

"He doesn't have a father," Aaron snarled, his tone a mixture of bitterness and rage. "I'm Tommy's closest relative now. I'll be there as soon as I can get a flight out. Where in hell is Apple Junction, New York, and what was she doing there? She's supposed to be in Manhattan."

"Apple Junction is in the Adirondack Mountains region of upper New York," the sheriff said. "The nearest airport is in Burlington, Vermont, just across Lake Champlain. You can rent a car there and drive to Apple Junction. You'd better get a pencil and paper and take down the directions."

Aaron did as suggested and made careful note of the instructions he was given. "When you get here, come right to the hospital and identify yourself at the admission desk. I'll give them your name and tell them to expect you." Aaron could hear him talking to someone beside him, then he spoke into the phone again. "The doctor wants to know how old your nephew is and if he's allergic to any medication or foods."

"He was born on Christmas Day last year, but I haven't the foggiest idea whether or not he has any allergies," Aaron admitted. "I haven't seen Eileen or Tommy since she took him and moved to New York when he was two months old."

"I understand," the sheriff said, and he sounded as if he really meant it, "but if you think of anyone later who might be able to give us that information please contact the party and ask them to phone the hospital.''

He gave Aaron the phone number, again offered his condolences and hung up.

Putting down the phone, Aaron dropped his head in his hands. Eileen. Willful, independent Eileen, whose worst fault was her cursed stubborn streak. She'd refused to tell him who the bastard was who got her pregnant, then disappeared. She'd dropped out of college and got a job at minimum wage until Tommy was born. Two months later, over Aaron's strenuous protests, Eileen took the baby and went to New York City at the urging of one of her flaky friends, an aspiring actress who had managed to get a job working backstage at a theater. She insisted it was the first step to being a star, and she had persuaded Eileen to come and try her luck, too.

Since their parents had died when Eileen was fifteen and he was twenty-five, the only family they'd had was each other. Now Eileen was dead. How had he failed her? What should he have done differently?

And his small nephew, Tommy. What would become of him? The poor little guy had nobody but his uncle, who'd already botched the raising of one child!

Chapter Two

Mariah shifted the precious burden in her arms, then rearranged her own position in the padded wooden rocking chair so as to be more comfortable. Eighteen pounds of sleeping baby could get pretty heavy after a while, but the nurse had put fluffy pillows on the seat, back, and both arms of the chair so Mariah could sit more easily.

A glance at her watch told her it was fourteen hours since Tommy had been admitted to the hospital. Now his temperature was within normal range, as were his other vital signs, and he was sleeping and breathing naturally.

It had been touch and go for a long time last night. She and her dad had paced around the waiting room while the medical staff worked to save the baby's life. Finally the doctor had come to tell them the child had no serious injuries, thanks to the fact that he'd been securely strapped into his car seat, and that he was responding to treatment for the hypothermia. The sheriff had left then to go back to the scene of the accident, where they were still searching for the woman in white and clearing up the wreckage. Mariah had convinced the physician to let her sit by Tommy's crib in the pediatric intensive-care unit for a while.

She'd felt strongly that Tommy have someone to touch him, talk to him, and somehow let him know, even though at the time he wasn't fully conscious, that he hadn't been abandoned. Apparently the doctor hadn't thought she was overreacting. Since there were no other patients in the pediatric ICU, he'd agreed to it without argument.

When Mariah had first entered the room, the child had had an IV in his arm and was whimpering and squirming restlessly. She'd pulled up a chair by the side of the crib and sat down, then took his tiny hand in hers. It had still felt cold.

He was a beautiful little boy with tufts of bright red hair. His features were still a little blurred with babyhood, but his cheeks were chubby, his eyes brown and well-spaced, and his mouth was neither too large nor too small.

With her other hand Mariah stroked his head through the soft wisps of red hair, and murmured simple words of reassurance and endearment. By the time the nurse came in to insist that Mariah go home and get some sleep, the baby had quieted down. "You've had a traumatic night, and you need rest," the nurse said. "You can't be any help to this little one if you're sick, too. Go home now and I'll leave orders for the next shift to call you when he wakens."

At around 2:00 a.m. Mariah had gone to her parents' house and encountered her father, who had arrived only minutes before. "We called off the search for the woman in the road," he told her in answer to her anxious questions. "We've done all we can until it gets light. We did get through to the woman's brother, and he's flying in from

Salt Lake City as soon as he can get a flight. He told us the baby's name is Tommy, and he's ten months old.''

The rush of adrenaline that had kept Mariah going since the accident had drained away and left her bone-tired and emotionally drained. She'd showered and crawled into bed and slept until around seven. Then she'd dressed and rushed back to the hospital to find Tommy conscious and crying with fright at the strange surroundings and people.

Mariah asked if she could hold him. The harried nurse said it would be all right, and Mariah had lifted the screaming child and held him against her chest with his head at her shoulder. She'd walked around the room rubbing his little back through the heavy, footed blanket sleeper that had been put on him to contain his precarious body heat.

She'd talked to him in a low, reassuring tone, and gradually he'd calmed down. When he was no longer crying she'd sat down in the rocker and offered him a bottle of water. He'd opened his little mouth, then closed it over the nipple and sucked contentedly.

"How come you know so much about calming fussy babies?" the nurse, whom Mariah had gone to school with, had asked.

"I've got a passel of younger brothers and sisters," she'd said with a laugh. "I've had lots of experience with cantankerous kids."

The nurse chuckled. "Well, you can come home with me and calm mine down anytime," she'd exclaimed as she left the room.

That had been several hours ago. Now it was noon, and Mariah had just finished giving Tommy a bottle of formula. A few upward strokes on his back and a pat or two brought up the desired burp. He snuggled his face in her neck contentedly.

A warm rush of emotion washed over her and she relaxed against the back of the chair and closed her eyes. What was going to happen to this poor little guy? Who would raise him now that his mother was dead? Apparently there was no father in the picture, but did he have loving grandparents who would take him in? What about the uncle . . . ?

A noise at the doorway interrupted her reverie, and she opened her eyes to see a man standing there, looking uncertain. He was tall and well built with thick black hair cut short in feathered layers. It was startlingly black when combined with a light complexion and deep blue eyes.

He took a few steps inside the room, then paused. "The nurse at the desk said Tommy Kerr is in here."

Mariah nodded, careful not to disturb the baby. "This is Tommy."

He walked closer. "I'm Aaron Kerr, Tommy's uncle."

So this was the uncle. Mariah hadn't expected him to be so young, or so devilishly handsome. She always thought of uncles as looking like her own, middle-aged and starting to thicken at the waist and thin at the hairline. This man wasn't much older than she was. In the blue jeans, sweatshirt and sneakers he wore, he didn't look more than thirty.

As if reading her mind he continued, "Sorry I'm not more presentable, but I didn't take the time to freshen up at the airport. I rented a car and drove immediately to Apple Junction and the hospital. I haven't even checked into a motel yet."

"You look just fine," Mariah blurted, then felt herself blush. "I . . . thank you for coming so quickly. I'm Mariah Bentley. My father is Sheriff Clifford Bentley. He's the one who notified you of the accident. Would you like to hold Tommy?"

"No." He sounded a little panicky. "That is, I'm...I'm not very good with babies, but if you'd lower him onto your lap I'd like to look at him. The nurse says he's going to be okay. Is he awake?"

She smiled. "He just had his bottle so he's pretty drowsy, but that doesn't matter." She turned the child and cradled him in her lap with one arm so that he could see his uncle, and his uncle could see him.

Aaron looked at the little child in the pretty young woman's arms and couldn't believe that Eileen's baby had grown and changed so much in just a few months. He'd at least doubled in size and weight, and his eyes were definitely brown. Except for the red hair Aaron couldn't see any resemblance to his sister so he must look like Eileen's lover. Some legacy, he thought grumpily.

He hunkered down and reached out to touch the tiny button nose. Tommy grabbed one finger in his little fist and pulled it into his open mouth. The contact brought a rush of tenderness to Aaron.

"Hi, buddy," he heard himself saying. "Hey, it's been a long time. Do you remember your uncle Aaron?"

The big brown eyes stared at him, and toothless gums bit down on his finger. "Taste familiar, do I?" he asked, feeling a little silly, but so overjoyed to find the boy relatively undamaged that he couldn't help himself. He had to establish contact in any way that a baby would accept it.

The sheriff's daughter, Mariah she'd said her name was, laughed lightly. "How long has it been since you've seen each other?"

"Almost eight months," he answered as Tommy began to suck. It was the strangest experience. He could feel the pull all the way to his toes. Could this be something like the way a mother felt when nursing her child? How very odd.

Mariah spoke again. "Well, a doctor would probably tell you that a two-month-old baby wouldn't remember that long, but I've been with him most of the time since he regained consciousness and I can assure you that you're the only person who hasn't sent him into a screaming frenzy when they came near him."

Her tone was low and husky, and her words were somehow comforting and most welcome. He looked up and for the first time really saw her. Up to now his attention had been entirely on Tommy, and his impression of her had been a fleeting one.

He must have been really upset! Otherwise he'd never have missed those huge warm brown eyes, that straight, slightly flaring nose, and the full, inviting lips. Neither would he have overlooked the honey brown hair with golden highlights that tumbled to just below her shoulders.

"Thank you for telling me that," he said. "I've been feeling so...so guilty."

"But you were hundreds of miles away," she exclaimed. "You couldn't have prevented what happened."

"Does the sheriff know yet just what did happen?"

She shook her head slowly. "Only that your sister went off the road at a particularly dangerous curve. They still don't know when. The car went over a cliff and landed in thick underbrush. It wasn't visible from up above, but it couldn't have been more than a few hours before or Tommy would have died, too. The temperature had been dropping all day, and, although he was securely strapped into his car seat and has no serious injuries, he was suffering from hypothermia."

Aaron shuddered. Poor, irresponsible Eileen. She was probably driving too fast. She always did, and no amount of scolding made an impression on her. He never should have let her take the baby and move so far away!

"How was she found, then?" he asked.

Mariah hesitated. She really didn't want to get into a discussion about the woman in white. "Well, I . . . I had an accident on that same curve at about seven-thirty last night. There was . . . that is, I saw something in my headlights and swerved but thought I'd hit it. I called my dad and it was while the deputies were investigating my accident that they found the earlier one."

He frowned. "What was it you thought you'd hit? An animal?"

"Possibly," she said evasively. "They still haven't found anything, and there was no damage to the front of my car, so I must have been mistaken."

Less than an hour before, Mariah's dad had come to the hospital to tell her they had been searching since daybreak and found no sign of an injured woman, or animal for that matter, anywhere near the road. "We also had a mechanic go over every inch of your car," he'd told her, "but the grillwork was undamaged and the headlights and bumper were intact. You can breathe easy again, honey. Whatever it was you saw, you didn't hit it. We're calling off the investigation."

Her momentary rush of relief was quickly eclipsed by her uneasiness. She *had* seen a woman standing in the road. There was no doubt about that in her mind, and the car had hurtled toward the woman when Mariah put on the brake so suddenly and lost control. She didn't see how she could have missed her!

"Do you mean they probably never would have found Eileen and Tommy if they hadn't been investigating your accident?" Aaron Kerr asked incredulously.

Mariah hadn't thought of it in just that way, but what he said was true. It's unlikely that he'd ever have known what happened to his sister and nephew if it hadn't been for that woman in white.

The thought made her skin crawl. If there had been someone in the road, where was she now? And if it hadn't been a person Mariah saw, then what was it?

"They very likely wouldn't have," she answered in a troubled whisper. "Have you...have you seen your sister?"

He looked down, probably unwilling to let her see his pain. "Not yet," he said. "As I told you, I came directly to the hospital to check on Tommy. Can you tell me where they've taken her? And how to get to the sheriff's office?"

"The morgue is in the basement of the hospital, and, if you'd like, I'll go with you to Dad's office."

"That's awfully kind of you," he said, looking up again, "but can you get away? I mean, aren't you a nurse?"

She smiled at his mistaken assumption. "No, I'm not a nurse, and I don't work here at the hospital. Up until a week ago I worked for the state in Albany, but I got caught in the latest recession 'downsizing' so right now I'm between jobs. I was in the process of moving my stuff back to Apple Junction when I had the accident."

"Oh," he said in a tone that sounded more puzzled than informed. "Then how come you're taking care of Tommy? I mean, are you a volunteer aide or something?"

Again she shook her head. "No, nothing like that. I was there when he was put in the ambulance, and I rode to the hospital with him. He was so little, I couldn't bear the thought of him not having anyone with him to care about him at such a crucial time."

"You mean you've been sitting here all night?" He sounded incredulous.

"No, I went home and slept for a while," she said, then explained how she'd stayed with the baby until he was out of danger and asleep, then was sent home by the nurse to get some rest.

"He...he seems to be less fussy when I'm here stroking him and talking to him. He wants his mommy," she said sadly, "but he's been accepting me as a poor substitute."

Aaron's features twisted with grief and again he looked away. Mariah had an uncomfortably strong urge to reach out and stroke him, too. Was he also alone? Or did he have a wife or girlfriend to comfort him?

Well, there was only one way to find out. "Is your wife with you, Mr. Kerr?"

He shook his head. "Call me Aaron, please, and I'm not married." He raised his face and looked at her. "My God, what am I going to do about Tommy? I've never even known any other baby, let alone tried to raise one."

Mariah blinked. "Doesn't he have grandparents or other relatives who could take him?"

"No. Eileen and I were all that's left of our family. Now I'm the only close relative the poor kid has, and I'm sure no bargain as a father."

Mariah silently disagreed. It seemed to her that little Tommy was a very lucky child to have his uncle Aaron to rely on. It was obvious that he loved the boy.

Unable to stifle the urge, she put out her hand and stroked his somewhat bristly cheek. "I suspect that you'll be a fine father," she said softly.

He put his hand over hers, then turned his head slightly and kissed the heel of her palm. "Thank you," he said shakily, "for everything."

Mariah felt the heat of that caress in places that no other light kiss had ever affected, and it disconcerted her. She gently withdrew her hand and looked at the baby in her lap. He was sleeping with the finger of Aaron's other hand still in his mouth.

"Tommy will sleep for a while," she said, "so if you're ready this would be a good time for us to go to the sheriff's station. Dad will need to talk with you, and I'm pretty sure he'll want to accompany you when you...um... identify your sister."

Aaron stood up. "Sure, I'm ready anytime you are."

A short time later, Aaron and Mariah drove up to the sheriff's station in Aaron's rented blue Cutlass Ciera and parked in front. The station was an old redbrick building in a rectangular box shape that housed the law-enforcement offices on the ground floor, and jail cells in the basement.

Fortunately the sheriff was in, and Mariah introduced the two men. "Thank you for coming so quickly," Cliff said as they shook hands. "I'm sorry about your sister."

Aaron's face contorted with grief, and both Mariah and her dad turned away to give him a little privacy as he fought for control.

"I...I appreciate all you people have done for my sister and her son," he said when he was able to speak again. "Eileen lives...um...*lived* in Manhattan. Have you any information as to why she was up here?"

The sheriff shook his head. "No, we don't. I was hoping you could tell us. But before we go any further with this, I'm afraid you're going to have to identify the...that is, your sister. I'm sorry to have to put you through this, but..."

"I know," Aaron said. "It can't be helped."

They drove back to the hospital, the sheriff in his white official car, and Mariah in Aaron's car. Aaron was glad she'd chosen to stay with him. He'd always prided himself on being self-sufficient, but her calm assurance and strong but silent compassion was what he needed at the moment. She didn't even have to talk. Just having her beside him gave him the support he required.

The hospital, a good half a century newer than the jail, was a modern, two-story building. Bright and clean, it served the medical needs of the whole county since Apple Junction was the county seat of government.

After leaving the cars in the parking lot, they all walked into the building together. With every step Aaron's heart grew heavier. He'd been ten years old when Eileen was born, and he'd been so proud of her. He used to take her for walks in her stroller.... He hadn't cried when his parents had died six years ago, but this was different. Eileen was so young. She'd had her whole life ahead of her.

"Mr. Kerr, it's this way," said the sheriff's voice, snapping Aaron back to the present. "I'd rather you'd wait out here, honey," he continued to Mariah.

She was more than willing to agree. In less than ten minutes the men were back. Aaron's face was white and lined with grief, and his eyes were red-rimmed and hollow.

Mariah put out her hands. He enfolded them and brought them to his chest. "Are you all right?" she asked softly.

He nodded. "I will be. Thank you for being here."

Their gazes held, and she knew he felt the force that radiated between them. It was no doubt compassion on her part, and a need to be comforted on his, but even so, it was scary. No man had ever stirred such deep feelings in her before, and this one was a stranger. Due to a twist of fate he'd appeared in her life less than two hours ago and would disappear in a matter of days!

Aaron didn't even attempt to resist the tug of the attraction that bonded him to the beautiful young woman with both his gaze and his hands. She was a very special lady to know intuitively how badly he needed someone to hold. To understand what this family tragedy was doing to him.

He took a deep breath, then broke eye contact with her. Turning his head, he faced the sheriff, careful not to dislodge Mariah's hands from his in the process. "When can I take Eileen back to Salt Lake City?"

"We can release her as soon as we get the paperwork cleared up," Cliff said. "But I don't know how long it will be before the baby can be released from the hospital. You'll have to speak to his doctor about that."

Aaron shook his head in an effort to dislodge the fog of shock and grief that clouded his ability to think clearly and make decisions. "Could we...could we get out of here? Go someplace else?"

"Yes, of course," Cliff said quickly as he turned and started up the stairs. Aaron and Mariah followed, hand in hand. Aaron wasn't going to let go of her until he had to.

When they got to the top, Aaron turned to Mariah. "I'd appreciate it if you'd come with me back to your dad's office. I also have to check into a motel and contact a mortician, and I don't know my way around the town."

To his relief she agreed and offered to drive his car since it was obvious that he was too shaken to be behind the wheel.

Neither of them spoke during the short drive. Aaron leaned back against the seat and closed his eyes as he fought for control. God, how he'd loved his little sister! Had he failed her somewhere along the way? Their dad and mom had indulged her every whim, and then when they died and she'd been put in his care it was easier to give in to her than to try to undo her self-centered nature. She'd been a difficult teenager, but surely no more than most. What should he have done differently?

The car suddenly stopped, jolting him out of his morose introspection. He opened his eyes to see that they were back at the sheriff's station, Cliff parked right next to them.

"I need to get a statement from you, and there are some questions you can answer for me," Cliff said as he led the way to his office situated in the far left corner. The two walls facing the rest of the large public area were enclosed to about waist height, then glassed the rest of the way to the ceiling. The sheriff could sit in his office and see everything that was going on in the building. The glass was covered with venetian blinds, but they were fully open so the view was only slightly obstructed.

Aaron had the distinct feeling that Sheriff Bentley made it a point to know what was going on in his domain at all times.

Cliff sat down behind his desk and motioned Aaron to the chair across from him. Mariah sat on a brown vinyl sofa on the other side of the small room. Aaron sorely missed her hand in his.

"Would you like some coffee?" Cliff asked Aaron, "or how about something stronger? We usually have a bottle of brandy around here somewhere. Strictly for medicinal purposes, you understand," he hastened to add, but with a twinkle in his eye.

"Thanks but no thanks," Aaron said. "I'll be okay, and I really need to keep my wits about me. You said you had some questions?"

"Yeah. We know almost nothing about your sister. The only address we had to contact was the one in Salt Lake City. It was on her driver's license. If she was living in New

York she hadn't gotten around to getting her license changed."

"Apparently not," Aaron said with a sigh. "The Salt Lake City address is our family home. She lived there with me until early March when she moved to Manhattan to pursue a career in show business. She and a girlfriend shared an apartment, but a couple of weeks ago the friend got married and moved out."

Cliff took notes. "I see. Do you happen to have this friend's new address?"

Aaron felt a flush of anger. "No, I don't," he snapped. "She's the one who convinced Eileen to leave Salt Lake City. I tried my damnedest but couldn't talk Eileen out of it. She didn't have either the talent or the experience to get a job in show business. She was pretty enough to get on at a second-rate modeling agency and seemed to be doing okay financially. At least, she never asked me for money."

"Do you want us to continue our investigation into her activities," Cliff asked, "or would you rather we just drop it? There's nothing to indicate that her death was anything but an accident, so we can go either way."

Aaron didn't even have to hesitate about that decision. "I want you to continue. Find out what she was doing here in the Adirondacks. Are you sure she was alone? I mean, no other adults with her?"

Cliff shrugged. "As sure as we can be. There was no sign that there was anyone else in the car, except, of course, the baby. We only found two suitcases, one containing baby things and the other adult clothes and cosmetics. Plus a couple of boxes of disposable diapers."

While the sheriff was talking Aaron remembered something Mariah had said...something about an animal in the road.... "Sheriff Bentley, your daughter told me she'd nearly had an accident on that same curve shortly before you found the wreckage. She saw something in the road. Could it have been another passenger from Eileen's accident—"

"We've thought of that and investigated the possibility," Cliff interrupted, "but there's no sign of the woman in white—"

Aaron blinked. "A woman in white?" He turned to look at Mariah. "Is that what you saw in your headlights?"

She sent her dad a scathing look before answering hesitantly. "I thought so, but—"

"There's no sign of anybody, woman or beast, being involved in Mariah's near-accident." Cliff hurried to say. "We searched for hours, first with artificial light and then by daylight. That's how we found your sister's wrecked car, but there was no sign of anyone else being there, or having been there. I don't know what it was Mariah saw, but I suspect it was some sort of illusion with the lights against the dark and the forest."

"Daddy, that's not true!" Mariah cried as she bounced off the sofa in agitation. "There was a woman dressed in white standing there. She was motioning me to stop with one hand, and pointing off to the side of the road where the drop-off is with the other. It was not an illusion. I saw her."

Aaron felt a jolt. Surely she wasn't implying...

"Good Lord, Mariah!" He hardly recognized his own voice. It was hoarse with a combination of disbelief and amazement. "You're not saying that a...a *ghost* intervened by stopping you and pointing to the wreckage in order to save Tommy's life?"

Chapter Three

Aaron's words exploded in Mariah's mind. Ghost? The idea had never occurred to her! There had been a *woman* in that road, damn it. A living, breathing woman!

The last thing she'd ever see was a spiritual being! She didn't believe in them. She didn't even go to church!

"No, that's definitely *not* what I'm saying!" she cried, and her tone sounded like a cross between a gasp and a screech. "I don't know what became of her, but that was no ghost I saw. Why won't anyone believe me?"

"Honey, no one doubts that you saw something," her dad explained. "But if it was a woman we would have found her. I swear we searched everywhere for miles up and down the highway, and as far as we could on both sides. There was no sign of either a moving or injured person or animal."

It was all so frustrating. Mariah knew what she saw, but she also had no doubts about the thoroughness of the search. Her dad never did anything halfway, so if he and his deputies didn't find anything it was a good bet there was nothing to find.

So what on earth had happened?

She sat back down on the couch and ran her hands through her hair. "I understand, Dad, but we both know that if she'd been injured and thrown over that cliff she could have flown or rolled so far that she'd never be found. A body is a lot lighter than a car with two people in it."

"Mariah, stop blaming yourself," Cliff insisted. "You couldn't have hit anything hard enough to throw it that far without damaging the whole front of your car, and there's not a scratch or dent or drop of blood on it. If there was something in your headlights you *did not* hit it.

Aaron was dumbfounded by what he'd unleashed with his startled inquiry. So this is what led up to finding Eileen and Tommy in their wrecked car. He agreed with Mariah, it couldn't have been a ghost she saw. Ghosts were just imaginary beings made up by kids to scare each other around a campfire, or on Halloween. Or by grieving adults who can't face the finality of the death of a loved one.

Mariah's experience didn't fit either criterion, and she seemed as sure as he that there was nothing supernatural about it, so just what in hell had happened?

"Mariah," he said quietly, "what did the woman look like?"

Mariah blinked. Look like? She hadn't given that much thought. She knew it was a woman and dressed in white....

"I...I'm not sure," she answered as she tried to focus her attention on that brief but mind-blowing glimpse. "It happened so fast and startled me so badly that I didn't have a chance to focus on details. The light was so bright that it washed out the colors. I was only aware of white."

"Was she young?"

"Oh, yes," Mariah answered quickly, then hesitated. "That is, she wasn't old. I mean...well, you know, she was just a woman."

"Women come in all sizes, colors and ages," Aaron said patiently.

"I'm aware of that," Mariah snapped, then immediately regretted her waspish tone. He was only trying to help.

"I'm sorry," she apologized. "It's just that women also do a good job of hiding their age, but I'd say she was in her twenties, or possibly thirties...." She shrugged. "Guess I'm not being much help."

The corners of his mouth turned up in a small, sad smile. "You're doing just fine. Do you know the color of her hair and eyes?"

"I told you, I wasn't aware of any color. It was like a black-and-white photograph."

"Then would you say her hair was blond?"

Mariah thought about that. "It must have been, because I don't remember any dark at all within the circle of light."

Aaron frowned. "The circle of light?"

"Well, you know...I mean, the headlights of my car." He was confusing her with his questions. "It was black all around but the lights were almost blindingly bright."

"That's odd," he commented. "Usually total darkness tends to dim the light. Could you tell how tall she was?"

"I'd say she was about average height."

"And weight? Was she slender or heavyset?"

"I...I couldn't tell. She was wearing a long, full, robe-type garment—"

"A what?" both Aaron and Cliff chorused in unison, startling her.

"You know, a loose-fitting, floor-length, white caftan. Now that I think of it it does seem like an odd thing to wear in a mountain forest—"

"Was it dirty, or torn?" Cliff asked.

"No, it was pure white and looked brand-new."

"Was she disheveled? I mean hair messed up? Makeup smeared?"

"No, Dad, nothing like that. She was really very beautiful even with the anxious expression on her face."

"You didn't mention an anxious expression before," Cliff accused.

"That's because I didn't think about it until just now," she said in exasperation. "Good heavens, Dad, she appeared all of a sudden without warning, and she was right in the path of my car. It scared the hell out of me, and I'm lucky I didn't go over the edge myself!"

Cliff got up from his desk and walked across the room to sit beside her and put his arms around her. "I'm sorry, honey," he murmured as she relaxed in his familiar embrace. "You've been through a bad experience, and I'm only making things worse for you with all these questions. Now that we've established the identity of the victims, and we know the baby is going to be all right, there's no hurry about the rest of the investigation. Why don't you go help take care of things. We can talk about this later."

Before Mariah could reply, one of the deputies walked in waving something in his hand. "Hey, Sheriff," he said, "did you know we made the Albany newspaper?"

He held out the paper folded to an inside page. Cliff took it, and together father and daughter spotted the item. It was a short three-inch column headlined, Fatal Accident on Suicide Bend, and was datelined Apple Junction. It was a short recounting of how, what, when and where, with a notation that the names of the victims hadn't yet been released.

Cliff grunted and handed the paper to Aaron. "Those reporters must stay up all night scanning the police calls."

Aaron took the paper and read the item. It said a motorist had swerved to avoid something in the road but thought she may have hit it. While searching for that object the sheriff's deputies found the wreckage of the other car. Aaron hoped that would be the end of it. He didn't want Eileen and Tommy's names splashed all over the papers, and certainly not in conjunction with any ghost nonsense.

Mariah followed her father's suggestion and, after a somber trip to the mortuary, she sat behind the wheel of Aaron's rental car and eyed his exhausted features. "Where to now?" she asked.

"I guess I'd better find a motel room," he said wearily. "Is there one you could recommend?"

She fitted the key in the ignition and started the motor. "Yes, there is, but first why don't you let me take you to my place for a drink? You look like you could use it. I can borrow a bottle of brandy, or bourbon if you prefer, from Mom—"

"Do you live with your parents?"

"Not really, but until I find another job I'm going to be living in the cottage at the back of their property. It was my grandmother's before she died. It's kind of a cluttered mess because I haven't moved in yet, but it's clean and furnished."

He settled back in the seat. "Thank you. I'd like that if it isn't too much trouble."

She grinned. "If it was I wouldn't have invited you."

Aaron felt as tired and dispirited as he apparently looked, but the enticing dimples that grin exposed made things seem a little less dark.

He gazed out the windows as the car sped through the town. It was a pretty little mountain village that didn't seem to have been touched by the passage of time. He hadn't seen any of the franchise fast-food drive-throughs, but there was a diner, an old-fashioned ice-cream shop, and a bakery that also sold sandwiches, according to the sign in the window.

Main Street, the primary business district, was about four blocks long, marked by the sheriff's office and County Courthouse at one end and a white clapboard church with a tall steeple at the other. Beyond the church was the nicer residential district with well-cared-for homes, large lawns, and big old shade trees.

They drove through this district and on to the outskirts where the lots were larger and the flavor more rural. Mariah turned into a gravel driveway that led to a detached garage a few yards from a green shaker-style two-story house. There were lots of trees and shrubs and flower bushes, dormant now, but Aaron could picture a beautifully sheltered and colorful setting from spring through fall when they were all leafed out and in blossom.

"Your parents have a nice place here," he said to Mariah as they got out of the car. "Do they have a large family?"

She chuckled and again flashed those distracting dimples. "Yeah, I have three sisters and two brothers. Sissy, seventeen, Betty Jean, thirteen, and Rob, the baby, who's ten, are still in school and live at home. Clifford Theodore, Jr. who's known as Ted, is twenty and in his second year at the university, and Linda, nineteen, recently married and moved to Virginia where her sailor husband is stationed."

Aaron felt a stab of jealousy as she rattled off the names and ages of her siblings. He'd never felt part of a family. A lonely only child until Eileen was born when he was ten, he'd always thought of her as "the baby" instead of "my sister." By the time she was old enough to be a companion he was in college. He'd never lived at home again until their parents died within weeks of each other when he was twenty-five and she was fifteen. By that time he and Eileen were strangers.

He'd been appointed her guardian and tried his best to raise her properly, but their relationship was more like father and daughter, and not a close one at that. He was always making rules and she was always breaking them.

Mariah got out of the car and Aaron followed suit. Although there was no snow yet, the mountain breeze was cold. He wished he'd brought a cap as well as the heavy jacket. They walked up the path to the cottage where she opened the door and let them in. Aaron was startled that it hadn't been locked, and said so.

"Oh, we seldom lock things up in these rural mountain communities," she said. "There's very little crime."

"You're extremely fortunate," he acknowledged, "but I wouldn't push my luck too far if I were you."

Mariah laughed. "Well, in our case, it sort of helps that Dad's the sheriff. I mean, who in his or her right mind would break into the sheriff's house?"

Aaron chuckled, too. "Who indeed?"

It was comfortably warm inside. The front door opened directly into a large room separated by the furniture placement into living area, dining area and kitchen, although the kitchen was tiny and set apart by a breakfast bar across the front of it. A door in the back wall of the dining area on the left opened into a bedroom, and Aaron assumed that the bathroom was back there, too.

It was, as Mariah had indicated, somewhat cluttered with unpacked boxes and suitcases, but it was a snug little home just big enough for one person.

"This is a great bungalow you have here," he said as Mariah led him over to the living area. "I'd sell my soul for a place just like it."

Again she laughed. "Oh, please, don't do that. I'm sure you could find something much cheaper than that. But, you might have trouble duplicating the view. Come look."

They stood in front of the wide sliding glass door that opened onto a redwood deck. Beyond that stood a dense forest of trees and brush. It was not only breathtaking, but calm and peaceful and inviting.

Mariah stood beside Aaron as they looked out at the beauty of the scene before them. She could tell that he was impressed. "Take off your jacket and sit down," she said as she walked over to the sofa and reached down to remove a filled packing box that had been set on it.

Aaron quickly removed the jacket and tossed it over the back of a chair, then hurried to help. "Here, let me do that," he said. "Hey, this thing is heavy. You shouldn't be carrying it around. Where do you want me to put it?"

"It's full of books," she explained, "so if you'll set it over there by the bookcase I won't have to move it again." She gestured toward the shelves built into the end wall to their right. "And if you'll excuse me for a minute, I'll go over to the big house and raid Dad's liquor cabinet. What do you prefer, whiskey, vodka, brandy...?"

He set the box on the floor by the wall. "Vodka with ice if you have it. Can I move the rest of this stuff for you?" He motioned to the other boxes and suitcases.

A wave of warmth mixed with compassion enveloped her, and she went to him and put her hand on his arm. It was hard and muscular, with the biceps of a man who kept in shape. "Aaron," she said gently. "In the last fifteen hours or so you've been subjected to a dreadful shock, a flight across the country and two time zones, and an ordeal here that nobody should have to face. I'll bet you didn't sleep at all last night. You're positively gray with exhaustion. Sit down and rest for a while before you collapse."

She hoped he wouldn't be offended by her brashness, but his handsome face was pale and pinched with fatigue and sorrow, and his deep blue eyes mirrored his overwhelming grief as his gaze melded with hers.

He swayed, she reached out, and then she was in his arms. He groaned and held her close, but there was nothing sexual about the embrace. It was a nonverbal plea for help from a man who had nearly reached the end of his endurance.

For a long time they just stood there holding each other, his face buried in her hair, and her hands gently caressing his broad back. The down-filled quilted car coat she still wore prevented any intimate contact, but she could feel the tension in him, and the shock that wouldn't let him relax.

"I'm sorry," he finally murmured close to her ear. "I have no right to touch you... To take advantage of your kindness..."

Although he apologized he made no move to pull away from her but continued to hold her and rub his cheek in her hair. "You'll notice I'm not complaining," she said softly. "Right now you need someone to lean on. There's nothing wrong with that, but I suspect it doesn't happen to you very often."

His arms tightened. "No, it doesn't, but that doesn't excuse me for coming on to you."

She raised her head and looked at him. "Are you coming on to me?"

"I hope not. That is ... I don't mean to, but neither do I seem able to let you go. I'm sorry...."

"Don't keep apologizing," she said. "I'm the maternal type, always bringing home stray dogs and lost children."

To her surprise he actually chuckled. "I have to tell you, you do not remind me of my mother!"

She laughed, relieved that he could find humor in her gaffe. "Oh, shucks," she drawled. "In that case, how about thinking of me as a bartender? I understand they're good at helping to chase away sorrow."

He hugged her close, then released her. "Not nearly as good as you are," he said raggedly, "but I would appreciate that vodka if the offer's still open."

She felt more than a little shaken, too, as she turned to leave. The man was a stranger, for heaven's sake. She shouldn't have found his embrace so ... so irresistible.

"Coming right up," she said lightly as she headed for the door. "So why don't you take my good advice and sit down and relax?"

"I wish I could," he answered, "but I'm too keyed up. I need to keep busy. Later, after I check into a motel, I'll probably crash and sleep all night."

Mariah left and returned a few minutes later with a bottle of vodka and a pitcher of orange juice to find that Aaron had moved her suitcases into the bedroom, and a heavy box of dishes into the kitchen.

"Well, I see you're extremely helpful around the house," she teased as she removed her coat, "but you don't take advice worth a darn. When you get married you'll probably drive your wife crazy trying to decide whether she should praise you or scold you."

She took her coat and his jacket and hung them in the closet by the door.

Aaron grinned. "I won't have to worry about that for a long time, if ever. I'm a confirmed bachelor, not accountable to anyone but myself. And I guess I like it that way."

Mariah wondered briefly where his small, orphaned nephew would fit into his bachelor life-style, but didn't comment. Babies take a massive amount of commitment, but that apparently hadn't occurred to him yet.

"I know how you feel," she said instead as she unwrapped two glasses from the box of dishes. "I've been on my own since I was nineteen. I graduated from business school and went to work in Albany. That was seven years ago, and I'm in no hurry to give up my freedom, but eventually I would like to have a husband and children."

"Of course you would," he commented as he opened the refrigerator door and put ice cubes in the glasses. "You're the nurturing type. You'll be a great mother someday, but I'm not good with children. Babies scare me, they're so tiny and breakable, and I don't relate well to adolescents. As for teenagers . . ." He shuddered and almost spilled the vodka he was pouring into one of the glasses. "Let's just say I'm not sure I could survive raising another teenager."

He glanced at her questioningly. "Would you like some vodka, too?"

She shook her head and reached for the pitcher of orange juice. "No, thanks, I'll just pour myself some juice."

They took their drinks to the sofa and sat down, he at one end and she at the other. "I take it Eileen was a typical rebellious teen?" Mariah asked.

Aaron grimaced. "I don't know how typical she was, but rebellious, definitely. She resisted my authority every step of the way from the time I became her guardian until she moved to New York. She kept telling me I wasn't her father and she didn't have to mind me. I'm afraid I wasn't very patient with her, either. She was never in any real trouble, no drugs or run-ins with the law, but when she got pregnant she wouldn't even tell me who the baby's father was."

He gulped the last of his drink and set the glass on the coffee table. "Don't get me wrong. I loved my little sister, but I had no idea how to handle her. I really messed up with her, and now I'm left with Tommy. What in hell am I going to do with him?"

He ran both hands over his face and through his hair.

Instinctively Mariah started to reach out to him, but the memory of what happened last time she did that held her back. It would never do to wind up in his arms again. He'd think she was deliberately coming on to him. Instead she wrapped both hands around her glass and took a sip of her juice.

"You could put him up for adoption," she suggested quietly.

He dropped his hands from his face and stared at her. "Adoption?" There was pain in his tone. "You mean give him away to strangers? I can't. He's my nephew, for God's sake. My sister's baby. He's the only family I have."

Mariah couldn't suppress a smile. "No, I didn't think you could," she said gently, "so stop flogging yourself over what you perceive as your failure with Eileen and face reality. Parents are never perfect, not even the most dedicated ones, and how many fathers do you know who have raised children all alone with no help?"

He frowned and hesitated. "None that I can think of."

"Right. I don't know any, either. That's because most single fathers share custody with an ex-wife, or marry again and raise the child with a present wife. Or, if there's no wife or girlfriend in the picture they have grandparents or other family who help out."

Aaron looked uncertain. "Yeah, but—"

"Now, how many brothers do you know who have taken on the raising of a young teenage sister by themselves?" Mariah interrupted.

"None."

"That's right. Neither do I. You had no guidelines, no one to turn to for help. Plus, this fifteen-year-old child had just been traumatized by losing both her parents...." Mariah paused. "What happened? Were they killed in an accident?"

He shook his head. "No, Mom collapsed one evening from a ruptured aneurism in the brain. She was dead on arrival at the hospital. Dad had been under treatment for a heart condition for several years and I guess the shock was too much for him. He died less than a week later."

"Oh, how awful!" Mariah exclaimed as the horror of such a dual tragedy washed over her.

"Yes, it was," Aaron murmured. "I don't think Eileen ever fully recovered her equilibrium. She was devastated."

"I can imagine. The poor child. I'm sure it took you a while to recover, too."

"Yes," Aaron agreed. "I don't want to make the same mistakes with Tommy, but I don't know anything about babies. I'm not at all the paternal type. I've never even especially wanted children of my own."

"The two situations are totally different," she explained. "Tommy is much too young to know what's happened now, or to remember his mother and the life he's led with her. He'll grow up thinking of you as his father, whereas Eileen knew you only as her big brother, and she wasn't about to let you take the place of her father."

Aaron nodded. "You're a very perceptive woman," he said, "and what you're saying makes a lot of sense. I'm sure there are books I can read, parenting classes I can attend. I just hope I'm up to the challenge."

"Don't sell yourself short," Mariah said. "If you didn't care so deeply you wouldn't be torn with doubts about your ability. You'll be a great father."

He looked at her and smiled. "I'm afraid your confidence in me is overly optimistic, but it makes me feel a lot better. Speaking of parents, am I going to get to meet your mother?"

She understood that he wanted to change the subject, and was happy to oblige. "You sure are. She was baking cookies, but she said she'd be over as soon as she takes the last batch out of—"

Mariah was interrupted by the ring of the doorbell. "Oh, here she is now," she said and got up to open the door.

Jessica Bentley had pulled on a quilted jacket over her sweatshirt and jeans, and she carried a Tupperware container. Mariah stepped back and smiled. "Hi, Mom. We were just talking about you," she said as Jess walked past her.

"Nice things, I hope," Jess said. "I brought you some cookies." She set the container on the coffee table, then looked at Aaron, who had also stood up, and held out her hand. "Hi, I'm Mariah's mother, Jessica. You must be Mr. Kerr."

"Aaron," he said and took her hand. "I was just asking Mariah if I was going to get to meet you, but I'd have known who you are even without the introduction. The two of you look so much alike."

Mariah had heard that often enough before. Although Jessica was about twenty pounds heavier, and six pregnancies had thickened her waist and abdomen, the resemblance between mother and daughter was still striking.

"I always take that statement as a compliment," Jessica said.

"So do I," Mariah said. "Can I get you something to drink?"

"I stocked your refrigerator yesterday with a few things you'll need until you have time to shop for groceries," Jessica told her. "I think I put several cans of cola in there, but I can get myself one."

She started for the kitchen but Mariah waved her back. "I'll fix it, and I've already inventoried the inside of the fridge. There's enough stuff to last me for a month. Thanks, Mom, you're a sweetie. Now, why don't you and Aaron sit down and get acquainted. I'll be right there."

The three of them relaxed with their drinks and conversation until Aaron reluctantly announced that it was time for him to check into a motel and then go back to the hospital. Mariah rode with him, and she directed him to the town's newest and most modern motel. He then drove her to the garage where her car had been towed the night before and given a thorough check-over.

"Will I see you at the hospital this evening?" Aaron asked as they stood between their cars on the garage property.

Reluctantly Mariah shook her head. "I don't think so. That is, not unless you need me to be there. I mean if Tommy's fussy. I still have to unpack and get settled into the cottage...."

Aaron had to stop himself from blurting, *Please come, I do need you, and not to comfort Tommy.*

This whole thing was getting totally out of hand. He wasn't in the habit of *needing* anybody, certainly not a woman he'd known for only a few hours and would never see again once he left to go back to Utah. It was just the aftereffects of shock and the fact that he couldn't remember when he'd last slept.

No way was he going to get involved with this sweet and compassionate little mountain maiden. Well, if she was twenty-six she probably wasn't a *maiden* in the traditional sense, but she was too innocent for him. She was the type who would wrap her soft warm hands around his heart and cling, and before he knew it he'd be trapped in a relationship he didn't want and had no intention of pursuing.

Quickly he thanked her again for all her help, then got in his car and drove off.

Chapter Four

Mariah went to bed early that night and slept soundly. She woke the next morning, Tuesday, feeling rested and eager to see Tommy again. She wanted to see Aaron, too, but tried not to think about that. He'd suddenly turned very businesslike and impersonal when they parted late yesterday afternoon, and she could take a hint. He was grateful to her, but that was all.

Well, that was fine with her. Getting emotionally involved with him would be a huge mistake. He'd told her bluntly that he wasn't interested in marriage, and obviously there was no future in a courtship when the lovers lived two thousand miles apart.

Tumbling out of bed, she pulled open the drapes and was greeted by the sight of snow on the ground and an overcast sky. It didn't surprise her. The weather people had been forecasting snow since Sunday, the day of the accident, and it had finally caught up with them.

Funny, she thought as she turned on the clock radio to her favorite news station in Albany, her point of reference now was the accident. Things either happened before or after it. The experience had shaken her up, and made some pretty big changes in her life, such as meeting Tommy and Aaron, and that business of the woman in white...

Her thoughts were interrupted by the newscaster speaking the same words:

"...woman in white that Mariah Bentley insists she saw standing in the path of her car. So far no trace of her has been found, but the condition of the child in the wrecked vehicle at the bottom of the cliff has been upgraded from critical to stable according to a spokesperson for the hospital.

"And now for the weather—"

Mariah switched it off. Darn, they were still covering the story! Why should the Albany newscasters be all that interested in a car accident that happened so far out of their area?

She dressed in a red wool plaid skirt and matching sweater, then heated a bowl of oatmeal in the microwave and ate it before leaving for the hospital. The newscaster had said Tommy was in good condition, but he might still be crying for his mommy.

Although it was only a few minutes after nine when she arrived at the pediatric ICU, Aaron was already there, walking the floor with a sobbing Tommy in his arms. He handled the baby as if he expected him to either break or blow up any minute.

Aaron looked up and saw her in the doorway and strode quickly toward her. "Here, take him," he said and thrust the child at her. "He won't stop crying. I was just about to call for the nurse."

Mariah took Tommy and spoke soothingly to him. He looked at her, stuck his thumb in his mouth and cuddled into her embrace.

A look of relief and amazement twisted Aaron's features. "How do you do that?" he demanded. "He screams every time I pick him up."

She sat down in the rocking chair and rocked slowly. "He probably senses your uneasiness when you hold him, and that upsets him. You're still a stranger to him."

"But so are you," Aaron protested. "I'm his uncle. I was there when he was born, and he and Eileen lived with me for two months afterward."

"He's too little to remember that," she said quietly so as not to upset Tommy again, "and he's used to a woman taking care of him. He doesn't seem to be familiar with men."

"He thinks you're his mother," Aaron said, and she detected a hint of accusation in his tone. "How am I going to take care of him when he screams every time I come near?"

"Don't take it personally. He knows I'm not his mother, but I'm the one who sort of took over that role after that awful experience in the car accident so now he knows me. It'll just take him a while to adjust to you. Have you talked to his doctor this morning?"

"Yeah, he says Tommy's doing great. If he continues to improve they're going to release him from the hospital tomorrow. But I don't know how I'm going to take him to Salt Lake City on a crowded airplane if he cries all the way."

The depth of the loss Mariah felt was scary. It shouldn't matter so much to her that a man and child she'd known less than two full days were leaving and she'd never see them again.

"I...I guess you two will just have to get acquainted fast," she said, striving for a light tone. "If you'd like, I can spend the day here and help. It shouldn't be too difficult to wean him away from me as he gets to know you better."

Aaron looked vastly relieved. "Would you? I hate to impose."

"You're not imposing on me," she assured him. "I'm 'between jobs,' so to speak, so I have plenty of free time. Besides, I've grown very attached to Tommy. I'm going to miss him when you leave."

I'm going to miss his uncle, too, she thought but couldn't say aloud.

"He's going to miss you, too," he said softly, but if *Aaron* was going to pine for *her* he wasn't admitting it, either.

A short time later Tommy drifted off to sleep, and Mariah put him back in his crib. She and Aaron were walking down the hall on their way to the cafeteria for coffee when a nurse caught up with them. "Excuse me, Mr. Kerr, but Mr. Warren, the hospital administrator, would like to see you in his office."

"Oh? Is there a problem?" Aaron asked.

"I don't know, but he said to tell you it was urgent. His office is downstairs on the ground floor and to the left of the elevators."

"I'll wait for you in the cafeteria," Mariah said as the nurse walked away.

Aaron caught her by the arm. "No, come with me. You've been in on this from the beginning. If there's trouble you're entitled to know what it is." His tone was insistent.

She didn't argue but went with him, her curiosity piqued and her imagination running riot. They found the door marked Oswald Warren. It opened to a small reception area.

Aaron identified himself to the woman behind the desk and was told Mr. Warren was expecting him and to go right on in. Another door led into a larger office. The chubby bald man at the desk stood and offered his hand. "Mr. Kerr, thank you for coming so promptly. I—"

He caught sight of Mariah and his cherubic face broke into a big smile. "Mariah Bentley. It's good to see you again."

Oswald Warren and her dad had gone through school together, and had known each other all their lives.

He shook hands with Aaron, then came from behind the desk to hug Mariah. "Hello, Ozzie," she said and hugged him back. "How are Evelyn and the kids?"

"Couldn't be better. And you? I understand you were responsible for finding our little miracle boy."

Her eyebrows raised. "Miracle boy?"

"That's what the news reporters are calling the baby found in the wrecked car. Don't you read the papers?"

Mariah shuddered. *Miracle boy?* She hoped this business wasn't going to get out of hand. "I haven't had time to read or watch television," she explained. "Tommy is all right, isn't he? The doctor said—"

"Oh, yeah," Ozzie said as he went back to his chair behind the desk. "Never saw a kid recover so quickly. Actually, that's what I want to talk to you about, Mr. Kerr. Please, sit down, both of you." He waved toward a couple of straight-backed chairs in front of the desk, then lowered himself into his padded executive chair.

When they were all settled Aaron spoke. "Please call me Aaron. Is there a problem with Tommy's recovery?"

"Not physically, no. The doctor just told us that, barring any setbacks, the child can be released tomorrow. That's what's causing the hang-up."

Aaron frowned. "I don't understand."

"Well, it's like this," Ozzie said as he settled back in his chair. "The night Tommy was admitted to the hospital we had no information on him, and the woman with him was dead."

Aaron winced, and Ozzie paused. "I'm sorry," he said. "I don't mean to sound unfeeling. I know now, of course, that she was your sister, and I'm real sorry about the accident."

Aaron nodded. "Thank you."

"Anyway," Ozzie continued, "the baby was brought in by the sheriff as an emergency, but we couldn't start any major invasive medical treatment without permission. There was nobody qualified to give that and his condition was critical, so we woke the judge up and asked that the child be made a ward of the court. That way the judge could give permission for us to treat him."

"I understand that," Aaron said, "and I'm grateful to you for your quick action. It obviously saved my nephew's life, but I still don't see—"

"The difficulty is that little Tommy is still a ward of the court, so we can't release him to you. I gather your intention is to take charge of the boy?"

"Yes, of course it is," Aaron said sternly. "I'm his uncle. His only living relative as far as I know."

"What about his father?"

"He doesn't have a father."

"Come on, now, Mr. Kerr...uh...Aaron—"

Aaron glared at him. "I don't know who the bastard is. Eileen wouldn't tell me, but I do know that he took off when he found out she was pregnant and she never heard from him again. I'll be damned if I'm going to look for him now. Whoever he is, he's not fit to raise my sister's son."

"Yes, all right, I see your point," Ozzie said placatingly. "But, if you want custody of Tommy you'll have to petition for it. Otherwise we'll have to release him back into the care of the court."

Aaron clenched his fists. "Just what does that mean?" he demanded.

"It means that he will be put in a foster home until someone claims him."

"But I'm claiming him!" Aaron bellowed.

"Fine. But you have to do it according to the law. Go over to the courthouse and tell the clerk you want to file a petition for custody. She'll give you the papers you need. You fill them out and file them. There will be a hearing with the judge—"

"How long is this going to take?" Aaron asked angrily. "I have a business to get back to in Salt Lake City."

"If you get right on it you should be able to take custody by the time he's released from here tomorrow. I know it's frustrating, but the laws of custody are set up to protect the child. Honest."

Mariah reached over and touched Aaron's arm. "He's right, you know," she assured him. "You have to prove who you are and why you have a claim on the child. You wouldn't want just anybody to be able to walk off with him."

Aaron sighed. "Yeah, I know. So how do we get to the courthouse?"

Mariah smiled. "It's right next door. We can fill out the papers and file them before lunch if we hurry."

Once the paperwork was completed and the petition filed, the clerk gave Aaron an appointment to meet with

Judge Gibson in his chambers at eleven o'clock the following morning. Aaron caught a look of dismay that flitted across Mariah's face when the judge's name was mentioned, and felt a twinge of foreboding. When they were outside he questioned her about it.

"Oh, it's probably nothing," she said. "It's just that I hoped you'd get Judge Paulson instead. Gibson must be pushing eighty, and he's getting crotchety and inflexible. He's been a judge here for almost fifty years, and he's beginning to think he's God. That his word is law. Dad gets so mad at some of his decisions. He and the two lawyers in town plus a few other concerned citizens have tried to talk Gibson into retiring, but he's not about to."

Aaron's sense of foreboding heightened. "Oh, great!" he muttered. "Just what I need. Is there any chance I could ask for the other judge?"

Mariah shook her head. "I wouldn't recommend it. If Gibson found out, he'd be even more impossible. Besides, your custody hearing is just a formality since nobody's contesting it, and you're Tommy's only relative."

Aaron wasn't so certain. So far, this week had turned out to be one long-running disaster, and he sure wasn't going to bet on anything good happening to him in the near future.

After lunch at the diner on Main Street, Aaron and Mariah detoured to her place where he called the airline to arrange for a flight back to Salt Lake City. His ticket was open-ended since he hadn't known how long he'd be in Apple Junction.

He'd hoped to leave as soon as possible after the hearing tomorrow morning, but his rotten luck held and he wasn't able to get a seat out until Thursday afternoon. He'd have the baby to look after in a motel room for a lot longer than he'd expected, and he didn't even know how to change a diaper or feed him.

Back at the hospital Aaron and Mariah spent the rest of the afternoon and early evening with Tommy. He didn't accept Aaron easily, but as the day wore on, and Mariah showed him how to change diapers and give Tommy his bottle, baby and uncle became more comfortable with each other.

Aaron was also getting altogether too comfortable with Mariah. She'd become indispensable to him. He'd never have survived this ordeal without her. Talk about angels! Maybe she *had* seen one. Maybe it takes one to know one.

He almost groaned aloud at the thought. It's a good thing he was getting out of here soon. His brain was turning to mush and it was all her fault! What was it about her that set her so far apart from the other women he knew?

She was beautiful, yes, but no more so than a lot of women he'd dated. She was sexy. God, was she sexy. But that didn't account for the tenderness he felt for her. He'd had his share of sexy women, but the main thing they aroused in him was lust. Not that there was anything wrong with lust, but it didn't inspire the depth of emotion that she stirred in him.

Yes, it was definitely time for him to get out of here. This mountain paradise was too isolated, too intimate, too picture-perfect. He needed to get back to Salt Lake City and the real world before he succumbed to Mariah's innocent charm and did something he'd bitterly regret later.

That evening he took her to the town's only upscale restaurant. A steak house on the outskirts of town called the Fireside that had carpeting on the floor, tablecloths on the tables, and a brick fireplace with a real fire.

They'd both changed clothes, and she looked stunning in a green, silky, two-piece outfit with a low-cut top that revealed her willowy neck and throat, a tantalizing bit of creamy shoulders and a now-you-see-it-now-you-don't glimpse of the beginning swell of her high, full breasts. The slender skirt was midthigh-length and showed off her long, shapely legs.

It was actually a very modest garment, but on her it stimulated in Aaron a powerful urge to stare, and touch, and nuzzle. Aaron gulped his first drink in an effort to calm his psyche and cool off his libido.

Mariah smiled as he set his glass down. "Are you nervous?" she asked sedately.

He felt himself flush. Damn, she must have read his mind. "You could say that," he said, trying to hide his embarrassment.

"Don't be." Her tone was low and husky. "I didn't mean to discourage you."

He blinked. "I beg your pardon?" Was she coming on to him?

She looked puzzled. "You know. This morning. I didn't mean to upset you with my misgivings about Judge Gibson."

Aaron was rocked by twin feelings of relief and disappointment. Relief was the strongest reaction, but he was jolted by the disappointment. How come? Surely he didn't want to take her to bed. Unfortunately, that's exactly what he wanted. He was practically drooling over her. But it was too soon after Eileen's death to think about these things.

On further thought, he was also frustrated. Any man in his state of arousal would be, but not many would be glad about it.

"I mean, his mind is still sharp," she continued, referring to the judge, "he's just opinionated, and sometimes he comes down hard on those that don't share his opinion."

"I'm sure you're right," Aaron said as he signaled the waitress for another drink.

The remainder of the evening was most pleasant. Their steaks were charcoal-broiled to perfection, the vegetables and salad greens were fresh, and the apple pie and ice cream were both homemade, using apples grown in the surrounding orchards.

It was a little before nine o'clock when Aaron drove Mariah home. There wasn't much happening in the small town on a winter weeknight. The one movie shown in the only movie theater was over by ten and after that the only thing for a dating couple to do was go to the local lovers' lane and neck.

He was too damn old for making out in the back seat of a car, and besides, making love with Mariah was not an option for him. Just two more days and he and Tommy would be on their way back to Salt Lake City and a new way of life, just the two of them. There was no place in that life for any woman except a nanny for Tommy.

Aaron pulled the car into the driveway, then helped Mariah out. He walked with her across the lawn to the cottage. It was snowing again and cold. Mariah wore a long heavy winter coat, but Aaron's short quilted jacket didn't offer much protection as the breeze whipped through his slacks.

He waited while she opened the door and turned on the light, but she didn't invite him in and he didn't suggest it. The whole scene was far too enticing, and his resistance was seriously impaired.

There was one more hurdle to get over, the hearing tomorrow, and he needed her quiet support when he faced that. He reached for her gloved hand and held it between both of his bare ones. In his hurry to pack and catch his flight he'd forgotten to bring gloves. "Thank you for having dinner with me," he murmured. "The food was great, but the company was a thousand times better."

The porch light was dim but he could see her sweet smile, and it was all he could do not to wrap her in his arms.

"I don't know how I can tell you how much I appreciate all you've done for me, Mariah," he continued somewhat shakily. "I couldn't have gotten through these last two days without you, and I...I hesitate to ask still another favor, but—"

Her exquisite brown eyes widened. "What is it you want, Aaron? I'll help in any way I can."

"Well, I... That is, would it be too much trouble for you to go to the hearing with me tomorrow morning?"

She blinked, and her smile broadened. "No trouble at all," she said happily. "I'd love to. To tell you the truth, I was beginning to be afraid you weren't going to invite me."

A surge of gratitude and yearning snapped his self-control, and he gathered her in his arms and hugged her. She hugged back, and in spite of the fact that once more there were heavy coats between them, a simple embrace had never affected him as deeply as the one they were sharing now.

He wanted to rain kisses over her face and murmur endearments: *I want you, I need you, Let me spend the night with you.* But he wasn't going to take advantage of her loving nature. Instead, he clamped his mouth shut and rubbed his cold cheek against hers.

Finally he managed to put her away from him. He hardly recognized his own voice when he spoke. "I'll pick you up here at a little before eleven tomorrow, if that's okay with you."

"Fine, I'll be ready." Her voice sounded shaky, too. Quickly, he turned and strode back to the car.

* * *

Aaron arrived on Mariah's doorstep right on time the following afternoon, but he wasn't alone. To her surprise Tommy was ensconced in a child's seat in the back of the car, and a middle-aged blond woman who was a stranger to Mariah sat next to him. "Mariah, this is Mrs. Atkinson. She's from the county's child-welfare department," he said as he helped Mariah into the front. "Mrs. Atkinson, Mariah Bentley."

The two women nodded to each other and murmured short greetings, but Mariah's mind was in a whirl. Child welfare! What was going on? And why was Tommy with them? She'd understood that he wouldn't be released from the hospital until the question of custody was settled.

"I...I don't understand," she said as Aaron slid into the driver's seat beside her.

"I know. I'm not sure I do, either. The judge's secretary called me this morning and said he wanted Tommy brought to the hearing, too. Mrs. Atkinson is his escort."

Mariah blinked, then turned to look at the woman in back. "Escort?" She heard the building anger in her tone. "Why is an escort necessary when the courthouse is right next door to the hospital?"

The woman's stony expression didn't change. "The child is a ward of the court, and cannot be taken from the hospital except by a court-appointed escort."

"Oh, for—" Mariah sputtered, and turned her head to talk to Aaron. "Why does the judge want to see Tommy? He can't testify. He can't even talk."

Aaron shrugged. "I don't know, but it wasn't a request, it was an order." He started up the car and backed down the driveway.

Shortly after they arrived at the courthouse they were ushered into the judge's chambers, a dark-paneled room that was furnished with a desk, a sofa and several chairs. Mariah carried Tommy, who was fretful in the unfamiliar surroundings but still preferred her to Aaron.

She hadn't seen Judge Gibson in several years, but she'd known him all her life and it was immediately evident to her that he was as pompous as ever both in looks and in personality. He was a small man with a big ego, and although age had lined his face, whitened his hair, and bent his once straight back, her dad had warned her that he still wielded his judicial authority with arrogance and a heavy hand.

After the introductions he looked at Mariah. "Bentley? Are you one of Sheriff Bentley's kids?"

She smiled. "Yes sir, I'm the oldest."

"Yeah, he has a passel of them, but I thought some of the older ones weren't living in Apple Junction any more."

"That's right," she said. "One of my brothers is at the university and one sister is married and living in Virginia. I've been working for the state in Albany until just recently."

When they were all seated, with Judge Gibson behind his desk, Mariah and Aaron on the sofa with Tommy, and Mrs. Atkinson in one of the chairs, the judge leafed through the papers in front of him and looked at Aaron through his heavy bifocals. "Mr. Kerr, you've stated in your petition for guardianship that you are the only close living relative of the child, Thomas Wayne Kerr."

"That's right, Your Honor."

"What about his father?"

"I have no knowledge of his father. My sister was a college student and unmarried when she got pregnant. She wouldn't tell me who the father was, and he never made himself known to me."

The judge scowled. "Have you made any effort to find him?"

"No, I have not." Aaron's tone was decidedly testy. "He's never attempted to see his son, nor has he offered to support him. As far as I'm concerned he has no claim on the child."

"I see. And what is your interest? Did his mother leave a sizeable estate?"

Mariah stifled a gasp as she tried to calm the wiggling baby. Her dad was right. Judge Gibson was argumentative and insulting.

"A sizeable estate?" Aaron hooted. "The only 'estate' Eileen left was a half interest in our family home in Salt Lake City. She was a student up to the time her baby was born, and here in New York she hardly made enough to pay her share of the rent and living expenses. Tommy's not going to inherit anything except possibly a batch of overdue bills."

The judge cleared his throat. "Are you married, Mr. Kerr?"

"No." Aaron was short and succinct.

"Are you planning to marry soon?"

"No."

Mariah was appalled at the judge's behavior. He knew the answers to all these personal questions. Aaron had explained all of this in the petition he'd filed, and Gibson had the papers right there in front of him.

"Do you plan to take this child back to Utah and raise him all by yourself?"

"Yes, I do," Aaron said, and she could hear the rising impatience in his voice. "With the help of a nanny, of course. I do have to work during the day," he added, unable to keep the sarcasm out of his tone.

Judge Gibson looked at Mariah. "Let Mr. Kerr hold the child for a while," he ordered.

She'd managed to get Tommy settled down while they'd been talking, but when she lifted him off her lap and handed him to Aaron he howled and kicked and held his arms out to her. Aaron sat him on his lap, but Tommy continued to fight him and scream until the judge motioned Aaron to give the baby back to Mariah.

It took a few minutes to calm him down again, but once they had, the judge looked at Aaron. "The child doesn't seem very fond of you." His tone was strident.

"That's not surprising," Aaron countered. "He doesn't know me well yet."

He explained how Eileen had taken the baby and moved to New York when Tommy was barely two months old. "He was severely traumatized by the accident and the resulting hypothermia, and the only person he's really bonded to now is Mariah."

Judge Gibson didn't look convinced. "Have you had any experience at raising small children?"

"I was legal guardian of my sister after our parents died when she was fifteen."

"Ah, yes, but caring for an infant is different from dealing with a teenager for three years. You'd be responsible for Thomas for *seventeen* years. Are you prepared to accept such a long period of parenthood for a child not your own?"

Aaron took a deep breath and leaned forward. "Your Honor," he said, "Tommy is my nephew. I'm the only family he has, and I love him. Eileen didn't know anything about taking care of babies either when he was born, but she learned. I can learn, too. I have a big home, a good income, and no major vices. I'm not only willing to raise Tommy, I'm eager to. He's the only family I have, too."

The judge was quiet for a moment, then he closed the folder containing the papers and folded his hands. "I'll take this under advisement and give you my decision this afternoon at two o'clock.''

He stood. "That will be all."

Aaron was deeply shaken as they walked out of the courthouse. If this had been an example of a "routine" hearing in this county he was sure glad he wasn't charged with murder. What was the matter with that old duffer, anyway? You'd have thought he, Aaron, was trying to abandon the kid instead of petitioning for custody.

Aaron had been instructed earlier to take Tommy back to the hospital when the hearing was over so he could be examined and then checked out. Thank God, they also got rid of Mrs. Atkinson and her sour disposition. She'd been instructed to tell the hospital administrator, Oswald Warren, that Tommy was to be kept there until the matter of custody was settled.

Aaron and Mariah again had lunch at the diner, and at two o'clock sharp were once more ushered into Judge Gibson's chambers.

There were no pleasantries or small talk as the judge got right down to business. "Mr. Kerr, I've gone over all the aspects of your petition for custody of Thomas Wayne Kerr, and I have grave misgivings about awarding this child to you."

Aaron's stomach dropped and he felt sick. "But, Your Honor—"

Judge Gibson held up his hand. "Please don't interrupt. Since the father is unknown, I'm willing to accept the premise that you are the boy's closest relative. However, that doesn't automatically make you a fit candidate for custody."

The temporary nausea Aaron had felt quickly turned to anger. What was the old fool getting at? There wasn't any other candidate. He was all Tommy had!

Before he could gather his wits about him and protest, the judge continued. "You aren't married, you tell me you have no plans to get married, and you have no experience in caring for an infant—"

Aaron clenched his fists and leaned forward in his chair. "What does my marital status have to do with this?"

The judge glared at him. "A great deal," he snapped. "A child needs a mother as well as a father."

Aaron's anger mounted along with his frustration. "Ideally that's true," he said as he fought to keep his tone calm, "but these days a lot of youngsters are not that fortunate. Tommy's mother was a single parent. She was raising him without a father."

"But he wasn't my responsibility while she was alive," the judge said sternly. "Now, unfortunately, she's dead and Thomas is a ward of this court. That makes me accountable for him, and I'm not willing to just let you take him so far out of the court's jurisdiction. Your petition for custody is denied, and Thomas will be placed with a foster family until we can determine your suitability for guardianship."

Chapter Five

Both Aaron and Mariah gasped, and Aaron jumped to his feet. "You can't do that!" he shouted. "Tommy is my nephew, the only family I have. Eileen would want me to raise him—"

"Sit down and be quiet, Mr. Kerr," the judge thundered, "or I'll find you in contempt."

Aaron wanted to wring his scrawny neck, but even through the haze of rage that clouded his vision and his judgment he knew he'd never get anywhere with the man if he let his temper get the better of him.

Although it galled him to do it, he sank back down in his chair and struggled to at least control his voice. "I'm sorry, Your Honor," he managed to choke out, "but I've just lost my sister, and now you want to take my nephew away from me. I don't understand. I can easily support the child, and I have a spotless record both at work and in my personal life."

Judge Gibson sat down, too. "I'm sure you can and have," he said in a tone laced with triumph. He obviously enjoyed the power he wielded over a younger man who dared question his decision. "But you can't give him an equally important advantage, a normal family life."

Aaron was puzzled. What in hell was he talking about? There wasn't anything Tommy needed that Aaron couldn't provide. "I don't know what you mean," he said.

Judge Gibson leaned back in his chair. "How old are you?"

"I'm thirty-one."

"Have you ever been married?"

So that's what he's getting at. My lack of a wife. "No, I have not."

"And you told me earlier that you're not contemplating marriage in the near future?"

Aaron devoutly wished that he'd retained a lawyer to handle this, but everyone had said it would be simple. Just a matter of filing the petition. That his gaining custody of Tommy was a foregone conclusion.

Damn! As a tax consultant he should have known that there were no foregone conclusions where the law was concerned.

"Your Honor, I haven't yet met a woman I want to spend the rest of my life with, but I don't see how that is relevant in this case."

Mariah cringed as she watched the judge's cheeks puff up and turn pink. That challenge was a bad mistake on Aaron's part.

"Oh, you don't, eh?" the jurist snarled. "Well, young man, perhaps I should remind you that I'm the law expert here, and I say it is relevant. What do you have against marriage and a normal family life?"

Mariah knew better than to interfere, even though Gibson was way off base. It would only make things worse. All she could do was pray that Aaron would accept his decision without an argument and then file an appeal.

Unfortunately that was strictly wishful thinking. "I have nothing against a so-called 'normal family life' but with nearly one out of two marriages today ending in divorce I'm not willing to up the odds by taking vows with a woman I don't love just to conform to your long-out-of-date sense of normal."

The judge lunged to his feet and sputtered, "Why you . . . you . . ."

Mariah had no choice but to intervene. She got up and stood in front of the desk, which put her directly between Judge Gibson and Aaron, who now was also standing.

"Your Honor," she said, "the sudden death of Mr. Kerr's sister has been a devastating shock to him, and now, only two days later, he's trying to do what's right by his orphaned nephew. He's understandably very upset—"

"I can fight my own battles," Aaron muttered from directly behind her.

She discreetly jabbed him hard in the ribs with her elbow as she continued. "Please overlook his outburst and give him a little time to calm himself before—"

"He can have all the time he wants to calm himself," the judge blustered, "but my decision is made and there's nothing more to talk about. The child, Thomas Wayne Kerr, will remain a ward of the court, and will be put in a foster home until an adoption can be arranged."

Mariah was stunned. Adoption! The judge was going to let strangers raise Tommy!

She turned to look at Aaron. He looked like he'd been poleaxed, and she realized that she'd better get him out of there immediately before he recovered from the shock of the judge's pronouncement and did something that would land him in jail, or worse.

She took Aaron by the arm. "Don't say a word," she whispered, "just come with me."

She might as well have been talking to a post. He stood firm and looked the judge straight in the eye. "You won't get away with this." His tone was low and chilling. "I'll hire an attorney and appeal."

Mariah was watching Judge Gibson while Aaron spoke, and she saw the look of fear that flashed across his face before he managed to control it. Aaron had hit a raw nerve in the other man, but how? Surely judges got used to their decisions being appealed.

She hastened to try to repair the damage Aaron had done to his case by daring to threaten the judge, although she knew Aaron had meant it as a promise, not a threat.

"Your Honor," she said carefully, "may I speak to you for a few minutes privately?"

Gibson shifted his glance to her and nodded. "You may." Then he looked back at Aaron. "And you are excused," he said in a voice that was cold and hard and final.

Aaron turned and stalked out of the room.

"Mariah, if you're going to plead on behalf of that arrogant son of a—" Judge Gibson stopped, coughed, and shrugged. "Well, you'll just be wasting your time. I've made my decision and it stands, even though I'll probably have to deal with the child-welfare people over it."

She was wading through a quagmire here, and she thought carefully before she spoke. "No, Your Honor, it's not Aaron I'm concerned about. It's little Tommy. He's been through a terrible ordeal. I know because I was there."

She went on to describe the scene of the wreckage, and finding Tommy cold and unconscious in the car with the body of his mother. The only thing she left out was reference to the woman in white.

"I rode with him to the hospital, and stayed there most of the night until they told me he would live. I've been there most of the time since, too, and he's come to know and rely on me. He wants his mother, but he seems willing to settle for me."

The judge cleared his throat. "That's very sweet and thoughtful of you, Mariah, but I don't see—"

"No, Judge Gibson, I'm not looking for praise. I'm just trying to explain why you should let *me* take care of Tommy instead of putting him in a foster home with strangers. I'm the only person he trusts and isn't afraid of."

The judge looked startled. "You? But you're not licensed for foster care, and I can't put him in an unlicensed home."

"I know that," she said earnestly, "but you could help me get a license. You've known me all my life. You and Grandpa Bentley were good friends. You know I'd take good care of the baby."

He frowned. "I'm not questioning your good intentions, but what do you know about caring for a baby? Have you had any experience at that sort of thing?"

"Of course I have," she hastened to assure him. "I've got five younger brothers and sisters. I was changing babies diapers and giving them bottles from the time I was in second grade. I earned my spending money in high school and college by baby-sitting other people's kids."

She put all her powers of persuasion in her voice. "It's true I've been working at another occupation for the past several years, but I was recently caught in the latest layoff of state workers. Now I'm living in Grandma's cottage on my parents' property until I can find another job. I could devote myself full-time to Tommy."

"Mmm," the judge muttered and rubbed his temples with his fingers. "I suppose I could get you a temporary license if you're sure..."

"Oh, I'm sure," she said, and the exuberance in her tone was real. "Tommy still needs a lot of special tender loving care, and he accepts me as a sort of substitute mother. Oh, please, Judge Gibson, I really want to do it."

He drummed his fingers on the desk for a few seconds, then looked up at her. "All right, I'll give it a try. Get an application from the clerk and fill it out before you leave, and I'll arrange for a restricted temporary license so you can take charge of young Thomas when he's released from the hospital, but now that won't be until tomorrow. Understand one thing, though. He is not to be taken out of the jurisdiction of the court until this case is settled."

Mariah agreed, thanked the judge profusely and left.

Aaron paced the floor outside the judge's chambers, alternately cursing him and uneasily wondering what Mariah was doing in there for so long. What had she had in mind when she asked to speak with the judge privately? How did Aaron know he could trust her? Apparently Judge Gibson's connection with her family went back a couple of generations.

A lot of small isolated towns were awfully clannish and tended to distrust strangers. Is that what was happening here? Was she going to side with the judge against him? But what would she have to gain? He wasn't a threat to anybody. There was no one else who wanted Tommy.

When the door finally opened and she walked out, closing it behind her, he rushed to her. "What were you doing in there?" he demanded.

"I was trying to repair some of the damage you did by threatening the judge," she said sternly.

"What do you mean, 'threatening' him? I simply told him what I intend to do. If I can find a lawyer in this town who's not senile or related to the judge I'm going to file an appeal and a complaint, just like I said I would."

"Well then you should have just gone ahead and done it instead of mouthing off to him," she snapped. "And don't judge the whole town by one of its elderly public servants who's outlived his ability to make good judgments, but can't bear to retire. You may be in the same position someday."

Aaron realized that he'd offended her, and that hadn't been his intent, but Gibson had really knocked the props out from under him. He wasn't going to give Tommy up without a fight no matter who he upset.

"I'm sorry," he said more gently. "I don't mean to talk like a jerk. Actually, the people in Apple Junction have been wonderfully kind and helpful, and I really am grateful."

Her expression softened. "I'm sorry, too. I know what a blow the judge's decision has been to you. You have a right to be angry. If you're looking for a lawyer, we have three of them in town. I'm sure Dad can recommend one. That is, unless you'd rather bring in someone from Salt Lake City."

Aaron took Mariah's hand and they started walking down the hall. "I do know several attorneys back home, but I think I'd have better luck with a local one. One who's well-known and trusted in the area."

"Fine," she said. "Come over for supper tonight, and we'll get together with Mom and Dad afterwards and talk about it. Right now, though, I have to stop in the clerk's office and file a request."

Aaron's uneasiness returned. What had she and the judge been talking about? "A request for what?"

"For a temporary license to take care of Tommy," she said happily. "I talked Judge Gibson into letting me care for him instead of putting him in a foster home with strangers."

Aaron was dumbfounded. He stopped walking and turned to look at her. "You did? But...but it could take quite a while to straighten out this mess. You said you were eager to find a job."

She grinned. "I was, and I just found one. I'll get paid for looking after him, and there's nothing I'd rather do. It would break my heart to see him turned over to strangers when he's bonded so well with me."

A warm tide of emotion swept through Aaron, and he squeezed the hand he was holding as he stroked her cheek with the other one. "I'm no longer surprised that you saw an angel in the road that night," he said shakily. "She recognized you as a kindred spirit. I...I don't know how I can ever thank you—"

Mariah put her fingers to his lips in a shushing gesture. "No thanks are necessary. I...I love the little guy. It's going to be hard to give him up once you've finally gained custody."

Aaron's heart was so full that it totally obliterated his better judgment. Right there in the hall of this small-town courthouse he kissed her fingers, then leaned down and kissed her on the mouth. It was only a quick brushing of lips, but it was almost unbearably sweet.

The sound of footsteps behind them broke the spell, and with faces flaming they stepped apart and headed for the county clerk's office.

When Mariah told her mother that Aaron would like to talk to her dad that evening after supper, Jessica invited them both to eat with the family. They were all seated around the big dining room table, and the meal was delicious but the atmosphere was a little strained. Aaron was obviously not used to the rowdy banter of a large family and seemed ill at ease as sexy Sissy flirted with him, sports nut, Rob, kept up a lively chatter about his favorite football players, and Betty Jean, who was at that painfully awkward age of acne and braces, refused to open her mouth and mumbled everything she said.

When everyone had finished eating Jessica charged Sissy and Betty Jean with doing the dishes while Rob was sent to his room to do his homework before his favorite television program came on. The rest of them took their coffee into the living room where it was reasonably quiet.

"I hope we haven't either driven you crazy or bored you to death, Aaron," Jessica said as she settled herself in the flowered chair by the fireplace, "but you should be around when the whole family is here. That's when things really get lively."

Aaron smiled from his seat beside Mariah on the brown velour sofa facing the warm, cheerful fire. "If you really want to know, I'm consumed with envy. I never had much of a family life. I was an only child until my sister was born when I was ten. I was pretty much raised by housekeepers. My parents were professional people, and we seldom all had a meal together. After Eileen came along they hired a nanny to work with the housekeeper, and I saw even less of them. Tonight you've given me a glimpse of all that Eileen and I missed. My admiration for the way you're raising your children is boundless."

Cliff, who had taken a leather chair on the other side of the fireplace from his wife, chuckled. "Take my word for it, son, it's not all beer and skittles. You should see us when all six of them are home at once and each one wants something someone else refuses to give up. It's bedlam, pure and simple. Makes you wonder why you were ever crazy enough to think you wanted a big family.''

They all laughed. "So which ones are you willing to give away?'' Aaron asked teasingly.

Cliff's expression sobered. "Sorry you asked that,'' he said, "because for a while there today I'd have given Mariah to the first person who bid on her.''

"Daddy!'' she protested.

Cliff grinned and winked at her. "Just kidding, sweetie, but you've had my telephone lines tied up at the station for most of the day. You wouldn't believe all the calls we've had from reporters wanting to interview you. Apparently you weren't home to answer your phone, so they called us.''

Mariah was stunned. "Interview me! But why?''

"They want to know about your woman in white. Apparently that's an angle that appeals to their imagination. A couple of the calls were from tabloids wanting to buy your story.''

Mariah blinked. "Buy it? What did you tell them?''

"I told them I didn't know anything about it and they'd have to talk to you. Something tells me that if you don't want to be bothered with them you'd better disconnect your phone.''

"Oh, darn,'' she groaned.

Cliff returned his attention to Aaron. "I was just teasing about giving her away, of course,'' he said seriously. "There's not a single one of my kids that I'd give up. I love all of 'em, even when they're the least lovable.''

Aaron nodded. "That's what I thought.'' His tone was also serious. "So maybe you know how I feel about that judge telling me I'm not fit to raise my infant nephew. Hell, I even agree with him. Right now I'm probably not, but I can hire help, and I can learn. Gibson has no right to say I'm not a fit guardian because I'm not married. That's the stupidest thing I ever heard of. I don't think it's even legal, and that's what I wanted to talk to you and Jessica about. I'm going to appeal his decision, and I need a lawyer. Mariah said maybe you could recommend one.''

"I agree with you," Cliff said, "and I think you're doing the right thing. If you want a local attorney, you only have three choices. One is approaching seventy and getting ready to retire. The second one is his son and partner, who's in his forties and good at corporate law. You know, contracts, property disputes, etc. Then there's Nathan Quimby. He's a newcomer in town.''

Cliff paused and grinned. "Well, that is, he's a newcomer according to Apple Junction standards. Five or six years ago the father of our father/son law firm had some extensive surgery and couldn't work for several months so they hired this kid right out of law school to work as a temporary fill-in and he's still here.

"When the old man recovered, Nate set up his own law office and handles most of the family type things, divorce, adoption, custody. He's the one most qualified for a case like yours.''

"Is he good?"

"Yeah, damn good. I can give you the names of some of his clients if you'd like.''

"Does he get along with Judge Gibson?"

Cliff frowned. "No. Nate's taken Gibson on before. He's gotten two of the judge's decisions reversed just lately, and I think Gibson's runnin' scared. That might work in your favor.''

Aaron felt a flicker of hope. "I really appreciate your help, Cliff. Mariah's, too. Has she told you what she's volunteered to do for Tommy?''

Cliff looked at Mariah and she was warmed by the pride in his expression. "Yes, she has, and you couldn't find a better foster mother. She was a big help to us with our other children.''

He smiled at Mariah and continued. ''I was in the army when Jess and I were married. That was during the Vietnam war, and shortly after Mariah was born I was sent over there. I was out of the country until the war ended, so Mariah was six years old before our second child was born. She insisted that we let her 'help' with the baby, and she got real good at it.''

He chuckled. ''So much so, in fact, that she was given the ongoing job of helping with all her younger siblings as they came along. I can vouch for her expertise in child care.''

Mariah felt a warm flush of embarrassment at her father's praise. She hadn't offered to keep Tommy in order to impress Aaron. She truly loved the little guy.

Aaron looked at her and must have seen her blush. He winked. ''You don't have to convince me. I've seen firsthand how great she is with Tommy. She works pure magic on him. Hell, he prefers her to me. Not that I can blame him, I'm all thumbs and screaming nerves when I try to handle him.''

A couple of hours later Aaron walked Mariah across the broad expanse of lawn to her cottage. As they stood on the step facing each other he wound a strand of her silky brownish gold hair around his cold finger.

''I suppose the hospital will call you tomorrow when Tommy is ready to be discharged?'' he said, although right at that moment his mind wasn't focused on the baby, but on the fine features of her moonlit face that was raised just inches from his gaze. He wanted to cup her delicately tinted cheeks, and cover her mouth with his, but knew that his hands and lips would be icy to the touch.

"I'm sure they will, but if I don't hear anything by eleven I'll call them." Her dewy breath misted in the frosty air.

"If you don't mind I'd like to go with you when you pick him up. I'm going to call Nathan Quimby's office first thing in the morning and schedule an appointment with him, but other than that I'm free. I have the child safety seat in my car, but if you'd prefer I can leave it with you now."

"No, please," she said. "I'd like for you to come with me. How about if I call you as soon as I hear from the hospital? You can pick me up and we'll go together. Do you have his clothes and things?"

Aaron nodded. "Yes, I retrieved them yesterday from the sheriff's station. There's not much, but we can go buy anything else you'll need."

The following morning Aaron called the lawyer's office, and explained who he was and what he wanted.

"Damn, I'm sorry you didn't let me handle this for you from the beginning," Nate Quimby said. "I might have been able to block some of Gibson's maneuvers."

"You're nowhere near as sorry as I am," Aaron lamented, "but everyone said it was just routine..."

Nate chuckled. "I know. All those readers of Perry Mason figure they know everything about the law. I'll be happy to meet with you. Let me turn you over to my secretary and she'll give you an appointment."

The meeting was scheduled for eleven o'clock, and Aaron immediately called Mariah. He told her about his conversation with the lawyer and invited her to go to the office with him.

Mariah was delighted that he'd asked her. "I'd love to. I haven't heard from the hospital about Tommy's release yet, but Dad was right about the reporters. They started calling before eight o'clock this morning.''

Aaron felt a shiver of foreboding. "What did you tell them?"

"I just told them what happened and refused to speculate. I hope this isn't going to be a big issue."

"So do I," he said emphatically. "I'd hate to have Tommy and Eileen linked to some supernatural nonsense."

"Me, too," she agreed. "Look, I'll call the hospital and arrange to have the baby released after lunch. Why don't you pick me up on your way to Nate's office? Then we can swing by the hospital and get Tommy later."

Aaron agreed, and Mariah broke the connection, then dialed the hospital.

When Aaron arrived two-and-a-half hours later she was wearing brown slacks and a rust-colored sweater. He wore the same dark slacks and gray pullover he'd worn the night before.

They greeted each other happily and drove to Quimby's law office on Main Street. Nate Quimby was about Aaron's age and build, but his hair was a medium brown and his eyes amber. He even had freckles that made him look boyish.

After the introductions, Nate invited them to sit down and took his own seat behind the desk. "You must be one of Sheriff Bentley's daughters," he commented as he smiled at Mariah.

"Yes, the eldest," she said as she and Aaron took seats in front of the desk. "I've lived in Albany for the past few years, but now I'm home again for a while."

His gaze shifted to Aaron. "And you're the uncle of the baby boy who was in the accident."

Aaron nodded. "That's right, and I don't intend to let my sister's son be adopted by strangers."

"Of course not," Nate said. "I have no doubt that the appeals court will reverse Judge Gibson's decision, but these things take time."

"I don't have time," Aaron protested. "Can you at least arrange for me to take Tommy home to Salt Lake City while the appeal is pending? I have to get back to work."

"I can't promise anything," Nate said sadly. "I realize you're not going to be moved by his plight, but Judge Gibson is really a pathetic case. He's always been a gruff, opinionated man, but until recently he was fair. I suspect he's been having small strokes that cloud his judgment, but he won't admit it.

"A number of the civic leaders here in town have urged him to retire. He's long past the retirement age, but he absolutely refuses. In the past few months he's had two rulings overturned on appeal. If that happens again, he could almost certainly be forced to retire. But, he's a stubborn old cuss and refuses to admit he could ever be wrong."

Nate agreed to handle Aaron's appeal, but warned him again that it might be months before a decision could be rendered.

As Aaron and Mariah left the office and walked to the hospital to get Tommy, Aaron suggested that they shop for whatever baby supplies she would need.

"I won't know until I go through the things his mother brought with her, but she probably packed everything she'd need for a while. You can't travel far or for very long with a baby unless you do. Mom's already loaned me the crib, playpen and stroller she used for Betty Jean and Rob, and you've bought a car seat so I'm pretty well set."

* * *

The phone was ringing when they arrived back at Mariah's cottage. She ignored it while they settled the baby in the crib for his nap and eventually it stopped, but by the time they got back to the living room it started up again. This time she answered it. It was a reporter from a national tabloid offering to pay her for exclusive rights to her story. She declined and broke the connection, then unplugged the phone.

He went to her and touched her arm. The long sleeve of her sweater felt soft and warm to his palm. "I'm sorry," he said apologetically. "I've never been able to accept the concept of supernatural or psychic beings, but I guess there are others that do. Anything to sell papers."

She smiled and seemed to sway slightly toward him as his hand automatically tightened on her arm. "I'm sorry, too. I don't believe in all that stuff, either. That's why I'm so sure that the figure in the road was a flesh-and-blood woman, not a phantom. It really bothers me that we can't find any trace of her. I wish that all these people would just leave us alone."

Aaron didn't know which of them moved first, but then she was in his arms and he was holding her soft, slender body gently but firmly against him. The faint scent of spicy fall flowers tickled his nose, and he didn't dare move or talk for fear he'd break the spell and remind her that she didn't know him well enough to allow him this liberty.

She settled her head on his shoulder, and he silently thanked God for the apparition, whatever it was, that brought them together.

Chapter Six

Mariah snuggled into Aaron's warm embrace and resolutely shut out the anxiously protesting good-sense part of her mind. If he wanted to hold her, she wasn't going to rebuff him by pulling away like a timid virgin.

No woman with a fully developed libido would. He was strong and muscular, and he smelled of pine and fresh mountain air. The soft wool of his sweater beneath her cheek was both comforting and arousing, and he apparently wasn't immune to her, either. She could feel his heart pounding against her breast. But with a heavy sigh he put her away from him.

"Mariah, there's something we have to talk about," he said. "Shall we sit down?"

Oh, dear, he sounded rather ominous. She nodded and they sat down together on the couch. "As you know, I was planning on leaving for home tomorrow," he said. "I've already made the arrangements for Eileen . . ."

His breath caught, betraying his grief over the necessity of his painful errand. "Although the judge has refused to let me take Tommy, I really must go back with Eileen. Will you... That is, is it okay with you if I leave tomorrow as planned? It means you'll have full-time care of Tommy with no help from me, but I'm more of a hindrance than a help anyway."

She felt a wave of disappointment. She'd known he'd go back to Salt Lake City soon, but she'd expected him to stick around for a few days until she and Tommy got settled in together. Not because she needed his assistance, but because she didn't want him to walk out of her life so soon.

"You're a big help," she said and hoped her regret wasn't obvious, "but this is something that can't be put off. Of course you must go. Just leave your address and phone number where I can reach you. Tommy and I will be fine."

He gave her a grateful look. "I don't know how long I'll be gone. There will be a funeral, of course, and a lot of paperwork to catch up on. If everything goes all right with you and Tommy here, I'd like to stop in New York City on my way back and take care of all the things that have to be done there."

"You're coming back?" The words were out before she could stop them.

He looked surprised. "Of course I'm coming back. Did you think I wouldn't? I'm not going to leave Tommy here for several months without a fight. Nate is petitioning the Court of Appeals to let me take the baby to Utah with me on a temporary basis until we get a permanent ruling on the custody matter, but I have to take Eileen home and get her affairs straightened out first."

He sounded so sad and forlorn that she couldn't resist reaching out to him. She slid closer and put her hand on his knee. "Aaron, don't worry about Tommy and me. I'm well qualified to take care of him, and if I have any problems Mom is just a few steps away. After raising six kids she's an expert."

He put his hand over hers, pressing it more firmly against him. "I can't even begin to tell you how much I appreciate all you've done for my little nephew and me. I hate to run off and leave you before you've even had a chance to see just how much time and effort all of your magnanimous gesture entails, but—"

"I know exactly what I'm letting myself in for," Mariah assured him, "but I love children. Especially babies. This is something I really want to do. Don't worry about us. Take your sister home, and feel free to call me anytime you want to. I'll always be happy to hear from you."

Aaron squeezed her hand, then released it. "In that case, I'll go to the motel and check out now. The forecast is for high winds and more snow tomorrow, so I'd like to get out of these mountains and across the lake this evening while the weather is still clear and calm. I'll call you from Burlington in the morning before my flight takes off."

The following week was both sad and busy for Aaron in Salt Lake City. Eileen's funeral was held on Wednesday and brought an outpouring of cards, letters, phone calls and visits, as well as flowers, food and donations to charity. Aaron was deeply grateful for the thoughtfulness and compassion of his neighbors, friends and business associates.

The other days were taken up with the chores involved in settling the legal matters pertaining to Eileen's death and trying to catch up on all the work that had piled up at his office while he was gone.

The one bright spot in his days was his nightly telephone call to Mariah. She was always so positive and cheerful, although he knew that looking after an active little guy like Tommy must be exhausting. She never complained, not even when she discovered that when she put the boy on the floor he got up on his hands and knees and crawled with both vigor and speed.

But it was her thoughtfulness that was Aaron's undoing. In a touching gesture she sent an arrangement of fall flowers to the funeral with a card enclosed that read, "For my Mommy, with love from Tommy."

Her sensitive tenderness was comforting. He tried not to think about how much he missed her and wished she were there with him. It would be a mistake for him to give too much importance to the strong attraction he felt for her. This was a difficult time for him and she soothed his aching heart. Once he got back to work and into the swing of his new life-style with Tommy and a nanny he wouldn't miss her anymore.

By Friday he had whittled down his backlog of work at the office to a manageable size and arranged for his secretary and one of the other accountants to take over what they could while he was away. On Saturday morning he caught a flight to New York City, then hailed a cab outside the terminal and gave the driver Eileen's address. Half an hour later the taxi stopped in front of a run-down brownstone on a dirty street littered with garbage and cluttered with ragged men and women milling aimlessly around.

Aaron was appalled. Surely this dump wasn't where his sister had lived! She'd been raised in an upper-middle-class area in an immaculate vintage house surrounded by green lawn and flower gardens. He doubted if she'd ever even walked through the slum area of Salt Lake City, and it wasn't as disgusting as this.

He checked the address with the cabdriver, and was assured that this was the place. Clutching his pullman case he walked up the rickety steps and tried the door. It was locked. Thank God for small favors. At least there was a modicum of security.

He took Eileen's keys from his pocket and tried them in the lock until he found the right one. Inside, the hallway was dark and smelled of stale cooking and other things he didn't want to identify. There was a row of mailboxes on the wall to his right, and he noticed that the one with Eileen's name on it was full. Selecting another key on her key ring, he opened the box and emptied it of its contents, then knocked on the first door he came to.

On Monday morning, Mariah woke while it was still dark to the sound of Tommy moving restlessly in his crib just a few steps from the side of her bed. The illuminated face of her alarm clock told her it was 6:32, and time to get up. She didn't need her alarm anymore. Tommy was more reliable than the clock.

She rolled onto her back and stretched. Today Aaron was coming back to Apple Junction! A warm glow of excitement and anticipation swept through her. He'd called from New York City last evening to tell her that his business there was taken care of and he'd made reservations on an early-morning flight to Burlington. He'd rent a car there and hoped to be in Apple Junction by noon.

She had a lot to do between now and then: clean the house, bake a cake, go to the grocery store... The list went on and on. Quietly, so as not to disturb the baby, she threw back the covers and got out of bed. Tommy was starting to wake up, but with a little luck she might be able to have her breakfast before he demanded his. She stepped into furry slippers, slid a velour robe over her head and zipped it up as she walked silently out of the room and closed the door behind her.

Half an hour later the house was warm, and Mariah had just finished her granola and toast when a loud wail shattered the silence. Tommy! She put down her mug and raced the few feet to the bedroom. Poor little guy, he often woke up screaming. She'd talked to Dr. Henderson about it. He'd said it was a lingering trauma from the plunge down the mountainside in the car, and his near brush with death.

She picked him up and cuddled him in her arms as she rubbed his back and murmured soothing assurances into his ear. "There, there, sweetheart, I'm here. Everything will be all right. It was all a bad dream."

She didn't know whether or not babies dreamed, but she was sure this one did. Or maybe it was that at the moment between sleep and waking he remembered the terror of being alone and cold and hurting. Of his mother slumped in the seat ahead of him but not responding to his desperate screams.

She took a blanket from the crib and covered him with it. He was wet and needed dry clothes, but first she had to calm him and take away his fears.

Walking into the living room she sat down to soothe the child in the old wooden rocker in which her grandmother had rocked her children. He sobbed but snuggled against Mariah and put his thumb in his mouth. She knew that thumb-sucking was considered a no-no, but it was a source of comfort for this traumatized little one, and she wasn't going to deprive him.

Gradually the sobbing stopped, and Tommy raised his head and looked at Mariah. "Well, good morning, my little darling," she said cheerfully and smiled. "Would you be interested in a bath and some dry clothes?"

A tentative smile banished the fear from his brown eyes, and he took his thumb out of his mouth and tried to put it in hers. "Thanks a bunch," she said dryly, "but I've al-

ready had my breakfast. How about you? Want some of
that wallpaper paste they call baby cereal and a bottle of
nice warm milk?''

He jabbed his finger in her mouth before she could shut
it, then laughed, lighting up his whole face. It was a beautiful sound, one she'd worked hard over the past week to
bring forth. For the last few days it had appeared more and
more often without coaxing, and she couldn't wait for
Aaron to hear it.

Aaron arrived about twelve-thirty. Mariah was feeding
Tommy his lunch of strained beef and vegetables when she
heard the car coming up the gravel driveway and stop.
She'd been listening for the sound, and her heart sped up
as she rose and hurried to the door.

She opened it to a blast of chilling fresh air and saw him
striding across the lawn. He was wearing a tan overcoat and
brown leather gloves. ''Hi,'' she called and saw his face
split into a wide grin as he closed the last few feet between
them and caught her in his arms.

''Hi, yourself,'' he said happily as he swung her around.
She wrapped her arms around his neck and hung on. ''God,
but it's good to be here,'' he said and hugged her close. ''It
seems like I've been gone forever. Where's Tommy?''

Tommy. Of course. It wasn't her he was glad to get back
to. It was the baby.

She tried to retain her bright smile and light tone, but her
disappointment was painful. ''He's fine. I was just feeding him his lunch.'' She backed out of Aaron's embrace.
''Maybe if you're good he'll let you share it with him.'' She
motioned toward the high chair in the kitchen area and the
child sitting in it with the last spoonful of pureed vegetables she'd shoved in his mouth now running down his chin.

"Yuck," Aaron said and made a face as he started toward the little one. "I'll pass on that if you don't mind."

He stopped beside the high chair. "Hi there, guy. Do you remember your uncle Aaron, or are we going to have to get acquainted all over again?"

Tommy looked up at him, his big brown eyes questioning, then let out a howl of displeasure. "Damn, I was afraid of that," Aaron grumbled as Mariah wiped the child's sticky hands and face with a warm damp cloth while he fought her every swipe.

"You've been gone ten days," she said, annoyed with Aaron because he seemed annoyed with the baby, "and you were still pretty much of a stranger to him when you left. You can't expect him to know you on sight and welcome you with open arms. He's still afraid of people he doesn't know."

She released the tray on the chair and lifted him up and into her arms. Poor little guy. It would take him a long time to get over all his fears.

Aaron looked startled. "I'm sure you're right." His tone was apologetic. "I'm sorry I upset him, but I'm totally out of my element around babies. Maybe I should go rent a motel room and get settled in, then come back later when he's asleep."

A wave of shame swept through Mariah. What was the matter with her, anyway? Why was she so quick to chide him for something that wasn't his fault, and that he was striving hard to overcome. She knew he was inexperienced and uncomfortable with small children. That had been one of the judge's reasons for denying him custody of his nephew. Aaron was looking to her to teach him what he didn't know, not scold him for it!

Tommy was still crying, but not so fearfully now, and she put him down in his playpen, then straightened and looked at Aaron. "No, I'm sorry," she said contritely. "I had no right to be sharp with you. You were so happy to see him, and it was natural that you'd be disappointed when he shied away from you. Please don't leave now. He'll quiet down when I give him his bottle. Besides, he'll never get to know you if you avoid him."

Aaron shrugged. "Whatever you think is best," he said, but she heard the hurt in his voice.

She picked Tommy up again and changed him, then warmed his bottle and settled with him in the rocking chair not far from Aaron, who sat on the couch. The child's mouth opened like a baby bird's and Mariah inserted the nipple. He closed his lips around it and sucked contentedly.

Aaron watched the peaceful madonnalike scene with both awe and dread. Awe that this young woman who'd never had children of her own could know instinctively how to handle them. Especially this small boy, who had a deep-seated anguish no baby should have to experience. Still she seemed to know exactly how to soothe, and calm, and banish the fears and pain that tormented the child. Was this true of all women? He suspected not, but on the other hand he had no way of knowing for sure.

Was Judge Gibson right? Did a baby need a mother in order to be happy and psychologically sound? He was beginning to suspect the judge knew what he was talking about after all.

The thought increased Aaron's feelings of dread. Was he wrong to insist on custody of Tommy? He'd felt so strongly that the youngster should be raised by his own family. If he'd known who the baby's father was, and his family were responsible people, Aaron would never have objected to the paternal grandparents or aunts and uncles adopting his nephew. He agreed that whenever possible it was better to be a part of an old-fashioned family—father, mother and siblings. But, lacking that, was he just being pigheaded to insist that the child would be better off with him than with strangers who could provide him that type of upbringing?

Mariah shifted uneasily as she rocked the suckling infant. The quiet in the house was becoming oppressive. Aaron hadn't spoken a word since she'd started giving Tommy his bottle. He just sat across from her looking sad and lonely and off somewhere in a world of his own.

Was he brooding over his nephew's continuing rejection of him? It was possible. She didn't really know him very well, but he didn't seem the type to be so thin-skinned. Was he resentful because Tommy so obviously preferred her? But it was only natural that the baby would. She was the one who took care of him, nurtured him.

Maybe Aaron was just exhausted. These past two weeks must have been pure hell for him.

"Aaron," she said softly. "Are you all right? You're so quiet...."

He looked at her and blinked. "I'm fine. Sorry, I was just thinking. Is the baby asleep?"

She glanced down at Tommy's closed eyes and busily working mouth. "Almost, but he's not going to give in completely until the milk's all gone. Your young nephew has a healthy appetite."

Aaron chuckled and his gloomy expression brightened. "I'm glad to hear it. He didn't get it from his mother. Eileen was always a picky eater. She practically lived on junk foods. Even when she was pregnant she wouldn't modify her diet to include healthy things."

His countenance darkened again, and Mariah knew it was difficult for him to talk about his dead sister. Still, he had to do it sometime, and avoiding the subject would only prolong his reticence. "Did you get answers to any of your questions about her while you were in New York City?"

He sighed. "I learned that she'd been less than truthful with me in her letters and phone calls about her living conditions," he said. "She'd indicated that she and her friend, Charlene, had a charming studio apartment in Greenwich Village. It turned out to be a studio apartment, all right. One dark, crummy room, with a dirty bathroom which they shared with the other tenants at the far end of the hall. The furniture was ratty and the only thing they had to cook on was a hot plate."

His expression turned grim. "Can you imagine trying to take care of an infant in a place like that?"

Mariah was shocked. "But why did she live there? You said she was a model. I thought they made good money."

"So did I," he said bitterly, "but it turns out that for every one who hits it big there are hundreds who just barely manage to survive. Eileen conveniently forgot to tell me she was one of those."

He ran his fingers through his hair. "I managed to track down Charlene. She'd gotten married and moved out a few weeks ago, but she's still trying to make it as a model and she explained the situation. It seems that rental space on the crowded island of Manhattan is so scarce that the rents are astronomical. Charlene told me what they were paying for that slum, and it was unbelievable. She assured me it was the best they could afford, and they were lucky to get it."

Mariah glanced down at Tommy, and he was sound asleep. She excused herself and left to put him in his crib. When she returned she sat down beside Aaron on the couch.

"I'm sorry to have interrupted you," she said. "Please go on."

He smiled at her and took her hand. "Tommy's a lucky little guy to get you for a caretaker. It's a pleasure to watch you with him. You're so loving, and so comfortable with him. Not like me. I'm scared to death I'll drop him, or hold him too tight, or not tight enough. No wonder he clings to you."

She thrilled at the feel of her hand in his. "Does it bother you that he clings to me?"

He thought for a moment. "No, at least not the way you mean. I'm not jealous, just upset because I'm so incompetent . . . so clumsy with him. I want to do what's best for him, but I'm not sure what that is."

She was touched by his uncertainty. "But you love him, don't you?"

He grimaced. "I don't know whether I do or not. I haven't had much experience with love, at least not the nurturing kind."

Mariah's eyes widened.

"I was never abused by my parents, but I never felt loved, either. Eileen and I were both well taken care of as children, but always by competent housekeepers or nannies. Our parents were busy working. Mom was a college professor and Dad a lawyer."

He looked at her and squeezed her hand. "I don't mean to sound like the poor little rich kid. For one thing, we weren't rich, just comfortably well-off, and for another I'm quite sure our parents loved us in their own way, they just never told us so. Neither of them was at all demonstrative, but they gave us everything material we needed or wanted."

Mariah had trouble empathizing with cold and unloving parents. Her own had always been so very warm and affectionate. Her family hugged and kissed each other every chance they got.

"But you nurtured Eileen after your parents died," she reminded him. "Surely you—"

"I didn't nurture her," he said flatly. "She was a teenager and I took charge of her. You can see how badly I screwed up on that. Maybe I'm not the right person to raise Tommy. It's just possible that judge was right in his assessment."

Mariah was incensed by his skewed reasoning. "I don't believe that for a minute and neither do you," she said hotly. "You took on the challenge and completed it. You did the best you could. It's not your fault your sister was strong-willed and stubborn. It was part of her character."

Aaron released her hand and put his arms around her, pulling her close against the muscled strength of his chest. "I knew there was a good reason I was in such a tearing hurry to get back here to you. It's because you're so sweet and warm and understanding. You make me feel so much more confident of my motives and better about myself."

Her heart sped up, and she snuggled into his embrace. "I'm only pointing out the obvious," she said dreamily. "You're a special type of man, who accepts responsibilities even when they're not really yours to take on, and then works hard to see them through. In the case of Tommy, that will take at least eighteen years, so don't tell me there's anything lacking in your character."

She raised her head and looked at him. "Aaron, don't you know you're the stuff that heroes are made of?"

She saw the blush that reddened his cheeks, but his expression told her it was a blush of pleasure rather than embarrassment. She was glad she could please him. He'd had so much grief lately, and besides, he pleased her every time he looked at her in that special way, or touched her.

"Believe me, I'm no hero," he said gruffly, but there was a touch of gratitude in his tone that he couldn't disguise.

She lowered her head to his shoulder again. "To my way of thinking you are, but we can argue about that later. Tell me what else you learned in New York City. Were you able to find out why Eileen was traveling in this part of the state?"

He settled back with her in his arms and sighed. "No, I wasn't. The apartment manager knew she was gone, but didn't know where. I talked to the people at the modeling agency that handled her, and they said she didn't have any out-of-town shoots. Charlene hadn't seen her in a while, but they talked on the phone now and then. She said Eileen had recently started dating a man that she was quite taken with. His first name was Rod, but that's all Charlene knew about him."

"But surely she must have told somebody where she was going and why," Mariah commented.

"If she did I couldn't find them. Manhattan is such a big, sprawling, impersonal place. Even the other tenants in the brownstone where she lived knew her only by sight, and to the people at the agency she was just another model. I doubt that she had any close friends in the city except Charlene, and they'd known each other in Salt Lake City before either of them ever moved to New York."

Mariah put her hand on Aaron's chest and gently rubbed it. "I guess it doesn't matter where she was going or why, but I can understand your frustration at not knowing. Will you return to Utah soon?"

His muscles tightened under her palm. "That depends on the court. If the appellate judge agrees to let me take Tommy back with me until the question of custody is settled I'll leave as soon as possible, but if he rules against me then I don't know what I'll do. Which reminds me . . ." He glanced at his watch. "I need to call Quimby and see how he's coming with the appeal, but he's probably still out to lunch...."

The sharp ring of the telephone made them both jump. "I'll get it." Extracting herself from his arms, Mariah reached for the phone on the small table at the end of the sofa.

A man's voice answered her greeting. "Mariah, this is Nathan Quimby. Do you know if Aaron's back in town yet? I can't reach him at his number in Salt Lake City."

Talk about coincidences! "He's right here, Nate. Arrived just a short while ago. Hold on just a second."

She handed the receiver to Aaron. "It's Nate. He's been trying to contact you in Utah."

Aaron was surprised to receive a call from the man he'd just been discussing, but all he really wanted was to get Mariah back in his arms again. She was so soft and round. She unknowingly did such erotic things to him by just putting her hands on him. It was almost as disturbing as it was exciting. It had been a while since he'd had a woman, but not *that* long. Why did he respond so quickly and so erotically to this one? He'd missed her, sure, but it wasn't as if they were lovers.

"Nate, hi," he said. "I was just telling Mariah I needed to call you."

"Speak of the devil, eh?" Nate said with a laugh. "I'm glad you're back. I have some good news and some bad news. Any chance you could come by the office right now? I have a few minutes before my next appointment."

"Be right there," Aaron said, and was just about to hand the phone back to Mariah when Nate spoke again.

"You may want to bring Mariah with you," he said. "This could concern her, too."

Oh, God, what now? Aaron thought as he hung up the phone.

Chapter Seven

Mariah asked her mother to come over and sit with the sleeping baby. Fifteen minutes later she and Aaron were greeted by Nate as they entered his office.

"Good to see you again," Nate said as they all shook hands, then settled down in chairs around the desk. "I'll come right to the point. The good news is that the appellate court has agreed to hear your appeal. The bad news is that they won't rule on your request to take the child back to Utah while waiting for their decision on permanent custody."

He settled back as if to give them time to digest this latest development. Mariah's head spun as she tried to figure out just what all this meant. It was great that the court was going to hear Aaron's appeal. Surely they would overturn Judge Gibson's narrow-minded decision, but why wouldn't they let Aaron take Tommy home with him? Surely it was the only sensible thing to do.

"What in hell is the reasoning on that?" Aaron said angrily. "I can't stay here until they review the case and rule on it, but neither can I just *leave* Tommy!"

"I know this has come as a shock," Nate said, "but to tell the truth I'm not surprised. The appellate court doesn't want to rule on the case piecemeal. It's not only time-consuming but it's also a courtesy to Judge Gibson. If it's going to overturn another judge's ruling it wants to do it all at once and not drag it out. Same thing if it lets the ruling stand."

"Gibson doesn't deserve any courtesy," Aaron grumbled.

Nate's expression hardened. "Yes, he does. Judge Gibson was a good jurist for a very long time. He deserves consideration for that if nothing else. He's also been an upstanding member of the community as well as his church. Unfortunately age and bad health have robbed him of his sharp mind and keen judgment. The law community in this district will take appropriate action, but it will be done with dignity and respect for the excellent service he has rendered in the past."

Aaron slumped in his chair. "Okay, I see your point, but you'll have to forgive me if I take exception to him putting me through this purgatory."

Nate's face brightened. "No one's blaming you. You've got a right to be upset, but we've got a sticky situation here. No one wants to see the old guy broken and humiliated. We just want to get him off the bench with as little damage to his past reputation as possible."

Aaron straightened. "Meanwhile what am I supposed to do? I have to work in order to support my nephew, but if he's here and I'm two thousand miles away it's going to be pretty damn hard to bond with him, as the psychologists call it."

Nate looked thoughtful. "It's a knotty problem no matter how you look at it. Too bad you're not married. Is there a special woman in your life? Someone you might be involved with in a long-term relationship? A possible fiancée? That might be enough to convince Judge Gibson to relent on letting you take the baby back to Utah while the appeal is being heard."

Aaron shook his head. "No, there's not. I've never been interested in getting involved in a live-in, or even a long-term arrangement, with any of the women I've gone out with. Besides I've already told Gibson I'm not planning marriage in the near future."

"Then I'm afraid you have no choice but to leave Tommy here with Mariah while you go back to Salt Lake City and wait for the court to rule on the custody issue," Nate said. "I'm sorry, but I just don't see any other way."

Mariah had been sitting quietly listening without interrupting, but the more the two men talked the more upset she became.

"How can a panel of people who are supposed to be intelligent enough to make life-and-death decisions about other people's lives, put an incompetent jurist's tender ego ahead of the welfare of an orphaned infant?" she demanded angrily.

Both men looked up, startled. "That's not exactly what's happening," Nate said. "They have no reason to doubt that you'll take good care of Tommy."

She pushed her chair back and stood. "Of course I'll take good care of him, but that's not the issue. It's his emotional well-being I'm concerned about."

She put her palms flat down on the desk and leaned over it as she glared defiantly at Nate. "The longer he stays with me the more dependent on me he becomes. Not just physically but emotionally, as well. He's been through a terrible experience. I don't know how much he remembers, but I do know that he wakes up at times screaming with fear and anxiety, and he clings to me.

"In several months, when he's taken away from me—and he will be, whether he's awarded to Aaron or put up for adoption by strangers—it will be like losing his mother all over again. He's too young to understand about death, but he'll recognize abandonment, and he may never recover from it."

Nate's eyes widened, but his voice was calm when he spoke. "You may be right, Mariah, but I've already explained this to the judges. They apparently didn't think it was too serious a problem because they ruled against us anyway."

"Then they're idiots," she exclaimed as she straightened up and began to pace. "They've probably never had children of their own."

"I hesitate to point this out," Nate said, "but neither have you. Also, you're not considered an expert on child development, so I'm afraid your words wouldn't hold any more weight than mine did. Besides, you wouldn't want to antagonize the appellate court. It's Aaron's last hope of gaining custody of his nephew."

She plopped herself back down in her chair. "You're right, the judges probably wouldn't take kindly to me pointing out that they can't tell the difference between the welfare of a baby and the conceit of an arrogant old colleague."

Nate grinned and looked at Aaron. "I'm afraid you hired the wrong advocate, fella. You should have let Mariah represent you. She'd have talked those judges into awarding you custody of every kid in the district who needs a home."

Aaron grinned back. "I'm sure of it. That's why I called you instead. One baby is all I can handle, and I'm not doing all that great with him."

He stood up and reached down for her hand. "Come on, Miss Counselor, I guess we've accomplished about everything we can here."

When Aaron and Mariah returned home, Jessica was walking the floor with a screaming Tommy.

"What happened?" Mariah asked anxiously as she took the child from her mother.

Jessica handed him over to her with alacrity. "I don't know. He woke up about ten minutes ago crying, but when I went into the bedroom to get him he took one look at me and started screaming. He's been like that ever since."

Mariah could barely hear her mother over the noise of Tommy's howls, but she caught the gist of it. "He's afraid of everybody but me," she explained. "I'm sorry, Mom, I shouldn't have left him." She never had before. Since bringing him home with her from the hospital, she'd been with him at all times.

Aaron stood by the door looking bewildered and concerned, but she didn't try to talk to him over the racket. Instead she sat down in the rocker and rocked the frightened child.

Gradually his crying subsided to shuddering sighs and then occasional hiccups. Mariah noticed that her mother had taken Aaron into the kitchen, and she smelled coffee perking. It reminded her that it was two o'clock and she hadn't had lunch yet. Probably Aaron hadn't either.

When Tommy started to wiggle and try to climb off her lap, she put him in the playpen, gently soothing him with soft words and his favorite toys. When he was settled and seemed content she went into the kitchen.

To her delight Jessica had just finished making a plateful of sandwiches and warming up chicken noodle soup. As they sat at the round oak table eating, Aaron told Jess about their visit with the attorney.

"You'd have been proud of your daughter," he finished with a twinkle in his eye. "If Nate had been a judge he'd have awarded me custody right then and there. You and Cliff really should have encouraged her to study law. She'd have been a great attorney."

Jessica laughed and patted her daughter's hand. "We always knew she'd excel at anything she tried, but she never indicated an interest in law. Have you decided what you're going to do now?"

Aaron shook his head. "I don't seem to have much choice. I have to get back to work. I'm a partner in the accounting firm, and I can't be gone indefinitely, but I hate to leave the full responsibility for Tommy to Mariah. Not that she's not capable. She is, much more so than I am. But I'm worried about what will happen when he's taken away from her and uprooted again. After the scene we walked in on just a short time ago, I understand even better what she was telling Nate."

"Have you registered at a motel yet?" Jessica asked.

"No, I haven't. I came right here when I got into town."

"Good," she said. "Cliff and I would like you to stay with us while you're here. We have the room now that three of our kids are no longer living with us. You're more than welcome to stay."

Mariah was both surprised and pleased. Neither of her parents had said anything to her about inviting Aaron to stay at the family home. She could see that Aaron was also surprised.

"That's awfully nice of you," he replied. "But are you sure?"

"Very sure," Jessica said with a smile. "You'll be close enough to get better acquainted with your nephew, and staying here with us should also put your mind at rest about trusting Tommy to us for the next several months."

"I've never doubted Mariah's ability to care for him," Aaron protested. "But if it won't put you out too much, I'd love to stay with you for a few days. I'll pay room and board of course."

"Don't be silly," Jessica said briskly. "You'll be our guest. You're welcome to bring your things over anytime."

Late that night, after Aaron had moved into the Bentley's comfortable guest room that, according to Mariah, had once been hers and her sister Linda's, he tossed restlessly in the soft warm bed. He'd been exhausted when he retired and was sure he'd sleep soundly, but every time he started to doze off the image of Mariah in Nate's office eloquently expressing her fears for Tommy jolted him fully awake again.

She'd been so passionately concerned about the baby's emotional welfare, and the things she said rang chillingly true. It was all such a mixed-up mess, and there only seemed to be one reasonably workable solution. *Find a woman to pose as his fiancée and tell the judge he was going to be married....* It was pretty weak, Aaron thought, but it just might work.

On the other hand, the scheme would be a lot stronger if he could convince one of the women he'd been dating lately to actually go through a wedding ceremony with him. A marriage of convenience! They could sign a prenuptial agreement that would release them both from their vows after Aaron was awarded custody of the child. It probably wouldn't be legally binding, but it would spell out the terms of the arrangement and what was expected of each of the parties in a divorce settlement.

Aaron rolled over and pounded his pillow. It was kind of a wild scheme, but it just might work. He'd think about it more tomorrow.

He burrowed his head into the pillow and realized that the wind had picked up and was rustling leaves and blowing tree branches against the house. Probably also ushering in another snowstorm. Were Mariah and Tommy all right over there in that little cottage by themselves?

He groaned and flopped over onto his back. Didn't he have enough to worry about without including a capable and independent woman like Mariah? She was twenty-six years old and had been taking care of herself since she got out of high school. Besides, she was used to mountain storms, and she sure didn't need him hovering over her.

He rolled over onto his other side and closed his eyes. He'd think of something else, such as which one of the women he knew intimately could be approached with his proposition of a temporary marriage of convenience. It would have to be someone willing to play the part of the blushing bride, even down to moving into his house. Although they'd be more than half a continent away from New York, Tommy would still be a ward of the Apple Junction court, and their child-welfare people would probably check up on him from time to time.

That would eliminate any woman with a big family, or a large circle of friends. There would be too many people to deceive.

Even more important he needed a woman who was good with infants. He wouldn't actually expect her to take care of the child. He'd hire a nanny for that, but Tommy had special emotional needs that only someone like Mariah could understand and soothe.

But where was he going to find someone like Mariah? She was an original—and what was she doing in his mental search for a wife, anyway? Even the thought of approaching her with such a proposition was unthinkable. She was too unsettling to his precarious peace of mind. Besides, she'd never go for it.

He punched his pillow and shifted to his other side again.

The image of an attractive blonde flashed into his mind. Polly. She was exactly the type of woman he needed, warm and cheerful, and she liked kids. She'd make someone a wonderful wife, but not him. She was the clinging type who'd never let him go once the marriage vows were said no matter what she agreed to beforehand. Come to think of it, that was the reason he'd eased her gently out of his life. She'd started talking about marriage, and he wasn't the marrying kind. He wouldn't hurt her by letting her expect more than he was willing to give.

So who? He had a lot of woman friends. Why did his mind keep coming up blank, or with unsuitable candidates?

The minutes ticked by into hours, and by the time the old grandfather clock downstairs chimed two he was no closer to a solution. He'd considered dozens of women, ones he knew well and ones he knew only slightly, but he was obviously hoping for the impossible. Someone who was innocent but mature, independent but willing to follow his rules, strongly maternal but able to step completely out of Tommy's life after a few months, and morally upright but eager to be a part of this unsavory scheme to deceive a sitting judge.

He snorted with self-disgust. Who did he think he was kidding? There wasn't a woman in the world who wouldn't run screaming in the other direction if he approached her with such a stupid list of requirements.

He took a deep breath and gave up all thoughts of sleep. So now he was right back to square one, and the only woman he wanted for the position. The woman he'd been resolutely pushing out of his mind and his heart because he could never present her with such a one-sided and self-serving brainstorm.

Mariah! The only person he knew who was so unselfish and innocent that she had an angel watching over her!

He sat bolt upright in bed and swung his feet to the floor. Damn. Where had that thought come from? He didn't believe in angels. So why did his subconscious badger him with such a possibility?

He propped his elbows on his thighs and dropped his head in his hands. It was probably because if there were such things as angels and one of them needed help on her earthly mission, Mariah Bentley was the person she would appeal to. He sincerely doubted that Mariah had ever turned anybody down when they asked for assistance, and that was the reason he couldn't enlist her in his proposed deception.

He wasn't going to be responsible for tainting that innocence.

The following morning Mariah received a call from Judge Gibson's secretary. She'd just finished bathing Tommy and was instructing Aaron in the proper way to put on a diaper when the phone rang. She quickly finished her task, then lifted the baby and carried him with her to the sofa where she sat down and reached for the instrument. The little guy had put up only a minimum amount of fuss when Aaron appeared on their doorstep shortly after breakfast, but she knew better than to leave him with his uncle while she was out of sight.

"Mariah, this is Edna at Judge Gibson's office," said the voice at the other end of the line.

Mariah's heart sank. Now what? "Yes, Edna, what can I do for you?"

"The judge would like to see you. Could you come in at eleven o'clock?"

A breath of apprehension blew across the back of Mariah's neck. "Well, sure, I suppose so." She managed to keep her voice calm. "Can you tell me what this is about?"

"No, I'm sorry, he didn't say." The secretary's tone was crisp but friendly. "We'll see you in about an hour, then?"

Mariah confirmed the appointment and hung up, then turned to find Aaron hovering over her. "Trouble?" he asked.

"It was Judge Gibson's secretary," she told him, then repeated Edna's side of the conversation.

Aaron muttered an oath. "What do you suppose he wants?"

"I haven't the slightest idea, but it's not likely to be anything good." She hesitated a moment, then asked. "Do you want to go with me?"

"I sure do," he said grimly.

When they arrived at the judge's office Mariah was carrying Tommy, and the three of them were ushered right in. Gibson looked up and eyed Aaron with distaste. "I don't remember asking you to come, too," he grumbled.

On the way over Aaron had been thoroughly briefed by Mariah about proper behavior, and he knew better than to antagonize the judge all over again. Instead he held his temper and murmured politely, "You didn't, sir, but if it's all right with you I'd very much like to stay."

"Oh, all right, but one peep out of you and out you go." He switched his gaze to Mariah and nodded toward Tommy, who was sitting on her lap. "Is he going to cry?"

She was equally anxious not to upset him. "I don't think so, Your Honor. Not as long as I'm holding him."

"Gonna make a damn mama's boy out of the kid," Gibson rasped.

"I'm not his mama," she reminded the judge, "but I'm trying to help him overcome the fears he's had since his mother was killed in the car accident."

Gibson cleared his throat. "Yes, well, that's what I wanted to see you about. What's all this nonsense I've been reading in the papers about you seeing an angel?"

She found it difficult not to cringe. "That's a lot of media hype, Your Honor. I thought I saw a woman dressed in white standing in the road the night of the accident that killed Tommy's mother. When I tried to stop, I was afraid I had hit her."

"Well, did you?" Gibson asked gruffly.

Mariah's heart was pounding, but she strove to keep her tone cool and her voice from shaking. "Apparently not. I called Dad, and he and the deputies searched the area but found no trace of the woman. They did find the wrecked car, though, with Tommy in it and just barely alive. That's what saved his life."

"Then why did you tell the reporters you'd seen an angel?" the judge asked. "If you're going to go around making statements like that I don't know if I can leave the child in your care—"

His words sent a bolt of shock down Mariah's spine. "Judge Gibson," she cried, "I've never told anyone I saw an angel."

Tommy let out a sharp yell, and she hugged him closer and lowered her voice. "I've denied it every time someone asked about it, but too often the newspeople don't listen. The angel story is much more dramatic than the real one, so they spread it all over the headlines. I'm as appalled as you are."

"That's the truth, Your Honor," Aaron said in spite of the judge's admonition to keep quiet. "She's denied it to me. That unfortunate interpretation was not her fault."

Gibson glared at him. "I told you to be quiet."

Aaron closed his mouth, but she could see his jawline clench in an effort to hold back a protest.

"Your Honor, please don't take Tommy away from me," Mariah begged, then repeated the same impassioned plea she'd given Nate about Tommy's emotional vulnerability.

When she'd finished the judge didn't speak for several minutes. When he did it was with a note of authority. "Mariah, because I've been a long-time friend of your family I'm inclined to believe you, but if these wild stories go on much longer I'm going to be forced to rescind your temporary child-care license and put the boy in a different home."

Mariah was too stunned to react, but Aaron wasn't. His face was red with anger as he jumped out of his chair. "Damn it, Judge, you can't do that. I won't allow it—"

"You are in contempt of court," the judge bellowed.

Tommy opened his little mouth and screamed as Aaron roared. "Oh, no, I'm not. We're not in court."

Gibson also stood. "When you're in my chambers you're in court," he said, and raised his voice to a shout that could be heard in the anteroom even above the baby's screams. "Edna, send a bailiff in here to escort this hot-tempered idiot to jail!"

Several hours later Aaron was sitting at a table in the public library with a book open before him. He had no intention of reading, but he needed a warm, quiet place where he could think without being interrupted.

His unfortunate outburst in the judge's chambers had cost him a lot of time and money before Nate finally managed to talk Gibson out of having Aaron booked into the slammer. He knew he hadn't done his petition for custody any good, but he didn't regret his protest. Tommy was his family, and he'd do anything to keep him even if it meant asking for help.

The judge's threat to take his nephew from Mariah and place him with strangers was totally unacceptable. Aaron had known his little sister well enough to know she'd want him to raise her baby now that she was gone and couldn't do it herself. He wasn't going to let her down, even if it meant clouding the rose-colored view of life enjoyed by another woman who was rapidly becoming very dear to him.

There was no way around it. He was going to have to ask Mariah to become a knowing accomplice in the deception he was planning. It was the only way he could be sure that she could continue to care for Tommy, and that Aaron wouldn't lose control of the child until the matter of custody was settled.

He thought about discussing it with his attorney first, but decided against it. He couldn't take the chance of word getting around about what he intended to do, and the best way to assure that was by not talking to anyone about it but Mariah.

He clutched the back of his neck in a gesture of anguish. The idea of asking her to participate in this little charade with him made his stomach turn. He doubted that she'd ever told a lie. Well…at least not a very big one. He felt like the devil incarnate for even thinking about asking her to tell a real whopper, not only to the judge but to her family and the whole town, then compound it by living with him for months.

Even worse, Mariah was a distinct threat to his well-being. She was becoming more important to him every day, it worried him. He wasn't ready to settle down permanently with a wife. To make matters worse, if she accepted his limited proposal he'd have to assure her it did not include the wifely duty of making love. With Mariah it would have to be strictly a marriage in name only. She'd never agree to a temporary sexual relationship, and he'd be a bastard if he tried to seduce her.

He wasn't at all sure he had enough self-control to live with her in the same house as man and wife for a prolonged length of time and not touch her. He sure didn't relish subjecting himself to that degree of torment, but if she would agree to help him he'd honor any restrictions she wanted.

Aaron had dinner with Mariah at her house that evening. She had invited him so that he and Tommy could spend as much time together as possible. So they'd get to know each other better. But in her heart she knew that was just an excuse. What she really wanted was for Aaron to spend more time with *her*, so he could get to know her better.

She knew he was attracted to her. The magnetism between them was not one-sided. When he touched her, held her, the enticement was too powerful to be a figment of her imagination, but she also knew that he fought that attraction. He didn't want to get emotionally involved with her. He'd made that clear.

Unfortunately, she wanted to get involved with him. She'd never met a man who affected her so strongly, and in such a short period of time. Aaron was everything she'd always wanted in a husband, handsome, well-educated, successful, and sensitive to her needs. She was very much afraid she was falling in love with him, and she wasn't willing to let him get away from her without at least exploring their feelings for each other.

She'd been as upset as Aaron earlier when the judge had threatened to take Tommy away from her. Since then, she'd been giving a lot of thought to the earlier conversation with Nate. If Aaron were engaged to be married, Judge Gibson just might change his mind about letting him take Tommy back to Utah. And if Mariah was the woman he was engaged to, it could make the argument even more compelling. She could go back to Salt Lake City with them and get a job and an apartment there, at least until the question of permanent custody was settled.

Just maybe during that time Aaron would discover that he loved her, too.

Tommy was much more cordial toward Aaron that evening, and even let his uncle spoon pureed vegetables and fruit into his mouth as he banged another spoon on the plastic tray of his high chair. Mariah was pleased to see that Aaron was really quite proficient at feeding, and seemed to enjoy talking nonsense to the child to get him to open his mouth.

When they finished eating Aaron cleaned up the kitchen while Mariah put the baby to bed. Afterwards they more or less collapsed on the sofa in the living room.

"I don't understand how Eileen found time to model," he groused as he relaxed against the cushions. "Caring for that little son of hers is like chasing down a whirlwind. Are you sure you have the energy and the time to look after him twenty-four hours a day for months? More to the point, do you want to, now that you've found out how much work it is?"

That was the opening Mariah had been waiting for, and she pounced on it. "Yes, I'm sure, to both questions. In fact, I wanted to talk to you about something. I can't let Judge Gibson take Tommy away from me, but neither can I control the exaggerations and excesses the tabloids seem determined to print."

He looked pensive. "I know. I've been thinking—"

"Please, let me finish what I was going to say," she interrupted. She was afraid she'd lose her nerve if she didn't tell him her plan right now. "Yesterday, Nate suggested you produce a long-term girlfriend, and see if that wouldn't satisfy Gibson's requirement so you can take Tommy back to Utah. It's really not a bad idea. But I've been thinking that it would be even better if you produced an engagement."

She took a deep breath and hurried on. "I think you should try it, Aaron, and if you'd like I'll volunteer to be the fiancée."

There, it was out, and it hadn't really been all that bad. He looked a little stunned, but all he could do was either accept or reject her offer.

He blinked, then stared at her as he slowly straightened up. "Mariah..." He sounded as if he'd just had the breath knocked out of him.

Again she interrupted to rush ahead. "If you have someone else in mind that's okay, but I just thought—"

"Mariah." This time he interrupted her. "I can't tell you how much I appreciate your sacrifice. I spent most of last night thinking about that possibility, but the more I examined it the more I realized that an engagement just isn't a strong enough reason for a judge as stubborn as Gibson to reverse his own ruling. Especially since I've already told him I hadn't yet met a woman I wanted to spend the rest of my life with."

Mariah crumpled like a pricked balloon. "Oh," she breathed as she sank back and rubbed her hands over her face. "You're no doubt right. I guess I just didn't think it all the way through."

Aaron moved closer and took her in his arms. He held her so tenderly, as if she were fragile and might break, and he rubbed his cheek in her hair. "There's nothing wrong with your thinking," he murmured softly. "You just didn't carry it to the next logical conclusion."

He raised his head, then put his fingers beneath her chin and lifted her face so he could look into her eyes. "Mariah, is there any chance you'd agree to be my wife instead of my fiancée?"

Chapter Eight

For a moment shock left Mariah speechless. She felt the color rush to her face, but all she could do was gape at Aaron.

Wife? Did he mean wife? As in husband and wife? Marriage?

Then it hit her. No, that isn't what he meant at all. He was talking about a sham marriage instead of a sham engagement.

She swallowed, then opened her mouth and prayed that she could form words that were coherent. "You can't be serious!"

Well, it wasn't exactly the most brilliant statement she'd ever made, but it sounded clear and concise.

She watched the blood drain from his face. "I'm sorry," he said anxiously. "I had no right to ask you that question. Just forget I said anything. You've already done so much for me."

"No, Aaron, that's not what I mean," she hastened to assure him. "I'd be willing to pose as your wife, but we'd never get away with it. We couldn't fake a wedding. The judge would want to see the marriage license, and proof that the vows had been spoken."

Aaron shook his head. "I'm not talking about a fake marriage, I'm proposing a real one. That is a...a marriage of convenience, I believe they're called. We'd have a wedding, all nice and legal, but with the understanding that neither of us were bound by the vows. That once the custody issue is settled, either for or against me, you would file for divorce or annulment and we could get on with our separate lives."

Mariah couldn't believe what she was hearing. He wanted her to go through a wedding ceremony with him, but only for a limited time and they would not consider themselves married? That was asking an awful lot of her!

The idea of being Aaron's wife was both intriguing and exciting, but not on his terms. When she took that important step she wanted a husband who loved her and was as determined as she to make their marriage rock-solid with children and a lifelong commitment.

A feigned ceremony such as he was proposing didn't fit that bill at all!

The touch of his hand on her shoulder startled her out of her musing, and she focused her gaze on his regretful expression. "Mariah, I've offended you," he said apologetically, "and that was never my intention. I'm so sorry. It's a stupid idea and I never should have brought it up."

He looked so tormented that she put out her hand and caressed his cheek. "I'm not offended, but I need a few minutes to think before I answer you."

He took her hand and kissed the palm. "Take all the time you need. Do you mind if I hold your hand while you think?"

"It ... it does make it hard for me to be objective," she confessed, then felt abandoned when he released her and moved a few inches away so they were no longer touching.

There was no doubt about it, Aaron was a good man and she was strongly attracted to him. It was also true that he was in an impossible bind. He was only trying to do what was best for his nephew. And it wouldn't disrupt her immediate plans, since she didn't have any. She'd just moved back to Apple Junction and had no job, so what harm could it do?

Besides, she loved little Tommy and was going to find it extremely difficult to give him up when the time came. This way she could continue to take care of him much longer than she'd anticipated.

There was one thing she had to know, though, before she made a decision. "Aaron," she said hesitantly, "what did you mean when you said we could get a divorce *or an annulment?* Would this marriage be consummated or not?"

He looked taken aback. "Well, that will be up to you. You're a temptingly warm and desirable woman and I would like very much to make love to you. But, you have to want it as much as I do. If you don't, I promise I won't bother you with unwanted attentions."

Unwanted? His attentions most certainly wouldn't be unwanted. In fact, dreaming of his passionate "attentions" had been all she could think of lately, but having sex with him on a temporary basis would be most unwise. He'd said nothing about love, and she wasn't sure of the depth of her feelings, either. She suspected that if the two of them ever became intimate it could easily break her heart when he sent her away.

Right now, though, she had questions of a different nature. "Just what does this involve? How deeply into deception would it take us?"

He shifted uncomfortably. "Much more so than either of us would want. Look, let's just forget about it. I'll find some other way to get around the judge's ruling."

She held up her hand. "Don't be in such a hurry to trash the idea. Tell me about it. Exactly what do you have in mind?"

For a moment she thought he wasn't going to answer, but then he sighed and met her gaze. "The way I've worked it out, we'll announce to everyone who will listen that we've fallen in love and are going to get married right away because I have to get back to Utah and my business and I don't want to leave without you. We'll invite everyone to the wedding, including Judge Gibson. Then he'll see that we can give Tommy the traditional family-type upbringing he feels is so important. If he won't reverse his original decision, hopefully he will at least let us take the baby with us when we leave."

She shook her head in dismay. "Aaron, do you have any idea how long it takes to put together a wedding of that size? Months! We'd have to reserve the church, arrange for attendants, shop for appropriate clothes for the wedding party, including us, and find a committee of people who are willing to cook a sit-down dinner reception for up to several hundred guests. And that's just the beginning. By the time we were ready to take the vows it would no longer be necessary. The appellate court would have already made a decision."

He groaned. "You're right, I wasn't even thinking about the mechanics involved. If we were to do this it would have to be in the next few days. I guess we might as well forget it."

Mariah was startled to realize that, instead of being relieved that Aaron's wild scheme was impossible, her mind was whirring like a computer, sorting and examining possible alternatives.

"Not necessarily," she said. "We could elope. That's always been a tried-and-true solution for couples who want to get married in a hurry."

He pondered that. "But wouldn't it defeat our purpose? Judge Gibson may be a tyrant, but he's not stupid. Surely he'd suspect right away what we were up to with that kind of maneuver."

She processed that through her whirring mind. "He probably would at first, but if we announced our marriage in the paper and invited everyone to an informal reception with just beverages and cake we could make a big production of spoon-feeding everybody there the story you suggested. You know, how we'd fallen in love and only eloped because you had to return to Salt Lake City very soon and we wanted to be married here before you left because you wanted to take me with you."

She sighed. "Everybody loves a romance. Look how the story of Cinderella has survived through the ages. The judge may be skeptical, but almost everyone else will be delighted to have a real life *affaire de coeur* happening in their midst. Since we would have fulfilled his original requirement for Tommy's guardian I don't think he'd risk having the wrath of the law community down on him again so soon."

"It just might work," Aaron said, sounding more optimistic, "but what about your family? People everywhere thrive on gossip, and few of them are able to keep a juicy piece of news to themselves, especially in a small town like Apple Junction. In order to make this succeed we can't tell anybody what's really going on."

She felt a twinge of annoyance. "Are you saying my family can't be trusted?"

He started to say something but she didn't give him a chance. "I agree that the kids might have trouble keeping it to themselves, but Dad and Mom would never give away our secret."

"I know that," he hastened to assure her, "but I don't think they'd approve of our deception, either. And it's not fair to burden them with our problems. For one thing your Dad's the sheriff. He could get into real trouble if it ever got out that he'd known we were less than truthful with the judge about our actions and did nothing. That would make him an accomplice."

Oh, God, she'd never thought of that! It would also mean that her mother would have to lie to all her friends, and everyone knew Jessica Bentley couldn't fib worth a darn. Besides which, Mom's conscience would bother her all the rest of her life.

"Mariah, this is getting too complicated," Aaron said. "I obviously didn't give it enough thought before approaching you with it. There are too many people who would be hurt if something went wrong. Let's just forget it. I'm not going to jeopardize your family's standing in the community. After all, Tommy isn't your problem, or theirs, he's mine, and I'll find a way to deal with it without involving others."

Aaron was right, the whole thing was just too unwieldy. It would require a major effort to bring off, and she had no right to put her own and her parents' reputations at risk for a man and child she'd never see again once it was over.

She opened her mouth to say so, and was dumbfounded at what came out. "I'm afraid Tommy is my problem, too, Aaron. I'm already too involved with him to just shrug him off as a lost cause. He needs you and I'd never forgive myself if he was passed around to foster-care parents and eventually put up for adoption by strangers. Not if I could possibly have helped to avert it.''

''Sweetheart, that's not likely to happen,'' Aaron said and sent pinpricks of pleasure down her spine with his casual endearment. She suspected he didn't even realize he'd done it, but she was going to pretend to herself that he did.

''Not likely, no,'' she agreed, ''but it could, and I'm not willing to sit back and take that chance. You're right, we can't tell anybody the truth about what motivated our sudden wedding. What do you have in mind once we get past that?''

He ran his fingers through his hair. ''If the judge gives me temporary custody of Tommy, we'll go back to Salt Lake City where I'll introduce you as my wife. We'll live together in my home until the appellate court gives me permanent custody, and then you can file for divorce and get on with your life.''

''And what happens if by some miracle Judge Gibson sets aside his original ruling and gives you permanent custody immediately?'' she asked.

Aaron hesitated. ''I think we can pretty well rule that out, but if it does happen I'm afraid we'd still have to put up a front of being a happily married couple for a few months. If I took the baby and left town without you right after the wedding, Gibson would know that we'd outmaneuvered him, and then even the court of appeals would throw my case out.''

It all sounded pretty cold and calculating. Not at all like the engagement and wedding she'd envisioned all her life. She quickly cut off that line of thinking. What nonsense. She wasn't a teenager anymore. It was time to give up her starry-eyed fantasies of Cinderella and the Prince. Or even Beauty and the Beast. Aaron was no beast, but neither was he a prince. He was just a nice man caught in a predicament he'd neither asked for nor wanted. And he needed her help to resolve it.

Besides, she strongly suspected that although he was neither beast nor prince, he was her Mr. Right. Shouldn't she be willing to gamble that after a few months of living together he would discover that he really did love her and didn't want a divorce after all?

So okay, it was risky, but so was just waking up in the morning. There was also the risk that if she played it safe this time another Mr. Right might never come along, and she'd have thrown away her only chance for a complete and fulfilling future.

Obviously it would be a mistake for her to make an on-the-spot decision about this—one that could affect all the rest of her life.

"I'm not going to give you a yes or no on this tonight, Aaron," she finally said. "I'd at least like to sleep on it. The Thanksgiving holiday weekend starts in just a couple of days, and we couldn't get married until after that, anyway."

Again he took her hand in his and smiled. "By all means take your time. I don't want to rush you into anything. If you decide against it I'll understand, really I will."

He squeezed her hand, then stood up. "I'll leave now and give you some space." He paused. "I'd ask if I could kiss you good-night, but I don't want to seduce or pressure you into making a decision you might regret later."

The offer was too good to resist. She grinned and stood up, too. "Oh, come on, ask. I promise I won't let you pressure me."

He didn't hesitate, but put his arms around her and drew her against him. "May I kiss you good-night, sweetheart?" he murmured into her ear, and this time she knew the endearment was deliberate.

She lifted her face to his and put her arms around his neck. "Please do." Her tone was barely above a whisper.

Their gazes locked, and she watched as he slowly lowered his head to cover her mouth with his own. It was firm, and warm, and her heartbeat jumped as the tip of his tongue rimmed her lips. They opened to him as she melted in his embrace and encouraged his exploration.

Mariah had never experienced anything like this before. It awakened nerve ends she didn't know she had, and she shyly responded.

With a low moan, Aaron broke the contact. "Ah, Mariah, I'm not made of stone," he said raggedly as he trailed kisses down the side of her throat. "I'd better leave now while I still can."

He slowly released her and walked out the door, shutting it quietly behind him.

It took Mariah most of the night to wrestle her libido into submission. Aaron was like playing with fire, and she understood that. But she was in far deeper than she realized. If she knew what was good for her she'd put a stop to this talk of a marriage of convenience and send him back to Utah with all speed. Let him find someone else to play the part of temporary bride. She wasn't tough enough to play games with him. He'd capture her heart and soul and tear her apart without even meaning to.

He wasn't a brutal man, Mariah thought in the early hours before dawn, just thoughtless, especially on the subject of love and matrimony. Obviously he'd never been in love himself. That was even more reason for her to get him out of her life and her mind. He had no idea what it was all about. That made him dangerous. The sooner she got rid of him, and his little nephew, the better.

But, she was hopelessly involved with Tommy. She couldn't love him more if he were her own, but he wasn't hers. He belonged to Aaron, and in order to take care of the baby she had to accept the uncle, too.

Mariah twisted and turned and cursed the dark, but when dawn finally crept over the horizon she reviled it. She'd never get through the day if she hadn't slept worth a damn all night.

Tommy awoke at six-thirty, and Mariah struggled out of bed to bathe and feed him. Fortunately he was happy and didn't object when she put him back down for a morning nap. She crawled into bed, too, and they both slept for a couple of hours. When she woke she felt much more rested and better able to face the difficult decision ahead of her.

She pondered the advantages and disadvantages of Aaron's scheme all day as she baked pumpkin pies and helped her mom get the big house ready for Thanksgiving dinner the following day. Her brother, Ted, the college student, and her married sister, Linda, and her husband, Victor, who lived in Virginia were coming in this evening to spend the long holiday weekend with their families. The couple would be staying with Vic's parents who lived only a few blocks away.

Mariah hadn't seen or heard from Aaron by noon, and his car wasn't in the driveway. When she inquired, Jessica told her he'd left right after breakfast, saying he wanted to explore the countryside.

The pressure to give an answer to his proposal lessened, and Mariah suspected that was why he'd made himself scarce. He didn't want her to think he was hanging around impatiently waiting for her decision. It was just one more indication of what a nice man he was.

About three o'clock Ted came rattling in in the old pickup truck he and Cliff had bought from a salvage company and rebuilt during Ted's last year of high school. They'd barely gotten their joyous reunion over when Linda and Vic drove up in their Classic Thunderbird, a wedding present from Vic's parents and their pride and joy.

Everyone oohed and aahed over Tommy, who seemed uneasily inclined to suffer the attentions of the strangers as long as Mariah held him and didn't let them get too close.

Jessica had already told Ted and Linda about Mariah's strange experience on the night the baby had been found, but now they wanted to hear all the details from her. For what seemed to her about the hundredth time she repeated the story of her encounter on the road as well as all that had happened since.

"Well, he sure is a cute little guy," Ted said, and smiled at Tommy who glared back and snuggled closer against Mariah. "But are you sure you want to tie yourself down for the next several months taking care of someone else's baby? I thought you were going to look for another job."

Patiently she explained that she loved caring for Tommy, and that she'd be paid for it, so it was a job as well as a pleasure.

"When are we going to get to meet Tommy's uncle?" Linda asked. "Mom says he's a real hunk."

Jessica gasped. "I said no such thing! Really, Linda—"

Linda giggled. "Well, not in those words, but I got that impression."

They all laughed except Jess, who blushed. "I'm sorry, Mom," Linda said contritely. "I didn't mean to embarrass you, but you should have gotten used to our slangy expressions by now."

She turned to Mariah. "Tell us about him. What does he look like, and what does he do?"

Mariah looked at her mother and grinned. "Mom's right," she said in a teasing tone, "Aaron is a hunk."

Jessica made a face at her but let it pass.

Mariah turned her attention back to her sister. "He's thirty-one, about six feet tall, slender, with black hair and the most gorgeous dark blue eyes. He's a partner in an accounting firm in Salt Lake City and appears to be doing very well indeed." She wrinkled her nose. "Have I left anything out?"

"Yes, where is he?" her irrepressible sister gushed. "Sounds like great husband material to me, and you're not getting any younger, you know."

Mariah blanched, but hoped nobody noticed. Linda was probing a little too deep into things Mariah didn't want to talk about. She'd forgotten what a tease her twenty-year-old sister could be. Although Linda had been married for nearly a year, she was still a kid at heart.

"I don't know where he is." It came out more snappish than Mariah had intended. "I'm licensed to look after Tommy, not Aaron, but he should be back soon."

"Maybe if you play your cards right you can get a license to take care of Aaron, too," Linda said playfully.

Mariah didn't know how to answer. If she denied any interest in him now, then decided to marry him in a few days, it would look odd, to say the least. On the other hand, if she confessed to an attraction and then decided not to marry him, it would look like he'd dumped her.

Fortunately for her the front door opened. Aaron and her father walked in and she breathed a sigh of relief as they all played the reunion bit with their dad.

Aaron headed for the stairs, presumably to go up to his room, but Mariah caught him by the arm. "Wait, Aaron, my brother and sister want to meet you."

He stopped and turned to face her. "I don't want to interrupt. I'm sure you all have things to talk about."

She chuckled. "Yeah, we do. You. They've been pestering me with questions and are eager to meet you. Please stay."

He chucked Tommy under the chin. "Hi, guy," he said, and got a sour look from the baby in return before he answered. "I'd love to meet the rest of your family."

She put her arm through his and led him back to the group. "Hey, you guys," she called over the talk and laughter, "I'd like you to meet Tommy's uncle." The racket stopped and she continued. "Aaron Kerr, this is my sister, Linda, her husband, Victor, and my brother, Ted."

Linda looked from Aaron to Mariah and impishly lowered her voice to a loud stage whisper. "Geez, Mariah, you were right. He is a hunk."

This time it was her turn to blush while everyone else laughed, including Aaron as he turned to her. "Did you really say that?" he inquired with a grin.

His grin was contagious and brought out one of her own. "What else could I say?" she asked with an elaborate shrug. "I couldn't very well lie."

He laughed again and hugged her and the baby against his side. "Your sister is a remarkable woman," he said to the group. "She's been a godsend to me, and I'll be eternally grateful."

She looked at him, wide-eyed with confusion. Was he just saying that to be polite? She enjoyed his admiration, but gratitude wasn't what she wanted from him. Was he reminding her that was all she was going to get? Or was he setting the stage in case she did agree to elope with him?

He must have read her mind, because as the others turned away from them he brushed her temple with his lips and murmured for her ear only, "No, love, I'm not just sweet-talking you in hopes of convincing you to say yes.

Nor is gratitude the only strong emotion I feel for you. I didn't sleep worth a damn after that kiss last night.''

She relaxed against him. "Neither did I," she confessed, but their close proximity must have squashed Tommy, who was between them, because he let out a yowl and they sprang apart.

Jessica fixed a large kettle of spaghetti, a tossed salad and garlic bread for supper. By the time they were finished eating it was after eight and Tommy was sleepy and cranky. It was definitely his bedtime!

Aaron insisted on carrying the baby across the dark and uneven terrain between the big house and the cottage, even though Tommy screamed until they got home and Aaron again handed him to Mariah.

"I'm afraid he's getting too attached to you," he muttered as the child clung to her and sobbed, "but I don't know what to do about it. You can't be with him twenty-four hours a day. That's not good for either of you."

She swayed and caressed the child soothingly. "You have to give him time, Aaron. He's still looking for his mother, and I'm the closest person he knows to identify with her," she said softly. "There's a bottle of Chardonnay in the cupboard if you'd like a glass while I put Tommy to bed."

"I've had enough to drink," he said, referring to the wine and beer Cliff had served with supper. "But I'll make coffee if it's all right."

"Fine," she said and headed for the bedroom.

Fifteen minutes later, surrounded by the smell of freshly brewed coffee, she stepped into the kitchen and shut the bedroom door behind her. Aaron poured them each a mugful and they carried them to the sofa and sat down.

"Do you know how lucky you are to have such a big and happy family?" Aaron asked as he sipped the hot liquid.

She nodded. "Yes, I do, but it's not always an unmixed blessing. Things sometimes got pretty rowdy around the house when we were all growing up, but I love every one of them, even bratty little Rob who was always telling me I wasn't his mother and he didn't have to mind me."

She laughed. "I was sixteen when he was born, and I'm afraid I was a tad overbearing."

Aaron's expression sobered. "But there was obviously a strong bond of love between you. I was ten when Eileen was born, and I hardly knew her until our parents died. By then it was too late to establish a loving relationship. Hell, we couldn't even manage to be friends."

And now you never will, Mariah thought. How tragic.

It was time to change the subject. "Well, you've sure made friends with my brothers and sisters," she said lightly. "My parents, too."

She almost faltered but took a deep breath and hurried on. "Once they get over the shock of our elopement they'll be delighted to welcome you into the family."

There, she'd said it, and there was no going back on her word. Now the ball was in his court. Did he still want her?

Chapter Nine

Mariah didn't have to wait long for Aaron's reaction. His sober expression faltered, then lightened as her words sank in.

"Are you saying that you'll accept my unorthodox proposal of marriage?" he asked haltingly.

She'd often heard the expression, "butterflies in one's stomach," and now she knew how butterflies felt. "I... I am, if the offer is still open. If you still want to carry out the plan you told me about last night, I'm willing to pose as your wife."

His countenance darkened again. "*Pose* as my wife?"

"I mean... I mean *be* your wife," she stammered. Oh, damn. She was so flustered she couldn't even talk straight. "Um... that is, temporarily of course."

He frowned and set his mug on the coffee table. "I think we'd better be very specific here," he said flatly. "We don't want any misunderstandings about this agreement. Now, tell me exactly what you're willing to do."

This wasn't going at all the way she'd expected it would. Why was he being so cold and impersonal?

"Don't be such a stickler," she admonished. "You know what I mean. I'm agreeing to what we discussed last night."

"And what was that?"

Damn him! He was playing games with her! Making her beg him to marry her!

She slammed her mug down on the table and jumped to her feet. "Forget it," she snapped angrily. "If you've changed your mind, fine, but do me the courtesy of just saying so. I assure you it doesn't matter to me one way or the other. I was only going to do it as a favor to Tommy anyway."

That was a lie, but she was in no mood to retract it.

Aaron stood also. "Mariah, please sit down." He made it sound like she was reluctant to buy insurance from him. "I haven't changed my mind. I'm deeply grateful to you for your willingness to help, but I have to know that you understand just what you are agreeing to."

His condescension was infuriating. "Oh, so now you think I'm stupid, as well as a love-starved spinster who'd do anything to get a man."

"Mariah, *sit down.*" He didn't raise his voice, but his tone was so commanding that she immediately obeyed without thinking.

"If this is the way you treated your sister I can see why she rebelled," Mariah fumed.

"That may be, but you're not my sister, and I'm not responsible for you," he pointed out reasonably. "You're of age. If you're willing to get involved in this questionable scheme of mine, then you must be made aware of the fact that it will require a great amount of your time and energy.

Are you sure you understand all the ramifications? If you don't then we'll just forget the whole business."

Business. That's all she was to him, just a business partner? Well, what had she expected? That's all he'd ever said she'd be, a wife in name only until her services were no longer required. Then the partnership would be dissolved because he'd have no further use for her.

He sat down again beside her. "If you're still willing to accept my proposal, we'll draw up a contract stating what is required of each of us. In order to make it strictly legal I have to ask Nate to do it, but I'd rather that not even he knows what we're planning. If we draw it up ourselves we'll both sign it in front of a notary public, but it might not hold up in court if we ever have a disagreement. I'll let you decide which way to do it."

Her mind was still reeling. She'd heard of prenuptial agreements, but never one like this! She picked up her mug and took a long swallow of the now lukewarm coffee. "I think it's best not to involve Nate."

Aaron looked at her, and for the first time since this discussion started he smiled. "Does that mean you're willing to go ahead with it even though I am a cold-hearted toad?"

It was scary the way he seemed to know what she was thinking. She lowered her head and ran her fingers through her hair, then looked up at him and smiled back. "Sure, why not? Maybe I can turn you into a warmhearted prince before we're through with this."

He reached out and stroked her cheek. "I don't know about the heart, but you have a real talent for warming me up in other places."

He leaned over and brushed his lips across hers, then back again. "It's getting late. Tomorrow is Thanksgiving and a big day for you and your family. I'm going to leave and let you get some sleep. We'll start drawing up the contract as soon as it's convenient for you.''

Again his mouth took hers, and this time it clung. It was a warm and wonderful kiss, and by the time he raised his head they were both breathless.

"Good night, love, and thank you," he said huskily. "I'll do my darnedest to make sure you never have cause to regret getting involved with Tommy and me."

Thanksgiving with the Bentleys was the largest family get-together Aaron had ever attended, and it was an experience he wasn't likely to forget. Not only were all the immediate members there, but an assortment of aunts, uncles, cousins and best friends trooped in and out all day long with noisy greetings and exuberant hugs. It surprised him how quickly he was accepted into the fold and made to feel welcome.

Outside, the ground was covered with a blanket of snow and the air was frosty, but there was no wind and the sun was bright and cheerful. The younger children frolicked with their sleds and threw snowballs at each other.

Inside, the giant television screen in the living room showed continuous football games while the smaller one in the family room was tuned to the Disney Channel. Both rooms were filled with spectators, while upstairs a different program could be heard coming from each bedroom on what he supposed were individual sets like the one in the room he'd been assigned.

At noon Aaron and Mariah took Tommy back to the cottage. After a quick lunch, Aaron volunteered to stay while the baby took his nap so Mariah could go back to the house and help with the dinner preparations.

"But you'll be all alone," she protested. "I can ask Betty Jean to baby-sit. She can bring some of the cousins with her."

He wasn't used to anyone being concerned about his aloneness, or lack of it, and it always touched him deeply when Mariah was.

"Honey, I'm used to being alone," he told her. "When I was growing up my family always sat down to a formal turkey dinner prepared by the housekeeper at exactly six o'clock, and that was the extent of our Thanksgiving celebration. The rest of the day was the same as any other day, with each of us doing our own thing. After our parents died, Eileen and I had Thanksgiving dinner in a restaurant."

A sorrowful expression crossed Mariah's beautiful face, and he knew it was caused by empathy for him. The last thing he wanted was for her to feel his pain.

"Actually, I prefer a little time to myself," he said, forcing a satisfied smile when what he really wanted was to keep her with him all afternoon. To take her in his arms and hold her close in the privacy of the empty cottage. To kiss her gently as he had last night. To caress her soft, round curves. To lose himself in the aura of sweetness and compassion that surrounded her.

Instead, he deliberately shattered that compelling illusion. "It's quiet here and I can start making notes for our prenuptial agreement. Then we can work out a plan that is satisfactory to both of us once the holiday is over."

She seemed to withdraw a little. "Well, all right, if you really don't mind—"

A knock on the door interrupted her. Before she could answer, it opened and Linda and Vic came in. "Hi," Linda said cheerfully. "Hope you don't mind, but we came over to talk to you without having to shout over all the background noise at the house."

"Sounds great," Mariah answered, "but I was just about to go over and help fix dinner."

"Oh, that's not necessary." Linda unzipped her quilted jacket. "Everything's under control. Aunt Judy and Aunt Kathy are helping Mom in the kitchen, and you know how it is when those three sisters get together. They don't want anybody else interrupting while they all talk at once."

Mariah laughed, but Aaron was a little jolted. He couldn't imagine ever talking about his mother that way. She'd been too dignified to be teased, especially by one of her children.

On second thought, he envied Jess's kids. The informality of her relationship with them was just one of the reasons they all adored her. She was never too regal to kiss a skinned knee, hug a crying child, or laugh at their jokes.

"In that case, take off your jackets and sit down," Mariah invited. "Would you like some coffee? Or cola? How about a glass of wine?"

They all opted for the wine, and after Mariah served it she settled down on the couch beside Linda while Aaron and Vic took the recliner and the rocking chair.

"So, how do you like living in Virginia?" Mariah asked. "Is base housing all you thought it would be?"

Linda shrugged. "It's okay, but that's not what I wanted to talk about. I want to hear all about the angel."

Mariah blinked. "Angel?"

"Oh, you know. The angel in the road who showed you where to find the wrecked car and the baby. God, I just shiver when I think about it."

Linda rattled on, but Aaron suppressed a groan. Oh, Lord, the woman in white again! Had Linda heard about it through her mother or in the media? Either way, she had the facts all wrong, just as everyone else in the country seemed to.

"Linda, for heaven's sake shut up and let me get a word in edgewise," Mariah commanded above her sister's continuing chatter. "You've got a lot of nerve making fun of Mom and the aunts," she said with a teasing smile as she lowered her voice. "You prattle on worse than all three of them. What makes you think the woman in the road was an angel?"

Linda's eyes widened in surprise. "What do you mean, think? Everyone knows it was an angel. It's been in the papers and on television for weeks."

"And you believe everything you read and see in the media?" Mariah's voice was heavy with sarcasm.

"Not everything, no," Linda said, her tone serious now. "But no one's disputing this. If you don't think it was an angel, why haven't you said so?"

Mariah threw up her arms in disgust. "I have. The appearance of an angel is a big story and nobody wants to hear it didn't happen."

Both Linda and Vic looked shocked, then Vic spoke. "Is that what you're saying? That it didn't happen?"

Aaron's heart bled for Mariah. She'd been over this so many times, and now members of her family were putting her through it again. He wanted to pick her up in his arms and carry her away from their insensitive prying, but he didn't dare offend them. Mariah wouldn't stand for it.

She sighed. "There was a woman in the road," she began, then repeated the whole incident over again. She'd done it so often that she could recite it by rote, just stopping now and then to take a sip of her wine.

"... the sheriff's department and even the state police have been over every inch of the area and found nothing," she finished several minutes later. "Whatever was in the road that night disappeared without a trace, but that doesn't mean it was an angel. It could have just been a trick of the lights."

Both Linda and Vic sat in silence for a few moments, pondering what they'd heard. Finally Linda spoke. "What do *you* think you saw, Mariah?"

Mariah leaned back and closed her eyes, and again Aaron had the urge to tell them to leave her alone. Couldn't they see how difficult talking about it was for her?

"I don't know." Her tone was devoid of emotion. "At first I was so sure it was a woman. I saw her so clearly, and yet I can't accurately describe her. I don't know if she was blond, brunette or redheaded. I can't tell you if her eyes were blue or brown or amber. She was beautiful, but the expression on her face was one of urgency."

She clenched her fists and pounded them on her thighs in frustration. "I saw a woman, damn it, but I'm beginning to wonder if I was hallucinating! It wasn't a trick of the lights or an illusion. It was a woman only a few feet away from the car anxiously motioning for me to stop. Either she was real or my mind was playing tricks on me, but I know what I saw!"

Aaron couldn't stand it any longer. He glared at Linda.

"Look, this has been an extremely upsetting experience for Mariah. Let's change the subject."

To her credit, Linda looked repentant. It was obvious that she hadn't realized she was being insensitive. "Oh, hey, I'm sorry. I didn't mean..."

Mariah reacted exactly as he'd feared she would. She frowned at him and immediately jumped to her sister's defense. "No, it's okay. It's only natural that you'd want to know the full story. I appreciate Aaron's concern, but I don't mind talking about it. It's just that I honestly can't explain why no trace of that woman has been found. My car tore right into the space where she was standing. It couldn't have missed hitting her."

Mariah's face was white and she twisted her hands in her lap, but Aaron knew better than to interfere again.

It was Vic who spoke next. "Since there doesn't seem to be any logical explanation for this...this image in the road, why are you so reluctant to consider the possibility of divine intervention? Don't you believe in spiritual beings?"

Mariah ran her fingers through her hair and shook her head. "I don't know," she said wearily. "I believe in a higher power, whether it be God or Nature, but ghosts and angels...? I've always been skeptical. Usually if you look hard enough you'll find a logical reason for most seemingly illogical happenings. I've always figured I'd better take care of myself, instead of relying on miracles or metaphysics."

A small smile twitched at the corners of Vic's mouth. "You won't get an argument from me there. I agree that people should be responsible for their own lives, but sometimes, in exceptional circumstances, the only way to avoid or reduce a disaster is by spiritual intervention."

Vic seemed well versed on the subject, and Aaron found himself listening with a great deal of interest.

"As you know, my family are regular churchgoers," Vic continued. "And Linda and I attend regularly. I have no problem with the concept of both ghosts and angels, but you don't have to be religious to accept the probability of their existence. There are a number of new and old books on the subject that have made the mainstream bestseller lists, and some of the most popular movies and television shows have been about them. You should read some of the books, watch some of the videos and think about it. It couldn't hurt, and it might help."

Mariah looked thoughtful. "I can't deny that what happened to Tommy was a miracle," she said thoughtfully. "There's no other explanation for him surviving the drop over the side of the mountain, and then being found in an area that was totally hidden from the road and the air. But an angel ... ?"

She paused, as if to give it some more thought. "If you'll give me the names of the books you recommended, I'll—"

"I can do better than that," Vic interrupted. "Mom has all of them. She'll be happy to loan them to you. Reading them might not make you an instant believer, but I think they'll leave you a little more open to the possibility, and maybe bring you some peace of mind."

Tommy woke Mariah up later than usual the following morning. It was nearly eight o'clock on Friday, the day after Thanksgiving. She'd fallen into bed late the night before, stuffed with turkey and all the trimmings, exhausted but happy.

Tommy must have been well content, too, because he slept clear through the night and woke an hour and a half past his usual time without screaming at the top of his lungs.

They had breakfast and then spent the rest of the day with her family. Aaron was again absent. Jessica said he'd left the house early after telling her he'd be gone all day and wouldn't be back until after supper. She was disappointed but tried not to let it show. She suspected that being cooped up with the whole Bentley family was more than a little unnerving for him, and he'd gone in search of some space.

On Saturday the sky was overcast and the forecast was for snow, but that didn't keep Vic and Linda from going skiing with their friends, or Ted from hanging out with his.

Aaron appeared on Mariah's doorstep early that morning with a cuddly teddy bear for Tommy and a beautifully gift-wrapped package for Mariah. He also delivered an apology. "Sorry I took off the way I did yesterday, but I knew you'd be tied up with your family and I wanted to check out Burlington."

"Burlington?" she said, as she slid the gold ribbon and bow off her package. "But you've been in Burlington several times."

"Actually only to the airport. This time I wanted to find out something about the town. Do you have time to go over this with me now?"

Mariah was only half listening as she carefully removed the gold foil paper from the white gift box. What on earth could he have brought her, and why?

With fingers that seemed to be all thumbs she pried the top off the box to reveal two jewelry cases nestled in white tissue paper. Her eyes widened. "Oh, Aaron," she said breathlessly as she picked up the larger, rectangular case and opened it.

Her breath caught in her throat. It was a pear-shaped emerald pendant on a gold chain, magnificent in its simplicity. "Ohhh," she exclaimed, totally unable to form coherent words.

"Do you like it?" he asked. She heard anxiety in his tone, but she couldn't imagine why. Surely he must know she'd never had anything like this before.

"Like it? Oh, Aaron, I've never seen anything so beautiful, but why...?" She still had trouble breathing.

He cocked one eyebrow. "Why? Because it compliments your beautiful brown eyes and brings even more sparkle to them. Because I want in some small way to express to you how very much I appreciate all you've done and are willing to do for Tommy, and most important, because you're very dear to me."

For just a shining moment she'd thought he was going to say, "Because I love you," but, of course he didn't. It was time to dispel that dream.

"I'm truly flattered," she murmured around the lump in her throat, "but you realize that I can't accept it."

She saw the look of disappointment that twisted his handsome features, and hastened to explain. "I mean, I appreciate your thoughtfulness more than I can say, but the necklace is much too expensive...."

"It's yours," he said sternly. "Do with it what you want, but I won't take it back. Now, open the other box. You won't be able to refuse its contents."

She heard the hurt in his tone, and chastised herself for not thinking before she spoke. She'd been rude without ever meaning to. "I...I'm sorry," she said carefully. "I didn't mean that I don't want the necklace. It's just that I don't accept such expensive gifts from men."

His stricken look softened. "But I'm not just any man, Mariah. I'm the one who's cheating you out of a proper wedding with a long white gown and flowers in your hair. I'm going to be your husband, and I want you to have something special to wear when we take the vows. Surely a man can give his wife-to-be a lavish gift?"

She couldn't argue with him. He was much too thoughtful, and the gift was too beautiful. She smiled. "Of course he can, and I accept it with joy. Will you put it on for me?"

He took the box from her, lifted out the pendant and fastened it around her neck. "For my lovely bride-to-be," he murmured softly, then put his arms around her waist.

She turned in his embrace and locked her fingers around his neck. "Thank you, my darling," she whispered just before his lips covered hers.

She closed her eyes and cuddled against him. His hands and face were still chilly from the frosty breeze outside, and he smelled of clean, fresh air and pine trees. Shyly she opened her mouth, and with a low moan he accepted her entreaty, but long before she was ready he broke the erotic contact and raised his head.

Involuntarily she murmured a rasp of protest and stretched upward to reestablish the caress, but he put his hand gently on the back of her head and guided it down to his shoulder. "I'd like nothing better than to kiss you all day," he whispered in her ear, then nibbled on her lobe, sending shivers to her core. "But, that wouldn't be fair to either of us. We have so much to discuss, and it won't wait. It's imperative that we be cool and clearheaded to make the decisions we need to make. And kissing you raises my temperature to the point of explosion and muddles my brain."

She knew he was right about them not getting too intimately involved, and she was embarrassed by her somewhat brazen behavior. She hoped she could make light of it.

"I know the feeling," she said breezily as she raised her head and flashed what she prayed was a grin at him. "You are a powerfully good kisser."

She pushed out of his embrace, putting a little distance between them. "Now, what did you want to talk about?"

A look of... what? Disappointment? flitted across his face, but was quickly replaced with something more neutral. "First, open the other jewelry case."

Good heavens, she'd forgotten about the second gift! She guessed that proved what a good kisser he was!

She picked up the small square box and lifted the lid, then gasped. It was a diamond engagement and wedding ring set! "Aaron, I... I don't know what to say. It's beautiful, but I... I didn't expect anything like this."

She looked at him and saw that he was smiling. "Why not?" he asked, sounding pleased. "We have to have a ring to get married."

A ring. For the first time she realized that there was no matching groom's ring. Apparently he didn't intend to wear a symbol of their short-term marriage. But then, why should he? It wasn't required for the ceremony, and he'd made it plain that he wasn't making a lifetime commitment.

She had no right to be hurt, and she wasn't going to let it ruin her day. "I know, but I never expected you to give me an engagement ring, too. I mean, ours will probably be the shortest engagement on record. Have you decided yet when you want us to get married?"

"As soon as possible," he replied, "and that's what we have to talk about. First let's iron out the terms of the prenuptial agreement. We've already concurred that it will be a temporary marriage of convenience...."

Aaron and Mariah were both surprised at how complicated a contract of this sort could be. They both had conditions they wanted to add, and they disagreed almost as often as they agreed. There was certainly nothing romantic about it. It was more like a business merger than a marriage.

By the time Tommy started banging on the bars of his playpen and fussing for his lunch, they'd finally wrestled the document into acceptable shape. Her job would be to stay at home and take full-time care of Tommy, and his would be to take an active part in the child's upbringing and to provide for them financially.

Aaron insisted that Mariah would be paid a monthly salary, which would be referred to as an allowance. Mariah was adamant that the engagement and wedding rings would revert back to Aaron when the divorce action was filed.

"If you don't like the rings, we can exchange them," Aaron had argued. "But I bought them for you, and I want you to keep them."

"I love the rings," she'd replied, "but they were never meant to be mine. They are just part of the charade, and I can't, won't, keep them once that is over. Please, Aaron, humor me on this. I'll wear them, and proudly, while we're together, but once the show is over I'll have no use for them. I certainly couldn't use them for another marriage."

"Neither could I," he snapped, but eventually he gave in and let the clause be included.

Both of them readily agreed that neither would become romantically involved with anyone else while they were living together, and they self-consciously agreed to leave the matter of consummation open for the time being.

After they'd had lunch and put Tommy down for his nap they tackled the plans for the wedding.

"Do you still feel it would be best to elope?" Aaron asked.

Mariah nodded. "Yes, I do."

"Okay, then I think we should define 'elope' so there won't be any misunderstanding. Do you see it as just going somewhere else to be married and taking some of your family and friends along? Or is it your intention to keep it secret and not tell anybody until it's an accomplished fact?"

She hesitated. Never in all her adolescent daydreams had she considered eloping. "I think we should get married first and then tell my family. It's a cruel thing to do. Mom will be heartbroken if we do it that way, but I know she and Dad and everyone else in the family will disapprove and try to talk us out of it if we tell them first."

She shifted uncomfortably. "Since we can't tell them it's only a temporary arrangement, they'll say we haven't known each other long enough to make a lifetime commitment, and of course they're right. On the other hand, if we have the ceremony first and then present it to them as a done deal they'll accept it. They won't like it, but they'll accept it."

Aaron put his hand on her knee, which immediately got her attention. "Sweetheart, I've said this before, but I'm going to say it again. You don't have to go through with this. If you want to back out I'll understand. I can't bear to be the cause of a rupture in your close-knit family."

She put her hand over his. "And I've told you before that I'm not going to back out. If there is some unpleasantness it won't last long. Mom and Dad don't try to live their children's lives for them. They like you, and they're wild about Tommy. They'll come around, you'll see."

He squeezed her knee, then took his hand away. "All right, if you're sure, but don't do anything you don't want to do. Promise?"

She nodded, and he changed the subject. "The reason I went to Burlington yesterday was to shop for the jewelry, but also to check the place out," Aaron began. "I discovered that we can get a license and be married in Vermont all at the same time. There's no waiting period. Also, I found several nice churches in town in case you—"

"No," Mariah interrupted firmly. "I won't take vows in a church that I don't intend to keep. I'd rather we just stood up before a justice of the peace and said them."

She hadn't realized she felt so strongly about this until he broached the subject. She wasn't a religious person, but going through a sham ceremony in a church with a minister officiating was offensive and disrespectful.

Aaron seemed rather startled by her vehemence, but he was quick to agree. "Whatever you want is fine with me. Would Monday be too soon for you?"

Monday? The day after tomorrow? The very thought took her breath away. That was awfully quick, even for an elopement. It was easy to talk about doing it, but to be faced with actually setting a date and going through with it...

Her misgivings lasted only a moment. If she was going to take part in this rash and unwise plan they might as well do it and get it over with. It would probably save her several sleepless nights of agonized soul-searching and, after all, time was of the essence.

"No, it's not too soon," she said haltingly. "We'll have to take Tommy with us, you know. I can't leave him with anybody else yet."

Aaron nodded his agreement. "I hadn't thought about that, but I guess we won't be the only bride and groom who ever took their vows with a baby in their arms."

Mariah smiled to cover the bleakness of her thoughts. That was another thing she'd never dreamed of in her wedding fantasies, but including the child in the ceremony didn't upset her. He was a joy, not an embarrassment.

What did leave her feeling empty and barren was the certain knowledge that the man she was marrying would never give her a son or daughter of their own.

Chapter Ten

Monday morning dawned bright and sunny. A beautiful day for a late-autumn wedding, thought Mariah as she dressed hurriedly in a winter-white wool dress, a chemise with long sleeves and a short hemline. She'd bought it in Albany last year to wear to a Christmas party, and it was the only outfit she had that even faintly resembled a wedding garment.

With it she wore patterned white stockings, off-white pumps, and, framed by the scoop neckline, the stunning emerald necklace Aaron had given her. He'd been right, it did make her eyes sparkle. Or was the sparkle caused by excitement?

She hadn't planned on being excited. After all, it was a wedding executed only for the sake of Tommy's welfare. Somehow, after the plans were made and the contract drawn up and signed, she'd began to look forward to it.

Her acceptance had grown to enthusiasm, and now that the day had arrived she was positively ebullient.

Well, why not? It would be her first marriage. That wasn't something to take lightly, no matter what the reason for entering into it.

She had Tommy all dressed in his new red corduroy overalls and matching red-and-white-striped shirt, and was checking the contents of his diaper bag and carryall when Aaron arrived. He was wearing an overcoat that was buttoned so she couldn't see what he had on under it except that his trousers were fine black wool.

He stood in the open doorway looking at her, and there was deep admiration in his twinkling blue eyes. "I've never seen a more beautiful bride, and that's the truth," he said huskily, then stepped inside and closed the door behind him. "Am I entitled to a prenuptial kiss?"

He held out his arms and she walked into them. His coat felt cold, as did his face and hands. She put her arms around his neck and raised her face to his. "How do you want it," she asked softly, "chaste or passionate?"

His arms tightened around her. "Both," he murmured just before taking her mouth with his own.

It started innocently enough with a soft brush of the lips and his hands gently rubbing her back, then progressed to warm as they nibbled and kneaded. Warm quickly became hot when their mouths opened and their tongues plunged and plundered, and finally passionate when his palm found the rise of her buttocks and pushed her against his unmistakable hardness while his other hand cupped her breast.

This time Mariah was the first one to pull away. It was either that or invite him to take her right there on the floor in front of the door. She'd never been so aroused before. Her whole body was trembling.

Aaron groaned when she broke the kiss, and he tried to hold on to her but she gently pushed him away. "I...I think we'd better leave if we want to catch the eleven o'clock ferry from Essex," she said unsteadily.

Passion clouded his eyes, and his lips were as swollen as hers felt.

They were both silent as they sped along the narrow road to the dock at Essex with Tommy waving his arms and jabbering with glee. They'd cooled off to some extent—at least Aaron had, and Mariah seemed calm again.

Damn! He hoped she wasn't going to put him through that kind of torment very often! He'd never survive several months of it! Not that it was her fault. He'd been the one to ask for the kiss, but he hadn't known it was going to turn into an inferno. He almost hadn't been able to stop.

He hadn't bargained for this kind of temptation when he'd proposed a marriage of convenience. Oh, he'd hoped she'd agree to sleep with him during the time they were together. There wasn't a man alive who wouldn't have, but he'd honestly believed he could control his desire for her if she chose not to.

Now he knew he couldn't, and it scared the hell out of him. It was too late to back out of the deal. He'd look like a fool if he did, and besides, he needed her to take care of Tommy.

If he'd been alone he would have hooted. Yeah, sure he needed her for that, but he needed her for a whole lot more, too! He needed her in his arms, in his bed, in his life, and that knowledge didn't please him at all.

He didn't want any woman to be that necessary to him.

They arrived in Essex in plenty of time to catch the ferry across Lake Champlain to Charlotte, Vermont. During the twenty-minute ride Aaron held a well-bundled Tommy as they stood at the rail in the cold, clear air and enjoyed the view of the mountain peaks and the blue water of the sixth Great Lake, as Lake Champlain was commonly called.

Even though Mariah was as familiar with this crossing as she was with the rest of the area where she grew up, she never tired of the view.

On the Vermont side they headed north on Highway Seven for the short drive to Burlington, Vermont's largest city. As they drove through a residential area, Aaron commented, "This town must be awesome in the summer and early fall when those massive elm trees that line the streets are all leafed out, and the lawns are green."

"It is," Mariah assured him, "and because it's located between the lake and the mountains the view is breathtaking in all directions. Did you know it's a college town? Both Champlain and Trinity Colleges have campuses here, and so does the University of Vermont. In fact, the university was the first in New England to admit women as regular students."

She always swelled with pride when she announced that fact. Although she wasn't a resident of Vermont, she lived close enough to it to consider it a second, unofficial, home.

Even though it was only four days past Thanksgiving, the pedestrian mall, which was within easy walking distance of both the lake and the university, was cheerfully festive with Christmas decorations, and there was plenty of snow on the ground to enhance the holiday look. It was past noon and Tommy was tuning up to demand his lunch, so they stopped at one of the upscale restaurants in the mall that Mariah knew had an excellent reputation for good food and service.

As soon as they were shown to a table, she took the baby into the women's lounge to change him.

Back in the dining room she took off her heavy coat and noticed that Aaron had removed his, also. He was wearing a black suit with a white shirt and a blue paisley tie, and he looked breathtakingly handsome. Exactly like the bridegroom she'd always dreamed of.

She told him so, and he looked a little flustered as he covered her hand on the table with his. "I've never envisioned a bride," he murmured softly, "but if I had, I couldn't possibly have dreamed up one as beautiful as you."

Tommy was surprisingly cooperative during the meal. The waitress heated his baby food and bottle, and he even let Aaron feed him so Mariah could enjoy her soup and salad. She was delighted to note that the child was warming up to his uncle. At least, as long as she was with them.

It was two o'clock when they arrived at the courthouse, and were directed to the room where marriage licenses were issued. Until now Mariah had managed to keep her reservations about what they were doing under control by thinking of their short trip as just a family outing, but the cold, formal corridors of this building dispelled her fantasy.

They were here to get married, and that was serious business. In some ways it would alter the whole course of her life, but whether for good or bad she had no way of knowing.

She was taking a big chance, and she suddenly had a wild urge to turn and run. Before she could act on it they arrived at the door and it was too late.

It took only a few minutes to get the license, and when Aaron inquired about arrangements for the ceremony the woman who waited on them was most helpful.

"There's a small secular chapel just a few blocks away that caters to couples who want to get married but aren't affiliated with a church. They supply the music, flowers and a minister or justice of the peace. It's really very pretty."

She gave them directions for finding the place. It was a small white building that looked like a church but with no steeple, cross or other symbol.

Aaron glanced over at Mariah. "Is this all right with you?"

"Oh, yes," she said, her relief evident in her tone. She hadn't wanted to admit, even to herself, how much she'd hated the thought of taking such important vows in one of the cold, colorless rooms at the city hall.

He smiled. "Well then, let's go in and see if they can accommodate us."

The inside was similar to a small church with a narthex, or small entryway, at the front, then a short aisle with pews on either side and an altar at the end. Flower arrangements banked the altar and even though they were silk they looked real. Soft strains of classical music floated on the air, and Mariah blinked back tears. It was truly a beautiful background.

A man and a woman greeted them and explained the procedure. They assured Aaron and Mariah that they could contact a justice of the peace and have him there in a few minutes. Aaron, who was holding Tommy in one arm, put the other one around Mariah. "Is this all right with you?" he asked for a second time.

"It's lovely," she said, and hoped he wouldn't notice the moisture in her eyes. "I couldn't ask for a more perfect setting."

Mariah took Tommy from Aaron and followed the woman to the Bride's Room, which was actually a large rest room with the addition of a full-length mirror and a sofa.

Aaron and the man disappeared in the other direction, probably to an office where he would pay for the use of the chapel and the services.

By the time Mariah got the baby changed again and herself freshened up, the woman came back to tell her they were ready anytime she was. She picked up the baby from the floor where he'd been crawling around and went back out to the entryway.

Aaron was waiting. He smiled and took Tommy from her as the wedding march began to play. Mariah took Aaron's arm and they walked slowly down the aisle together, all three of them.

It was a very short but impressive service, and when it came time for him to put the ring on her finger he put Tommy down on the floor. She held her breath, afraid the child would cry, but he immediately got up on his knees and crawled off.

Aaron took her hand and repeated after the justice as he slipped the ring on her finger, "With this ring I thee wed."

Then, to her surprise, he slid the engagement diamond on the same finger. "And with this ring I pledge my deep devotion."

The tears that had been threatening spilled over as the justice pronounced them man and wife, and Aaron took her in his arms. It wasn't a declaration of abiding love, but she knew he meant what he'd said and that was enough.

The kiss they shared was one of affection and commitment, along with a carefully controlled touch of yearning. The tender warmth of it forced Mariah to face the fact that she wished the vows they'd spoken were real and not just pretend.

They parted slowly, reluctantly, and were confronted with congratulations and best wishes by the justice and the managers, who had also acted as witnesses. When it was over they rounded up Tommy, who had crawled between two of the pews, and left.

Tommy fell asleep in his car seat before they made it to the city limits. Aaron reached across and took Mariah's hand. "I hope you never have cause to regret this." His tone was strained with emotion. "I'll never forgive myself if I make you unhappy, even for a short while."

She smiled and squeezed his hand. "You won't," she assured him, although it wasn't quite so easy to assure herself. "I know exactly what I'm getting into, and I made the choice of my own free will."

That probably wasn't altogether true. Her good judgment had been obscured by his startling good looks, and her free will had been clouded by her overactive hormones, but still it had been her decision. He hadn't coerced her.

"It was a lovely wedding," she continued. "So much nicer than just saying our vows at the courthouse. Thank you for making it such a memorable occasion."

He turned his head to look at her. "No, thank *you*," he said firmly. "Tommy and I owe you more than we can ever repay."

She found it hard to hang on to her smile. She wished he hadn't said that. If she couldn't have his love, she didn't want his gratitude. She didn't want him to be indebted to her.

"I wish you wouldn't feel that way," she said. "Actually, you're doing me a favor, too. You're going to provide me with a home, financial support, and the pleasure of taking care of the little fellow I love most dearly. Not only that, but you're giving me a chance to travel. I've never done much of that. The farthest west I've ever been is Chicago, and I was only there once. I'm really looking forward to living in Salt Lake City. Tell me, is the lake really salty?''

Aaron laughed. "It sure is. The salt content is twenty-five percent, six times as salty as any of the oceans, and just west and south of it are four thousand square miles of flat salt beds known as the Salt Flats. They are hard as concrete, and famous for the speed races held there."

Her excitement was building again. "There, you see, it's not only going to be fun, but also educational. You will take me sight-seeing, won't you?"

He sobered. "I'll take you anywhere you want to go, sweetheart, and that's a promise."

Tommy slept through the return ferry ride, and once they were back in New York Aaron switched the conversation to a more immediate topic. "When are we going to tell your folks that we're married? Do you want to do it as soon as we get back, or wait a few days? I'll have to tell Nate fairly soon so he can set up a hearing with Judge Gibson. Once he does that, the whole town will know about it. It will be a matter of public record."

Mariah's spirits plummeted. The wedding had been beautiful, but the honeymoon would probably be a romp through hell. She hated having to hurt her family, but there was no way out of it.

Come to think about it, what were they going to do about sleeping arrangements! Somehow they'd managed to shove that little complication aside and ignore it. As soon as they broke the news Aaron would have to move in with her. It would look mighty odd if they continued to sleep in separate houses!

She cleared her throat and tried to keep her voice from shaking. "I...I guess you're aware of the fact that we haven't settled the matter of...of whether or not we're going to...um...sleep together."

She knew she was blushing, and she turned her face away so he wouldn't see. She hated being so unsophisticated.

"I'm very much aware of it, yes." His tone was kind but firm and unembarrassed. "I suggest that we not make that decision right away. This has been an emotional day for both of us, and I'm not going to ask you to commit yourself one way or the other until I'm sure you don't feel coerced."

Her head swam with relief. "I'd appreciate that, but are you certain you don't mind?"

"It doesn't matter whether I mind or not," he said tartly. "This is your decision, and I'm not going to try to influence you. When we get back to Apple Junction I'll go over to the big house and spend the night there. Then some time tomorrow we'll make our announcement to your family and the local newspaper, if that's all right with you. After that I'll move in with you and Tommy and sleep on the sofa."

He picked up her hand again and looked at it. "Meanwhile, you'd better take off your rings before we get home. You won't want anyone to see you wearing them until tomorrow."

Aaron didn't sleep easily that night. Every time he closed his eyes he saw Mariah looking like an angel in her white wedding clothes. She was so beautiful, and so eager to please, and so damn trusting. He felt like the lowest form of life for taking advantage of her sweet nature.

At least he hadn't taken advantage of her sexually. Not yet, but given half a chance he would. He couldn't help himself, and that excuse was totally unacceptable to him. He'd never had any use for men who claimed they couldn't control their sexual urges, but he'd never been tempted beyond his endurance before.

He wanted his wife with a heat that burned and tormented, but Mariah wasn't really his wife. He'd been the one who'd suggested a marriage of convenience, but there was nothing convenient about the way he was feeling now.

If he was having to struggle to keep himself from stumbling barefoot across the dark lawn in near-zero weather to claim her, how was he going to restrain himself when she was in the bedroom next to his in the same house?

What in hell had he gotten himself into?

The following morning Tommy woke early as usual. Mariah had just finished dressing and feeding him when there was a knock on her front door. She answered it, still clad in her faded old robe and slippers, and found Aaron standing there wearing jeans and his heavy jacket. He didn't look as if he'd slept much.

It struck her then that she didn't look all that great, either. She hadn't even brushed her hair yet.

"Aaron, come on in," she said and stepped back to let him enter, then closed the door. "You're out early this morning. Is everything all right?"

For a moment she thought he was going to take her in his arms. The magnetism between them was compelling, but instead he unzipped his jacket and walked over to where Tommy sat in his high chair making a gooey mishmash of a piece of toast.

"Everything's fine, but your dad was called out in the middle of the night and didn't get back until early this morning, so he's sleeping in for a while. I thought that when he wakes up would be a good time to tell your parents that we're married."

Oh, dear! She hadn't had a chance yet to think about what she was going to say to them, how she could make them understand without actually telling them the truth.

She'd been tired when she went to bed last night, and both she and Tommy had slept clear through without waking until morning.

"Sure," she said. "We might as well get it over with. Will you watch Tommy while I get dressed?" She put her hands to her hair. "I must look like a mess...."

His expression softened. "You look just the way I thought you'd look first thing in the morning. Cuddly, disheveled and sexy..."

His words trailed off as his glance roamed over her baggy attire, then he straightened and changed the subject. "Go ahead and dress, I'll wash the baby."

Ten minutes later Mariah and Aaron pushed Tommy and his stroller across the lawn to the big house. Mariah was still trying to sort out in her mind how she'd tell her parents, when they opened the unlocked back door and walked into the big, cozy kitchen that smelled of home-baked cinnamon rolls.

Jessica looked up from loading the dishwasher to greet them with a happy smile. "Well, hi there. You're just in time. The rolls are still warm, and I've made fresh coffee."

She hunkered down in front of Tommy. "And how's my sweet baby?" she asked as she chucked him under his double chin.

Much to Mariah's amazement he actually held up his arms to Jess. Usually he eyed her balefully and fussed if she tried to touch him.

She swung him out of his stroller and up into her arms. "Well, bless your little heart, you finally decided you could trust me, didn't you?" She nuzzled his neck and he laughed and clutched her hair in his fists.

She played with him for a few minutes, then put him in the jumper chair Aaron had bought so Tommy would have something to play in when Mariah brought him over.

"Sit down at the table," Jess invited, "and I'll get the coffee and rolls—"

"Does that invite include me?" asked Cliff's voice from the dining room.

"Sure does," Jess said, and stretched up to kiss him when he reached her side. "Did you get enough sleep?"

Cliff kissed her back, said he had, then turned his attention to Mariah, Aaron and the baby until his wife finished serving the refreshments and sat down at the table with them.

Mariah took a deep breath and dived in. "Dad, Mom, Aaron and I have something to tell you."

"What is it, dear?" Jess asked absently as she poured cream in her coffee.

"Well...uh...Aaron and I spent the day in Burlington yesterday." She didn't know how to soften the shock of what she was going to tell them.

"Aaron told us that last night," her dad offered. "He said you had a great time."

She wished they'd both be quiet and just listen. "Yes, we did, but something happened—"

"You mean an accident?" Jess asked in alarm.

"No, no, nothing like that," Mariah assured her, as she forced a big smile and tried to sound joyful. "It was something wonderful...."

She glanced sideways at Aaron, and he put his hand over hers on the table. "Very wonderful," he said with a twisted smile and a catch in his voice.

She couldn't look at any of them as she hurried on. "We...that is, Aaron and I got married."

Aaron squeezed her hand as they heard the shocked intake of breath from both her parents.

"Married!" Cliff and Jess spoke the word in unison.

Aaron quickly took over the conversation. "We knew it would be a shock, and we're really sorry we had to do it this way—"

"What in hell is going on?" her dad asked angrily as he pushed back from the table and stood. "You two have known each other for less than a month," he said to Mariah. "And he was gone for at least a week of that time."

He shifted his glance to Aaron. "If you're playing games with my daughter, I'll—"

Mariah jumped up in alarm. "Daddy, no, it's not like..."

Before she could finish Aaron was on his feet. "I'm not playing games with Mariah," he said adamantly. "I'd never do anything to hurt her. I made sure she knew exactly what she was doing when I asked her to marry me. I'm sorry we found it necessary to do it the way we did, but we thought it best."

"Best!" Jessica echoed. "Sneaking off to another state as if getting married was something to be ashamed of..."

She stopped in midsentence and stared at Mariah, her mouth still open. "You're not pregnant, are you?"

For a moment Mariah could only stare back. The possibility that her family, as well as all their friends, might think that had never occurred to her. It was too ludicrous. She and Aaron had hardly even kissed!

"No, Mother, I'm not pregnant," she said when she finally caught her breath. "I haven't known Aaron long enough to know it even if I were, but I swear to you there's no possibility of that. We've never...uh..."

While she floundered, searching for words, Aaron put his arms around her and finished the sentence. "Mariah and I have never been intimate. In fact, we haven't even consummated the marriage. If you'll remember, I stayed here last night."

Jessica sank back in her chair, and there were tears in her eyes. "I . . . I'm sorry," she stammered. "I shouldn't have jumped to conclusions, but why . . . ?"

Her voice broke, and Cliff hurried to her side. "There's no need for you to apologize, honey," he said and patted her shoulder caressingly. "It was a natural assumption, one that everyone is bound to make."

Mariah rubbed her face in Aaron's shoulder. "Oh, Mom, Dad, I'm the one who's sorry. I didn't even think of that possibility."

"Neither did I," Aaron said and cuddled Mariah closer. "It seems like an obvious suspicion now that you've brought it up, but I guess since we knew it wasn't possible it just never crossed our minds."

Mariah nodded in agreement, but she knew the oversight went deeper than that. They'd been so busy planning ways to keep the judge from suspecting the real reason for their sudden, secret wedding ceremony that a pregnancy scandal was too mild to merit consideration.

It wasn't mild to her parents, though, who had old-fashioned values, as did most of the other citizens of this small mountain community. Mariah deeply regretted putting her dad and mom through the hurt and embarrassment of being the butt of town gossip.

"Then why did you feel it was necessary to elope without a word to anyone?" Jessica cried in a voice that trembled. "Didn't you want your family with you when you took such an important step?"

Mariah felt worse by the minute. "Of course we did, Mom, but we . . . we . . ."

Aaron stepped in and took over. "It was my fault, Jess. I talked her into it."

"No! Aaron—" Mariah couldn't let him take the blame. It had been her idea, not his.

He put his finger to her lips. "Hush, sweetheart, let me tell it. Mariah would have liked to have had a big wedding with bridal showers and all her family and friends present, but I have to get back to my job in Salt Lake City as soon as possible and I want her to come with me. We knew you'd be shocked to hear that we wanted to get married, and we anticipated that you'd be against it."

"Damn right we are," Cliff interrupted. "You haven't even known each other long enough to get acquainted, let alone married. What on earth were you thinking of?"

"We were thinking that we didn't want to be separated by two thousand miles," Aaron said reasonably. "Even if you'd eventually given in and agreed, you couldn't possibly have arranged a formal wedding in the next few days. It just seemed more expedient to elope and then tell you."

Mariah was crying openly now, and so was her mother. Her dad and Aaron had their hands full trying to calm their sobbing wives. Mariah was almost as upset over Aaron taking the blame for their elopement as she was over hurting her parents. He didn't need to do that. She'd been the one who argued in favor of it, not him, but how like him to deflect the blame from her and onto himself. No wonder she loved him.

She put her arms around his neck and sobbed while he caressed her back and rubbed his face in her hair. She'd noticed that her dad had hunkered down beside her mom's chair and was holding her.

Come to think of it, it was no wonder she'd fallen in love so quickly with Aaron. He had a lot in common with her dad. They were both strong but sensitive men, intelligent, successful, and compassionate. What was not to love?

She only wished Aaron loved her the way her dad loved her mother. They'd been married twenty-eight years, raised six children, and still acted like honeymooners most of the time.

That thought brought on another round of sobs. She'd found the man who was right for her, but she wasn't right for him. He didn't want her for a lifetime partner. He only wanted her for a part-time baby-sitter.

Chapter Eleven

It took Aaron and Cliff about twenty minutes to calm their wives enough to carry on a lucid conversation. Then they all went into the living room and made themselves comfortable while they talked.

It was Cliff who asked the first question. "Now that you're married, what are your plans? You said something about going back to Salt Lake City?"

Jessica looked as if she were going to lose control again, but managed to control herself as Aaron answered. "If it's all right with you, we thought we'd put an announcement in the local paper and invite everybody to an informal reception here at the house on Saturday afternoon."

That brought a little of the brightness back to Jessica's expression. "Of course. I'll get Loretta Rockford to bake a wedding cake, and we'll serve champagne punch—"

Cliff held up his hand. "We'll plan the reception later,

honey. Right now I'm more interested in our daughter's immediate future."

He turned again to Aaron. "If you take Mariah back to Utah with you, who's going to look after the baby? The judge has forbidden you to take him out of the court's jurisdiction."

Aaron had known that question was coming, and he'd dreaded it. How could he answer it without giving away their real reason for getting married?

"We're going to talk to Judge Gibson and try to get him to change his ruling on that," Aaron said carefully. "We hope that when he sees how happy Mariah and I are, and how much we both love Tommy, he'll at least let us take the child to Utah with us until the appellate court rules on our appeal."

Aaron saw the storm clouds gathering behind the question in Cliff's eyes, and hastened to deflect it. "Look, Cliff, why don't we go into the family room to talk and let the women stay here and plan the reception?"

Cliff's expression was a study of conflicting emotions— doubt, curiosity and anger—but he apparently recognized the urgency in Aaron's tone and nodded curtly.

As they stood up Mariah looked as if she were going to object, but Aaron frowned at her and shook his head. She closed her mouth and settled into her chair.

The family room was far enough away that they could speak without being overheard. Cliff took a position in front of the fireplace. "If you're using my little girl to get custody of your sister's son, I'll come down on you with the full force of the law." His tone was cold with fury.

Aaron stood at the window looking out over the forest in back of the lot. "I've already told you, I'd never hurt Mariah. We are both adults, and we went into this marriage knowing exactly what we wanted from it. I'm not going to tell you what that is. It's personal and private, just between the two of us. Mariah's very dear to me, and she loves Tommy and wants to take care of him. If you're really concerned about her happiness, and I know you are, you'll accept what we are telling you and not stir up questions and doubts.''

He turned and faced his reluctant father-in-law. ''I'm asking you to trust Mariah and me to make decisions that are right for us and not voice your doubts to the rest of the family. It's important to Mariah that all of you be happy for her.''

Cliff scowled and hesitated. ''I have no reason to trust you,'' he finally said quietly. ''I don't even know you.''

''I know you don't, but despite what you think, Mariah knows me well. You can rely on her to be sure of what she wants.''

Cliff shook his head. ''I don't like this, but I'll go along with it for now. Just make damn good and sure you never give me cause to regret it.''

While Aaron and Cliff talked in the family room, Mariah reassured Jessica in the living room. She described the wedding for her mother, and convinced her that it had indeed been a proper one with music and flowers.

''But why didn't you have a minister instead of a justice of the peace?'' Jessica asked.

''Neither Aaron nor I belong to a church, and the justice of the peace was handy,'' Mariah answered truthfully but with a lot left unsaid.

''I . . . I just can't believe that you'd rather be married in a hurry-up ceremony among strangers instead of a beautiful wedding here at home with all your family and friends present.'' Jessica's voice was shaky again.

Mariah couldn't help feeling guilty and selfish, even though her motive at the time had been pure. "It's not what we preferred, Mom, but we didn't have time for a big wedding. Aaron wants to leave as soon as we can get another hearing with the judge about Tommy's custody. He's been away from his accounting firm for weeks, and it's not so big that it can run smoothly without him."

Much to Mariah's relief, Aaron and her dad reappeared just then. Her dad still looked grim, but he didn't ask any more questions.

Shortly after that Mariah and Aaron took Tommy and went to the weekly newspaper to give them the announcement of their marriage and an invitation to the open reception at the Bentley home on Saturday afternoon. They were assured it would run in this week's edition, which would come out on Thursday.

After lunch Tommy was put down for his nap and Mariah stayed home with him while Aaron went to see Nate Quimby at his office. He'd made an appointment earlier that morning, and Nate greeted him somewhat anxiously. "Hey, man, what's up? You wouldn't tell me a damn thing on the phone. Is there a problem?"

"No problem," Aaron said cheerfully. "Just the opposite. Mariah and I were married yesterday in Burlington."

Nate's jaw dropped. "Married! You and Mariah? But I thought you didn't know each other before... I mean... Well, hell. Congratulations!" He came around the desk with a big smile on his face and shook Aaron's hand while pounding him on the shoulder. "Mariah's one fine lady."

"Yes, she is," Aaron said matching the size of the other man's smile. "The Bentleys are having a reception for us on Saturday. We'll expect to see you and your family there."

"Wouldn't miss it. Does that mean you'll be staying here in Apple Junction until we get a ruling from the court of appeals?"

"That's what I wanted to talk to you about," Aaron said.

"Okay," Nate said, obviously puzzled. "Sit down and tell me what you have in mind."

He motioned to the chair in front of the desk as he settled into the one behind it.

"I can't stay here any longer," Aaron began. "I have a business to run back in Salt Lake City, and every day I'm away is costing me money. But even more important, I don't want to leave until I can take Mariah and the baby with me. What I want you to do is set up another hearing with Judge Gibson. He wouldn't give me custody of Tommy because I wasn't married, but now that's changed. I am married, and to a woman he approves of, so I don't see how he can refuse me at least temporary custody until the appellate court rules on the appeal."

Nate's smile had disappeared and was replaced by a frown. "Good Lord, man, I didn't mean for you to go out and get married...."

Aaron held up his hand. "Hold it right there," he ordered. "I have deep feelings for Mariah, and I don't want anyone thinking otherwise. I proposed to her and she accepted, and I'm sure we're going to be very happy together. Now do you want to continue to handle this for me, or would you rather I found another attorney?"

Nate didn't answer right away, and Aaron's apprehension increased. This was going to be even more difficult than he'd expected it would be. If he couldn't convince his father-in-law and his lawyer of his good intentions how could he ever convince that mule-headed judge? Had he and Mariah made things worse by getting married instead of better?

His musing was interrupted by Nate's voice. "I'll handle it," he said reluctantly, "but we need a few ground rules. I won't ask any more personal questions, and I don't want you to volunteer any information on the subject. As far as I know, you and Mariah fell in love at first sight and couldn't wait to become man and wife. Now, I gather you want this renewed hearing to take place yesterday?"

Aaron nodded, extremely relieved. "Yes, certainly no later than tomorrow," he said with a small smile. "Thanks, buddy, I don't know how I can tell you how much I appreciate this."

Nate stood. "You can pay my bill in full and on time," he said with a grin. "Now get out of here while I make some phone calls."

While Mariah waited for Tommy to wake up and Aaron to come back from the lawyer's office she made an apple pie and prepared a meat loaf to bake later. She couldn't get used to the fact that now she had a husband and baby to take care of.

It was the *take care of* that gave her goose pimples. Just what all did that include? Aaron had made no secret of the fact that he wanted to make love with her, and she hadn't been able to hide her heated responses to his tentative overtures. But did she really want to get that involved with him in this very limited marriage?

Of course she wanted to. Have sex, that is. He was, as her mother and sisters all agreed, a real hunk. Just thinking about going to bed with him made her squirm with prickles in erotic places. But wouldn't that be a stupid thing to do?

On the other hand, Mariah wondered to herself, would she be able to resist? He'd said he wouldn't seduce her against her will, but she didn't have any will where he was concerned. She loved him, and was only too eager to give him anything he wanted. She'd already tasted his kisses, felt his hands cup her breasts, and brushed up against the heat of his hard arousal....

She realized that her hands shaping the meat loaf were shaking, and her heartbeat had sped up alarmingly. *Get a hold of yourself, girl! You don't want to pounce on him the minute he comes through the door.*

Mariah finally managed to get control of her thoughts and turn them to plans for the reception she and her mother were working on. By the time Aaron returned, Tommy was awake and she was ready to help Aaron move his clothes and things from the big house to the cottage. He didn't have much to move, so it didn't take long. As they were getting ready to leave the house for the last time Jessica stopped them.

"I have just one more question for you two and then I promise not to pry any further." She looked directly at Mariah. "Mariah, are you in love with Aaron?"

Mariah had expected the question earlier, but when it came it caught her off guard. Her mother knew she'd never been able to lie to her successfully, and this time she didn't even try. She looked straight at Jessica and answered. "Yes, Mother, I am."

Out of the corner of her eye she saw Aaron looking at her speculatively and she couldn't face him, but Jessica did. "And you, Aaron, are you in love with my daughter?"

He met Jessica's gaze, but his answer wasn't quite so short and simple. "I care deeply for Mariah," he said. "I'll do everything in my power to make her happy. I'll swear to that, Jess."

He'd sidestepped an actual declaration of love, but her mother didn't seem to notice. She looked convinced, and hugged and kissed them both.

At the cottage the atmosphere got a little tense as they made a place in Mariah's closet for Aaron's clothes and in her dresser drawers for his underwear and socks. The sight of his shirts and trousers next to her dresses and skirts was so intimate!

They laughed and joked and tried to make light of the situation, but the tension between them built steadily, no matter how much they tried to deny it.

Later that evening they had just finished supper when the phone rang. Mariah was busy cleaning Tommy who had been fussy during the meal, throwing his food around and creating a mess instead of eating it. Aaron answered the phone.

Tommy objected to Mariah's efforts and started to cry so she missed Aaron's side of the conversation, but it was obviously for him since he didn't call for her to come. By the time he hung up she'd got the baby cleaned up and quieted down.

"That was Nate," he told her. "Good news. He says Judge Gibson has agreed to see us in his chambers at eleven o'clock Thursday morning."

"That's great," she said. "Did Nate tell him what we wanted to talk to him about?"

"Only that something had come up. Nate thought it better that we tell him ourselves. That is, on the off chance that he hasn't heard the gossip by then, or read the paper, which will be out that morning."

The baby started to fuss again and squirmed in Mariah's arms. Aaron eyed him anxiously. "Is he always this cranky?"

She walked over and sat down in the rocking chair. "No, he's not. Especially not when he's being fed. Maybe he's getting another tooth."

She put her finger in the child's mouth, much to his howling indignation, and felt his gums, but they didn't seem to be swollen any place. "I guess he's just worn out from all the activity he's been exposed to over the Thanksgiving holiday, and then the trip yesterday. I'll get him into his pajamas and give him his bottle. That should put him to sleep."

It was an hour or better before they got Tommy settled and the supper dishes cleared away. Mariah sat on the couch and Aaron settled into the lounge chair. After politely consulting each other about who wanted which section, they read the Albany *Times Union,* the daily newspaper Mariah subscribed to.

She read it from the first page to the last, but then couldn't remember what she'd read. She was too uptight to concentrate.

When they'd gotten all the mileage they could from the paper, they politely argued over which television programs to watch. Aaron said it didn't matter to him, and Mariah said it didn't matter to her so they wound up watching something that neither had seen before. She had no idea whether it was good or not, because her nerves were about to snap.

When that program ended, the discussion started all over again until Aaron suddenly stopped talking and stood up. "Mariah, are you afraid of me?" He sounded as exasperated as she felt.

Unwittingly she cringed. "No, of course not. Why do you ask?"

He reached the couch in two strides and stood looking down at her. "Because we can't go on like this, treating each other like strangers, or worse yet, predators. I'm not going to throw you down and rape you."

That elicited a sharp gasp from her. "Oh, Aaron, it never occurred to me that you might! It's not you I'm afraid of. It...it's me. I...I'm strongly attracted to you, and—"

He sat down beside her and she promptly forgot what she'd been saying.

"And what?" he murmured softly as his gaze caught hers and hypnotized her with its understanding.

"And I didn't want you to think I was coming on to you," she finished in little more than a whisper.

He reached out and took her in his arms, and she moved closer and snuggled against him. "Whyever not?" His lips nuzzled her hair, sending tremors to all her quivering nerve ends.

"Because... That is, I don't go to bed with the men I date."

He tensed and raised his head. "Are you telling me you're a virgin?"

She shook her head. "No. There was a man in Albany when I first went to work there. We had a relationship, but it turned out to be a passing attraction instead of the real thing. I haven't met anyone since that I wanted to be that intimate with."

He relaxed and rubbed his cheek against the top of her head. "You're not dating me, Mariah. I'm your husband. If you want to make love with me there's no reason to hold back, is there?"

She wasn't sure how to answer him without letting him know she didn't want their marriage to end when the custody situation was settled. She'd agreed to that arrangement knowing exactly what she was doing, and she intended to keep her word.

"No, I guess not. I just don't want you to...to use me as a...a temporary convenience until you're free to choose a woman more to your liking."

He muttered a low oath, but it was one of sadness rather than anger. "Sweetheart, what have I ever done to give you such a low opinion of me? I don't *use* women, and I don't have sex with every woman I take out. The few relationships I have had were fairly long-lasting and both the attraction and the arrangement were mutual. I thought you understood—"

Now she'd really mucked things up! "I do understand," she said forcefully as she sat up and pulled partially away from him. "And I don't have a low opinion of you. I lo—" She bit back the word "love" so quickly that it nearly choked her, and started over. "I like you very much, but I guess I'm afraid of getting that involved with a man again."

He gathered her close to him once more and rained soft little kisses on her eyes and temples until she almost purred with contentment. "Tell you what," he murmured, "why don't we just take it slow and easy? Get to know each other a little more intimately. Do a little kissing and cuddling without either of us feeling pressured to go any further than that and see what happens."

She knew what would happen. After the first few minutes they'd go up in flames, and then wonder afterward how things got so out of hand. However, she was willing to try anything.

"That's fine with me," she said as she kissed the side of his neck.

"That's my girl." He fondled the lobe of her ear with his tongue.

She felt all quivery inside and instinctively clutched at his shoulder when he took her lobe in his mouth and sucked gently.

"You're so soft and snuggly," he said huskily as he caressed her in slow circles that moved closer and closer to the rise of her breast until she was breathless with anticipation.

"And you smell so good," he continued, "like an elusive potpourri. What is that fragrance called?"

She moved her hand from his shoulder to the back of his neck and massaged it. "English Garden," she told him. "I'm glad you like it."

She felt him shiver under her touch. "I like *you*." His voice dropped to little more than a whisper. "The cologne is an added plus, but it's your sweet and loving warmth and your fresh, natural beauty that entices me and makes you so irresistible."

He dropped one hand to her thigh and caressed it lightly through her red slacks. His palm was big and warm and sent heat straight up her inner leg to the core of her being. It was thrilling but, surprisingly, not threatening as it had been when other men did the same thing.

She rubbed her palm over his chest and kissed his throat at the V-opening of his shirt, then caressed it with her tongue and kissed it again. She could feel his heart beating against his ribs and knew she was pleasing him.

That knowledge excited her even more, and she moved her hand to his shirt buttons and unfastened the next two. He wasn't wearing an undershirt, and there was soft hair on his chest. She rubbed her face in it.

The hand that was doing provocative things to her thigh moved up and across her belly to inch under her blouse and cup her lace-covered breast. She gasped and clenched her teeth in an effort to keep from crying out as a wave of exhilaration melted any lingering resistance and left her weak with longing.

Eager to pleasure him as he was pleasuring her, she tore open the rest of his shirt and put her hand inside to stroke his bare chest. Her caresses brought a groan from deep in his throat and he pulled her to him so that their bodies fit tightly together.

She could feel his throbbing hardness against her pulsating heat. She raised her head and his mouth came down on hers, hard and insistent. Lips parted and his tongue plundered and explored before allowing hers to do the same to him.

At first Mariah thought the noise coming from the background was the sound of the tumult her body was experiencing, but gradually she recognized it as a baby crying.

Tommy! The wailing registered in her mind, but it was a few seconds before she could pull herself together enough to respond to it. When she did, and tried to pull away from Aaron, he seemed unwilling or unable to let her go. His arms tightened around her and he muttered frantically, "Oh, God, sweetheart, please..."

She knew how he felt. Those had been her very thoughts when she first realized the baby was crying, but obviously Aaron still wasn't aware of the noise.

She continued to struggle. "Aaron, something's the matter with Tommy," she said loudly. "I'm sorry, but I have to go check on him."

His eyes were glazed with passion, but he released her and shook his head as if to clear it. "What? Tommy? What's wrong with him?"

Mariah was on her feet, but her knees shook and she wasn't sure she could walk. "I don't know. I have to go and find out."

She made it to the bedroom and flicked the light switch. Tommy was sitting up in his crib screaming at the top of his lungs. She rushed over and picked him up. "What's the matter, baby," she said soothingly and cradled him to her. He was hot! Probably running a temperature. He must be getting a new tooth, after all.

"What's wrong with him?" Aaron asked again, and she looked up to see him standing in the doorway.

She told him what she suspected, and he grimaced and walked over to put his hand on the baby's temple. "Geez, kid, you sure know how to shatter a man's nervous system," he said somewhat shakily.

Mariah giggled. "I guess this is why pregnancy has a nine-month gestation period. It gives the newlyweds a little time to... um... mess around without interruption."

He leaned over and kissed her. "A wise idea, my darling, but we're starting our marriage with a ready-made baby, which, if this is any indication of what's ahead for us, could severely damage my whole outlook on family life." He removed his hand from Tommy's forehead. "He feels pretty hot. Shall we call a doctor?"

She headed for the door. "I'll take his temperature, but I think half an acetaminophen tablet and a bottle of warm water will hold him over until morning. That's what Mom used to do when one of her babies woke in the night with a slight temperature.

"There's bedding in the linen closet," she called over her shoulder. "You can make up your bed on the couch, and I'll try not to disturb you."

He grunted. "Don't bother. That's a lost cause. You've disturbed me from the day I first set eyes on you."

Tommy was fretful off and on all night, and the next morning when Aaron and Mariah took him to the doctor they were told he had roseola, a childhood illness that was bothersome but seldom serious. Mariah was up and down with him for the next three nights, though, so Aaron continued to sleep on the sofa.

Word about their elopement got around with record speed, and Mariah and Jessica were kept busy answering the phone and the doorbell. Everybody they talked to said they wouldn't miss the reception and the chance to meet Mariah's new husband, so they upped their order for champagne, and the ladies of the Eastern Star Lodge volunteered to make finger sandwiches.

On Thursday Aaron and Mariah kept their appointment with Judge Gibson in his chambers. With the doctor's permission, they took Tommy along. By then his temperature was normal and he was no longer contagious. He was still cranky, though, and while he'd learned to accept Aaron and Mariah's family as long as Mariah was in sight, she couldn't leave him with anyone else.

Nate met them at the courthouse and they were all ushered into the judge's chambers. He stood and scowled at them while they were being seated, with Mariah holding the baby on her lap, then sat back down behind his desk.

"You have an awful lot of explaining to do, young man," he said, looking directly at Aaron. "I suggest you get started."

Aaron opened his mouth to say something, but Nate quickly intervened. "Your Honor, Mr. Kerr is petitioning to have the original decision on the custody of the child, Thomas Wayne Kerr, set aside now that he has fulfilled your requirement—"

"Does your client have a speech impediment, Mr. Quimby?" the judge interrupted.

Nate looked startled. "No, Your Honor."

"Then let him speak for himself." He turned to Aaron. "I understand you've taken a wife since I last saw you. Is this so?"

Aaron nodded. "Yes, sir." He looked over at Mariah and smiled. "Mariah Bentley and I were married in Burlington, Vermont on Monday of this week."

"How convenient," Gibson said sarcastically. "Perhaps you would explain why."

Aaron blinked. "I beg your pardon?"

"It's a simple question, Mr. Kerr." The judge's voice was laced with steel. "Why have you run off to Vermont and married a woman who, by your own sworn statement, you'd never laid eyes on until earlier this month, when your sister was killed and you needed someone to look after your infant nephew."

"Your Honor...!" Nate had half risen from his chair.

"Sit down, Mr. Quimby," Gibson thundered.

Nate didn't give up easily. "But Your Honor, I'm here on behalf of my client—!"

"Fine. So sit down and listen to what he has to say for himself."

Deliberately Nate stood up straight. "Judge Gibson, I object. Mr. Kerr has a right to legal counsel—"

"And he has legal counsel, as you are taking such pains to let me know. Your objection is noted and overruled."

Nate sat down, his face flaming with indignation.

Unperturbed, the judge turned again to Aaron. "Now, Mr. Kerr, I want you to tell me, in your own words, about this wedding you and Miss Bentley have entered into. Be advised that this is all on the record." He motioned toward the court reporter who was busily recording everything that was being said.

Aaron felt tendrils of panic claw at his nerves. Nate had said he'd do most of the talking, so Aaron hadn't prepared a scenario or given much thought to defending his actions. After all, how many bridegrooms had to defend themselves on a charge of getting married? Wasn't matrimony an inalienable right or something?

He settled back in his chair and laced his fingers together across his stomach. "I'm not sure what it is you want to know, Your Honor. Mariah and I have become strongly attracted to each other in the short time I've been here, and I realized I didn't want us to be separated when I go back to Utah. She admitted she felt the same way about me, so we...we decided to get married."

Damn, it sounded like he was talking about hiring a secretary, or worse, a nanny, which in its purest form was exactly what he was doing!

"How nice," the judge muttered, "but aren't you forgetting something? I didn't hear a word about undying love, or sizzling passion."

Nate jumped to his feet. "Your Honor, I object. Their feelings for each other are personal and private. There is nothing in the law that says a man and a woman have to profess sizzling passion in order to marry!"

"That's true," Gibson agreed amiably, "but review your own marriage vows, Counselor. I don't think there's any doubt that you and your wife vowed to *love*, honor, and...whatever. Every married couple vows before God and the law that they will love each other."

He shifted his gaze to Aaron and Mariah. "What I want to know is, when you vowed to love each other were you being truthful or merely trying to circumvent my custody ruling?"

Chapter Twelve

Aaron and Mariah looked from the judge to each other and back to the judge, too flabbergasted to speak. Even Nate stared in disbelief, but it didn't take him long to find his voice.

His gaze locked with the judge's. "Judge Gibson, I object." His tone was level but deadly serious. "And before you rule on my objection I must tell you that no matter what that ruling is, I'm not going to let my clients answer that question. There's not a precedent anywhere in law that will allow it, and I'll take full responsibility for my clients' silence. If you find them in contempt I'll have no recourse but to take it to a higher court."

Aaron stifled a gasp. He didn't know a lot about the law, but he knew that Nate had just put his career in jeopardy. Now it was a battle of wills between the judge and the attorney.

Gibson's expression was as cold as his tone. "I believe you and some of your fellow lawyers have already done that, Mr. Quimby."

Nate didn't even blink. "Yes, sir," he admitted. "We have, with reluctance, taken that step, but the complaint can be amended to include this, and I don't think you want that."

"Is that a threat, Mr. Attorney?"

"No, Your Honor, that is a promise."

The two men glared at each other in stony silence until the very air vibrated with unbearable tension.

It was Gibson who finally looked away. "The objection is sustained," he said, but not giving an inch in tone and demeanor. "You need not answer the question, Mr. Kerr. I assume you have a marriage license?"

"It's right there with the other papers on your desk, Your Honor." As if the unpleasantness between them had never happened, Nate's voice resumed its respectful sonants.

The judge seemed calm and controlled as he glanced through the papers, but Aaron noticed that his hands shook. Aaron felt a twinge of sympathy for the elderly man. Growing old could be difficult.

Gibson finally put the papers down and looked at Aaron. "Mr. Kerr, I'm not convinced that this marriage of yours was undertaken in good faith, or that you are the right person to have full custody of the child Thomas Wayne Kerr."

He paused, and Aaron's heart sank. Was the judge really intent on putting Tommy up for adoption, even though Aaron had complied with his highly controversial conditions for custody?

"However," he continued, "in the absence of proof of my suspicions, I will rescind my order that the boy not be taken out of the jurisdiction of this court. I'll give you temporary custody of him for one year. If, at the end of that time, you and Mariah are still married and able to produce proof of a happy and stable home life, the arrangement will be reviewed for the possibility of making the custody permanent. Meanwhile, you may take him back to Salt Lake City with you."

It took Aaron a couple of minutes to sort out what had happened. He didn't know whether to celebrate or protest.

He glanced at his nephew curled up on Mariah's lap. He'd won custody of the little guy, but only for a year. If he and Mariah weren't still together at that time, he could lose Tommy altogether!

Aaron was vaguely aware that Nate had somewhat curtly thanked the judge as they got up to leave. Aaron followed the attorney and Mariah, who was carrying Tommy, out of the room and down the hall.

"I'm late for another appointment," Nate said as he looked at his watch, "but I'll get together with you later to discuss this."

Mariah and Aaron spoke little on the way home. He assumed that she was as stunned by the turn of events as he was, and he fumed at the smug maliciousness of the judge's ruling. The man was thoroughly incompetent, but still he was allowed to sit on the bench and make chaos of people's lives. It was bad enough that he was manipulating Aaron's freedom and using his love for his nephew to do it, but now the old coot had caught Mariah in his web, too.

Now, if she still wanted to help him keep Tommy, she'd be tied to him for a whole year! Maybe more.

Not only that, but if she decided she didn't want to consummate the marriage how could he live in the same house with her for a year or more and not make love to her? He was quite sure that would take more self-control than he was capable of. These past few nights of abstinence with only a thin wall between them had shown him that.

It wouldn't be long before he tried to seduce her, and he suspected that he'd succeed. That would make him a real bastard, since he'd promised not to do just that.

No, he couldn't ask her to carry on with this sham of a marriage for so long a time. But if he didn't, if she didn't continue the charade, he'd lose Tommy for sure!

When they got home Mariah changed and fed the baby and gave him his bottle, as her thoughts kept going back and forth over the scene in the judge's chamber. She'd been delighted when he'd said he'd give Aaron temporary custody of the baby, but then he'd made it plain that he'd rescind that custody if she and Aaron weren't still living together at the end of a year.

Her first reaction to that had been one of hope. She had a whole year to make him fall in love with her! But Aaron was clearly upset by the need to prolong their marriage so far beyond what they'd originally expected.

Her hopes were quickly dampened by Aaron's disappointment. He didn't want to be stuck with her that long. He was obviously eager to get her out of his life and go back to his carefree bachelor status.

Once she had Tommy tucked sleepily in his crib, she fixed tuna-fish sandwiches and coffee and carried them on a tray to the coffee table in front of the couch where Aaron was sitting. He looked at her and smiled as she sat down beside him.

"Thank you," he said and reached for a sandwich. "I'm making a lot of extra work for you, aren't I." It wasn't a question.

"That's what wives do," she said. "They look after their husbands."

He put the sandwich back down. "But I never expected you to fuss over me. All you signed up for was to care for Tommy for a few months."

Mariah's stomach knotted and she looked at her own sandwich with sudden distaste. "I did more than just 'sign up.' In case you've forgotten, I also took the vows of marriage. Don't you want me to take care of you?" She sounded as hurt as she felt.

To her surprise he looked stricken. "Oh, hell, I'm sorry. I've always been clumsy with words. It's a good thing I'm an accountant and not a lawyer. What I'm trying to say is that I don't want you to feel obliged to perform wifely duties...." His voice trailed off.

His message was coming across loud and clear. "In other words, you don't want me in your personal life. I'm just the nanny and I'm to remember my place."

"Damn it, that's not what I said or meant." He ran his fingers through his hair. "I just don't want you to feel trapped in this marriage."

"You mean the way you do," she said, finishing for him.

He looked at her with an expression of surprise and disbelief. "You're the one who's trapped. Not me."

Now she was surprised. "Have I ever indicated to you that I feel trapped?"

"You haven't had time. We only just learned of the judge's custody ruling, but you never agreed to stay with Tommy and me for a whole year. I wouldn't have asked that of you. No, make that I *can't* ask that of you. I'll agree to an annulment right away if that's what you want."

"An annulment!" The thought of getting out of the marriage so soon had never occurred to her, and it was the last thing she wanted. She hunched over in an effort to alleviate the pain of his rejection.

"Is ... is that what you want?" she stammered.

He seemed almost as upset as she was. "No, that's not what I want! I need you. Tommy needs you. But I'm not going to hold you to an agreement you never made. I can't let you give up a whole year of your life in order to solve my problem."

I need you! Did he mean that personally, or just expediently? "If you and Tommy need me, as you say, then why are you so eager for an annulment?"

He sighed, and she heard the exasperation behind it. "Mariah, I do not want an annulment. I can't seem to bear the thought of losing you so soon, but neither do I want to hold you to your wedding vows if you feel that the rules have changed. I'll say it again—I don't want you to feel trapped by an agreement that went wrong."

He sounded sincere enough. Maybe he really meant it. "Our agreement didn't go wrong, Aaron. It's true that the judge's decision made it necessary to lengthen the time frame, but don't forget the appeal. We should be hearing from that within a few weeks, or possibly months, and the appellate court is almost certain to throw out Gibson's original ruling, which will also invalidate the second one. I don't see where anything's changed, honest I don't."

Aaron looked somewhat relieved but still doubtful. "And if they let the original decision stand? What then? Will you still be willing to spend the rest of the twelve months' time limit with us to convince Gibson that we have a happy and secure marriage?"

Mariah didn't have any doubts at all. The longer she stayed, the more time she'd have to convince him she was the only wife for him. "Of course I would. I love Tommy. I wouldn't do anything to put his well-being at risk. There is one thing I want to ask of you, however."

A look of uncertainty replaced his relieved expression. "Anything."

"If I'm going to be in your home mothering Tommy then I want to take care of you, too. I don't want us to live like two separate tenants renting the same house. I feel strongly that we must make a home for Tommy, not just a shelter. Will you agree?"

Aaron leaned back on the couch and held his arms out to her. She didn't need any coaxing, but snuggled happily in them. "Mariah, my love, how could I help but agree?" He nuzzled her exposed cheek. "There's nothing I want more than for you to take care of me, but it seems so selfish. You'll do all the work, and I'll get all the benefits, all the sheer joy of having you fuss over me. You're so extraordinarily good at that."

He put his fingers under her chin and raised her face for his kiss. It was almost like a spiritual experience rather than a physical one, gentle and soothing, and so very needy. It reassured her more than all the words he could say that he really did want her to stay with him even if it took an entire year to settle the custody problem.

It gave her renewed hope that he wouldn't be able to let her go when the time came.

She twined her arms around his neck and nibbled at his lips. He responded eagerly, but within seconds he raised his head and pressed her face back into his shoulder. "I... I think we'd better eat our sandwiches before they get soggy," he murmured raggedly.

Saturday morning was gray and windy, but by two o'clock when the guests started to arrive the sun had come out and made the snow sparkle. The wind had died down, and the air was crisp and fresh and invigorating.

Mariah and her mother had chosen red, green and white as their decorating colors since it was now the early part of December and Christmas was on everyone's mind. Red poinsettias and holly berries, green leaves and ivy, and white bells and candles festooned every room in the house.

Mariah, Aaron and Tommy wore their wedding clothes, and her parents and all five of her brothers and sisters were present and elegant in their best outfits. Jessica had insisted on having a photographer there to record the occasion since they had no pictures of their wedding.

Mariah had made a few arrangements of her own for later on, but no one knew about them but her. She'd share them later, but only with Aaron.

The guests, unable to curb their curiosity, started arriving a few minutes early. The invitation in the paper had specified an open house so they tended to come and go in bunches all afternoon. That was fortunate because the house would never have held them all at once.

The ladies of the lodge were kept busy in the kitchen dispensing champagne punch and finger sandwiches, keeping crystal and silver bowls filled with nuts and candies, and cutting the beautifully decorated cake.

The younger cousins kept Tommy entertained in one of the bedrooms upstairs, while Mariah and Aaron made the rounds downstairs so she could introduce her groom to the guests coming in, and thank those who were preparing to leave. He was charming and seemed right at home with the crowd of strangers. They were all genuinely impressed with her choice of a husband.

It was dark by the time all the guests had left, but the family insisted that they open the large stack of beautifully wrapped gifts that had been so generously showered on them. They'd requested "no gifts" in the invitation published in the paper, but apparently nobody had paid any attention.

Mariah felt badly about that because the marriage was to be such a short one, but it was exciting to open the packages while the camera continued to flash and click. Tommy had joined the group by then, and he had the most fun of them all, sitting in the middle of the discarded wrappings and squealing with delight as he scattered them around.

One of the gifts was a sexy black chiffon-and-lace nightgown. It brought a chorus of hoots and whistles, and Mariah hid her flaming face in it while everyone laughed.

By the time Aaron and Mariah managed to break away and get to the cottage it was past Tommy's bedtime. It was also time for the surprise she'd arranged for Aaron. When she was planning it, it had seemed like a romantic way to let him know what she wanted. But now, while she undressed Tommy and got him ready for bed, all the doubts she'd shoved into the background surfaced.

What if she'd misunderstood his signals and it wasn't what he wanted at all? She'd make a fool of herself and embarrass him. Maybe she should just forget the whole thing. He seemed reasonably content to go on the way they were.

When she had finished with the baby, she carried him out to kiss his uncle Aaron good-night. Aaron had removed his suit coat and tie, unbuttoned the first two buttons of his white shirt, and was watching a football game on television. Should she just leave well enough alone and let him enjoy the game?

He took Tommy from her and played with him for a few minutes, then kissed him and handed him back to her. Mariah took Tommy back into the bedroom and shut the door. Instead of putting him in his crib she lowered him to the floor and let him crawl around.

Now was the time. Mariah either had to go through with her plan or forget it altogether. She removed her dress and hung it carefully in the closet, then took off her white lace slip and her panty hose.

Now what? She could pull on jeans and a T-shirt, or...

Her gaze fastened on the new black nightie that she'd laid out across the bed. There could be no mistaking the message if she went back to the living room in that!

Walking to the closet she pulled out her purple velour robe. It zipped up the front and had a violet appliqué across the low-cut bodice. Her parents had given it to her for Christmas last year, along with matching furry slippers, and it was very beautiful. It covered almost every inch of her, but still somehow managed to be sexy.

She studied both garments. Should she or shouldn't she? She wanted to send him the message, but maybe this wasn't the way.

Her nerves were beginning to fray. What was the matter with her, anyway? It wasn't as if she was a teenage virgin! She was twenty-six years old and married to the man. The only reason the marriage hadn't been consummated was because she'd been reluctant, so now the move was up to her.

Quickly she finished undressing and slid the silky nightie over her head. The skirt fell to the floor in soft folds, and the bodice was just tantalizing enough to drive a man crazy without being brassy. She put on the robe, brushed her hair until the golden highlights glowed, then settled Tommy down in his crib and rubbed his back as she crooned soft lullabies to him until his tired little eyes closed.

Quickly she turned down the bed covers, then tried to calm her pounding heart as she walked across the room and out the door, pulling it almost shut behind her. Aaron was still sitting in the chair watching the ball game on television as she came up behind him. A fresh wave of shyness swept over her, and she almost turned and bolted, but managed to control the urge.

Deliberately lowering her voice she asked, "Would you like me to make some coffee?"

A shiver feathered over her skin when he turned his head to look at her. "Not for me, thanks, I'm about coffeed out..."

His voice broke and he blinked. "Mariah!"

He continued to stare as she moved to stand in front of him. "Do you like it?" This time her voice lowered all by itself.

"I like it very much," he rasped. "What have you got on under it?"

His expression quickly changed to one of regret, and she knew the question had slipped out accidentally.

She allowed the corners of her mouth to turn up in a tiny smile. "Why don't you take it off me and find out?"

He reached out for her hand, and with a gentle tug pulled her down onto his lap. "Do you know what you're doing?" he asked unsteadily.

"I think so." She leaned over to kiss him on the cheek. "But I'm not very experienced." She kissed the other cheek. "If I'm not doing it right, please tell me."

He put his arms around her waist and tumbled her so that she lay across his lap with her head on his shoulder. "You're doing just fine, sweetheart," he said against her ear. "But you'd better understand that if this goes any further I won't be held responsible."

"I sincerely hope you won't," she whispered and started to unbutton his shirt.

His eager hands were stroking her all over, her breasts, her waist, her hips, her legs. It was like a tender assault that took away her breath and left her aching for more.

Her fingers trembled as she wrestled with the tiny buttons until she finally got them all open. By then he had lowered the zipper on her robe, and she could feel the exciting warmth of his palms through the thin protection of chiffon.

"You have a body that could drive a man right out of his mind," he murmured as his hand pushed aside the wisp of material and cupped her bare breast. "Have you any idea how badly I've wanted to do this? What hell it's been for me to resist?" He rolled her nipple between his thumb and finger, causing her to shiver with pure ecstasy.

"I...I know how hard it's been for me not to touch you," she confessed shakily.

He nibbled at the side of her neck. "Where did you want to touch me?"

Her fingers dug into his nape. "Anywhere. Everywhere." A picture of him walking ahead of her in his tight jeans flashed into her mind. "You've got the cutest rear end—"

He threw his head back and laughed. It was a joyous sound. "So have you, my darling, so have you." He stroked the area he was talking about. "Please feel free to touch mine anytime."

She chuckled. "Anytime?"

"Absolutely anytime, but if you do be prepared to take the consequences. My self-control with you is all used up."

To prove his point he raised her slightly and took the hard, rosy nub of her breast in his mouth. He teased it with his tongue then sucked gently, causing tiny explosions in her most intimate recesses.

Mariah felt the shuddering groan that started deep in her chest and was muffled in his shoulder as she moved her head back and forth in ecstatic torment.

He trailed one hand slowly down her stomach and stopped, then let his fingers roam lower, making her reflexes jump and her lower body squirm in his lap.

He squirmed, too, and bit tenderly at her breast before releasing it. "Sweetheart, stop wiggling like that," he groaned. "I won't be able to hold back if you do."

She felt his hardness beneath her, but his fingers were driving her crazy. She couldn't stop bucking into them. "I . . . I can't," she panted.

Much to her dismay he removed his hand and zipped her robe. "We need a bed." His voice was raspy. "But what are we going to do about the baby? We don't want to wake him."

Reluctantly she sat up. "I already thought of that," she said through lips swollen by his kisses. "We can move the crib out here."

He grinned. "You've been planning this whole thing?"

She grinned back. "Uh-huh. I hope you don't mind."

"Would I mind blundering into heaven?" he asked, then carefully pushed her off his lap and stood up. "I just hope Tommy doesn't wake up and cry."

Tommy slept peacefully as they rolled his crib out into the kitchen area, and Aaron turned off the lights as he and Mariah returned to the bedroom. The full moon was glowing outside the window and bouncing moonbeams off the snow. There was enough illumination for them to walk around without bumping into the furniture.

"Do you want the lights on or off?" Aaron asked huskily as he closed the door.

"I . . . I like to look out and see the moon shining in the window and all the snow-laden trees," she told him. "That is, if that's all right with you."

His hands cupped her shoulders and drew her close. "I'm not going to be looking at anything but you," he murmured. "So whatever you prefer is fine with me."

He found the pull tab at the top of her zipper and lowered it, then slid the robe off her shoulders and let it fall to the floor around her feet. They were close enough to see each other in the moonlight, and his glance devoured her.

"Ah, the black nightie," he breathed. "When you unwrapped the package you couldn't have known how fervently I prayed that very soon I'd get to take it off you."

She was sure she blushed even though it was dark. "Do...do I get to undress you?" she stammered, and felt her blush grow hotter.

"I hope you will." His voice shook slightly. "I love having your soft little hands on me."

He had a way of saying things that made her melt in all the right places, but now she didn't know where to start. His shirt was already unbuttoned, but it was still tucked into his pants. It would be easier to pull it free if she removed his belt and unfastened the top button, but that seemed awfully forward.

"Honey, you'd better get on with it." His tone combined both humor and impatience. "I'm not a robot, and I'm getting hotter by the minute."

She knew she was taking too long, but she wasn't going to let him know how flustered she was. Deliberately she moved a step closer which put her body flush against his, then rubbed her face in his chest hair. "Really?" she asked innocently. "But we have all night."

She moved her face to one side and licked circles around his hard male nipple.

His arms closed around her and crushed her to him while his hand pushed her groin into his throbbing hardness. "You may have all night, but I don't," he muttered. "I don't know how much more of this I can stand."

She didn't have a lot of firsthand knowledge of men's sexual responses, but she knew he wasn't exaggerating. She tried to push herself back so she could get started on her exciting task, but he hugged her closer. "No. Don't pull away from me!" he whispered raggedly.

"But I have to unfasten your clothes," she protested.

He didn't speak for a moment, then took one arm from around her waist and held up his hand. "Here, take out my cuff link."

She did, and he put that arm around her again and held up the other one. "Now this one."

She was getting into the spirit of it. She took out the second cuff link and tossed them both on the floor. They could search for them later.

She wedged her hand between their entwined bodies. "You'll have to give me some space so I can unbuckle your belt," she murmured as she again laid her cheek on his bare chest.

His heart was pounding, but he loosened his hold on her enough so she could unfasten and remove his belt. Then she fumbled with the button. He groaned, and a tremor ran through him as he bunched up her nightgown and caressed her bare bottom.

Mariah was as heated as he was, and she ripped the shirt out of his pants and slid it off him. When she reached for his zipper he captured her hands and held them against his chest. "Just a minute, love," he said in a strangled tone. "I want to take that nightie off you, and I know that once you start grappling with that zipper I'm going to forget everything else."

He released her wrists and stepped back, then reached down and slowly drew the hem of her gown up her legs, her hips, her breasts, and finally over her head. Touching her only with his hands, he let them roam over her naked body, caressing her firm high breasts, spanning her small waist with his two palms, stroking her quivering belly and tenderly kneading her derriere.

He was handling her as he would a delicate work of art, and she squeezed her eyes shut to concentrate more fully on the ripples of pleasure that swept through her and left her helpless and trembling in their wake. She ached with wanting him.

Without further delay Aaron swept her up in his arms and laid her down on the bed. He swiftly finished undressing himself and leaned over her. She held out her arms and he lowered himself on top of her, then captured her mouth. In a frenzy of desire her legs encircled him and he entered her, carefully at first but when she arched her hips and dug her fingers into his back he lost control and thrust deeply into her throbbing heat.

The whole world exploded, and for a long time Mariah was lost in the ecstasy that buffeted her again...and again...and yet again.

The euphoria lasted all night as she slept in Aaron's arms. She'd never experienced anything like it before.

Toward morning she wakened to the delicious warmth of his body curled around her back, and his hands working their magic on her, and she turned to him eagerly.

This time they were able to go a little slower, and it was every bit as good as before. Aaron's lovemaking was all Mariah had imagined or hoped it would be. Wonderful. Satisfying. How could she ever let him go?

If only... if only he loved her....

Chapter Thirteen

Aaron, Mariah and Tommy left Apple Junction early Monday morning amidst many tearful goodbyes from the Bentley family. They drove to Burlington where they dropped off the rental car and caught a commuter flight for Albany on the first leg of their journey to Salt Lake City.

It was an exciting trip for Mariah, who had never flown before. O'Hare Airport in Chicago where they changed planes the second time was positively mammoth. The hike between concourses seemed like miles with her carrying her hand luggage and purse while Aaron balanced Tommy in one arm and assorted baby paraphernalia in the other. Because of the holiday season they'd been unable to secure an extra seat for Tommy so they took turns holding him on their laps during the flight.

It was midafternoon when the plane approached Salt Lake City for a landing. As it came out of the clouds, Mariah could see the snow-covered city nestled at the foot of the Wasatch mountains with the Great Salt Lake visible to the northwest and the salt desert to the west.

"Oh, Aaron, it's beautiful!" Her tone was filled with awe. "Such wide-open space. I've never seen a desert before. New York is so crowded, and the mountains are mostly heavily forested."

Aaron smiled indulgently and squeezed the hand he was holding. "Utah has a diverse landscape. Two mountain ranges, vast salt and alkali deserts, and an inland sea. The various regions also have different climates. The desert is dry and hot, while the mountains have cold winters with spectacular snowfalls."

He shifted Tommy from one knee to the other when the child started to fuss, probably because the change in altitude hurt his ears. "The Great Salt Lake was discovered in the early eighteen-hundreds," he continued, "by a couple of trappers who reported they had found an arm of the Pacific Ocean. Salt Lake City was founded about twenty-five years later by Brigham Young and the Mormons, who had come west in search of a place they could settle and be safe from religious persecution."

The plane finally landed and pulled into the boarding gate. Aaron and Mariah gathered up Tommy and their belongings and slowly made their way down the crowded aisle and up the ramp into the terminal. They were headed for the baggage department when a young woman caught up with them and put her hand on Mariah's arm.

"Excuse me," she said, "but aren't you Mariah Bentley? Or, I guess I should say, Mrs. Aaron Kerr?"

Startled, Mariah stopped and turned to face her. The woman was wearing khaki slacks and an unbuttoned trench coat, and had a notepad and pencil in her hand.

Mariah groaned inwardly.

"Yes, I'm Mariah Kerr." Even through her exasperation she felt the thrill that always went through her when she said her new name.

The reporter beamed and looked at Aaron, who had Tommy strapped to his back in a canvas carrying seat. "And this must be the dying baby whose life was saved by the angel," she cooed. "Isn't it miraculous how she not only saved the child, but brought you two together? It's so romantic!"

Mariah had heard all of the drivel she could stand. Apparently Aaron had, too, because he glared at the woman. "Look, miss, we've had a long trip, and the baby is tired and hungry. We're eager to get home, and we'd appreciate it if you'd just leave us alone."

He motioned to Mariah to follow him, since all his hands were full and he couldn't take her arm, then started walking again at an accelerated pace.

"Oh, but I... At least let me take your picture," the reporter called as they strode off.

They didn't slow down or talk until they reached the baggage claim and stood waiting for their luggage to come out.

"I wonder how she found out we'd be arriving on this flight," Aaron grumbled. "We didn't broadcast our itinerary."

Mariah sighed with resignation. "No, but I'm beginning to think reporters have a sixth sense. What I can't understand is why she would seek us out. I mean, it's been a month since the accident, and it's not as if there wasn't any other news going on in the world."

Aaron set the diaper bag and carryall on the floor at his feet. "Your mysterious lady in white is the type of thing that sells papers. At any given time there's a lot of misery going on in the world, and I think we all like to believe that if the going gets too tough we can hope for some type of divine intervention to help us through it."

She set her makeup case and weekender bag on the floor, too. "I can understand that, but I've never indicated that what I saw was an angel."

"I know, love, but be truthful with yourself. Haven't you sometimes wondered if there wasn't something ... something supernatural about your experience?"

Mariah started to shake her head, then stopped. Why was she so adamant in her denial that it wasn't a spiritual being? Maybe it was Tommy's guardian angel who appeared to her and, through her, saved the baby's life?

Well, for one thing, the whole idea scared her. She didn't want there to be anything guiding her life that she couldn't see, hear or feel.

But she had seen the apparition in the road. Be it physical or spiritual, she *had* seen it. Denying the possibility of its being mystic in nature wouldn't make it go away.

She sighed. "Oh, I don't know. I admit it was a miracle that we found Tommy, but it would still be a miracle if it was a real, live woman, or even a trick of the lights that distracted me. Why is it so necessary to people that it be an angel?"

Before he could answer the luggage began to appear, and Aaron moved closer to watch for their suitcases.

After hailing a taxi, Aaron asked the driver to drive through the center of town so Mariah could see the city in which she'd be living. Even though the daylight was waning into dusk she could see that it was beautiful, especially with the brightly lit Christmas decorations that were now out in all their glory and the shoppers carrying colorful shopping bags and gaily decorated packages.

They took a turn through Temple Square, home of the Mormon Temple and the Tabernacle among other intriguing structures, and high atop Capitol Hill they glimpsed the State Capitol building with its massive copper-covered dome.

A short while later Aaron pointed out the campus of the University of Utah. "This is my alma mater. It's the oldest state university west of the Mississippi," he said proudly, but his tone changed to sadness as he continued. "Eileen finished her sophomore year before she dropped out."

Mariah heard the grief in his tone and put her hand on his thigh, knowing that it would distract his thoughts from his sorrow.

It was almost dark when they pulled up in front of Aaron's two-story white house set in the middle of a large lot on top of a hill in an affluent neighborhood. Inside was a wide rectangular entry hall with a staircase up the left wall. Aaron turned on lights as he led Mariah from room to room, the formal dining room and the kitchen on the left, a large living room and an office on the right, and a glass-walled sunroom and a bathroom at the end of the hall.

"There's a laundry room and another bathroom off the kitchen," he explained.

Mariah was more than impressed, she was amazed. "Your home is lovely, and so big," she told Aaron.

"Yes," he said. "Far too big for me. After Eileen left I started making plans to sell it and move to an apartment closer in, but now, with Tommy..."

His voice trailed off and he turned the heat thermostat higher, then took her upstairs to see the four bedrooms and two baths. "I think this would be a good place for the nursery," he said as they stood in the room next to the master bedroom. *Their bedroom,* she thought happily.

"It's perfect," she said, surveying the graceful old mahogany furnishings which would probably have to be put in storage to make way for the tiny-tot equipment they'd need for Tommy. "I won't have any trouble hearing him when he wakes up in the middle of the night, but maybe you should have an intercom system put in so I can be sure of hearing him during the day when he's napping up here and I'm downstairs."

He nodded. "You're right. I'll make arrangements first thing tomorrow to have it done. Fortunately I still have the baby furniture that I bought for him when he was born in the attic. Eileen didn't take it with her. It would have cost almost as much to ship as to buy new stuff when she got to New York."

He held out the child to her. "Here, why don't you take him downstairs and feed him while I go up and bring down the crib? We can get the other things tomorrow."

Much later, after they'd settled the baby in the crib, eaten the chicken dinners Aaron picked up from a nearby fast-food restaurant, and unpacked and put away their clothes, they climbed the stairs again and entered the master bedroom. The antique grandfather clock in the living room had chimed midnight just minutes before.

Aaron closed the door and leaned back against it with a sigh. "God, but it's good to finally have a little privacy," he said. "I hadn't realized how disruptive a child can be until I started sleeping with you. I felt as if I was about to do something really sinful every time we pushed Tommy's crib out of the bedroom so we could make love without waking him."

She chuckled. "Actually, I thought it added a little spice to our lovemaking. Not that we needed any," she hastened to explain, "but the forbidden-fruit element is kind of exciting."

He smiled and held out his arms to her. She came to him and snuggled into them. "Sweetheart, I don't need any more excitement when I'm with you. It's all I can do to control myself as it is."

She loved it when he held her like this, so warm, and caring, and . . . and possessive. "Why do you feel that you have to control yourself?"

He rubbed his cheek in her hair. "I don't when we're alone like this, but you arouse me without even trying, and in some of the damndest places. We would have gotten cold and wet tumbling on the snowy ground on the streets of Apple Junction, and there wasn't any room to maneuver on the airplane. Besides, we don't want to be arrested for outraging public decency, they wouldn't let us share the same cell."

She laughed, but a wave of heat washed over her. If he thought he was the only one who had trouble controlling himself he was wrong. He aroused her just talking about it!

Mariah tightened her arms around his neck and rubbed her groin against his. "Oh, my," she said, trying hard to keep her voice from quivering. "You do have a problem, don't you?"

His hand pressed on her derriere, holding her in place. "No problem," he assured her shakily. "The front door's locked and we have the house to ourselves. We can do anything we want."

She thought about that for a moment. "Anything?" She nibbled at the side of his neck.

He shivered. "Absolutely anything. What did you have in mind?"

That stumped her. She'd never played erotic games. She'd had no idea that making love could be so consistently mind-blowing. And things had been so hectic since their first explosive lovemaking on Thursday night that they hadn't had the leisure or privacy to attempt any kind of sexual love play.

They'd made love every night, but had been too afraid of being interrupted to prolong it. And it would have been an exercise in futility to try, anyway. They were always too turned on by the time they got to bed to hold back.

Aaron lifted Mariah and she raised her legs and locked them around his waist. Quickly he clutched at her bottom to support her then drove his hard length against her clothes-covered heat. Their muscles clenched and their arms tightened around each other as they moved in glorious unison.

It took every bit of Mariah's willpower to stop responding and murmur in Aaron's ear. "I hate to break this up, but we'd better get out of our clothes."

His fingers dug into the flesh of her buttocks, but he managed to slow down. "You've been taking lessons from Tommy on how to shatter my complete nervous system," he accused lovingly. "Between the two of you you're going to make a eunuch of me."

He lowered her to her feet, then took her hand and walked with her to the bed. They sat down on the side and took off their shoes and socks, then stood and removed their slacks and shirts.

When they were down to their underwear, Aaron turned to her. "Let me," he said huskily and reached for the fastener on her bra. He undid it and slipped the bra off her arms, then hunkered down and put his fingers under the waist of her panties. Slowly he slid them over her hips and legs, tenderly kissing his way down her stomach as he uncovered her bare flesh inch by inch.

Mariah gasped and her muscles twitched as he came closer and closer to his final goal. Just before his mouth touched her soft short thatch of hair, he stood up and gently lowered her across the bed. He stepped out of his briefs and followed her down to lie between her legs and start all over again from the top.

He cupped her face with his hands and kissed her, a long, deep, erotic kiss that left her breathless when he broke it off to nuzzle first one side of her throat, then the other. The blood pounded in her ears and she twined her legs with his.

Lowering his head he licked at one of her straining nipples, then took it in his mouth and suckled. She writhed beneath him and ran her fingernails up and down his back as the tension building in her most feminine parts escalated.

He seemed to know just how far he could go without driving her over the edge. By the time he started moving slowly downward, nibbling and licking his way across her belly, she was tossing her head from side to side and clutching at his bare back and shoulders as she begged for release.

"Just hold on a minute longer," he said, and with a final shove downward, his mouth found what it was seeking and his tongue plundered her hidden erotic folds and creases.

With a cry of exaltation she lost all control and was catapulted into swirling, mindless rapture. Aaron joined their bodies with a deep thrust and together they soared.

The following morning Tommy woke Aaron and Mariah early with a frightened scream that sent them both scurrying out of bed and into the nursery next door. He was sitting up in the crib crying at the top of his lungs with tears streaming down his chubby little face.

Mariah reached him first and swept him into her arms. He clung to her and trembled as he sobbed on her shoulder. "What's the matter with him?" Aaron shouted over the noise.

"I'm not sure," she answered as she patted and soothed the terrified child. "I suspect that he woke up and found himself in a strange place and all alone, like he did in the hospital after the accident."

She kissed his soft, wet cheek and paced slowly around the room. "The poor little guy has been subjected to so many frightening experiences in the past month, and now he's been uprooted again and put in another unfamiliar environment."

Aaron looked both frustrated and helpless. "Maybe we'd better take him to a doctor. Eileen had him in the care of a pediatrician from the time he was born until she took him and went to New York. The guy's name is Foster, and his number is in the Rolodex by the phone in the office downstairs."

"I think he'll quiet down once he trusts the fact that we're here with him," she said. "I agree that we should take him in for a checkup, but unless he's sick, I suspect it would be better to stay here and let him get used to the house before we introduce him to even more strange people and places. He won't remember the doctor or the doctor's office, and he'll just be scared all over again when we take him there."

Aaron could see the logic in that, and went downstairs to make coffee and warm the baby's bottle while Mariah continued to ease and reassure Tommy. Thank God for her maternal instinct and good common sense! What was he going to do when she left him alone with the child and went back to New York?

The very thought terrified him. He knew absolutely nothing about taking care of babies. When Eileen had brought Tommy home from the hospital after he was born, Aaron had provided them with all the material things they'd needed, but he left the care and nurturing of the child to Eileen. She seemed to know what to do for him, and Aaron had left her to it. He'd never changed a diaper or given a baby a bottle until Mariah showed him how and insisted that he do it.

He took the baby bottle out of the pan of hot water and tested the milk temperature on his wrist. It felt about right, but he decided to leave it in for a while longer since he didn't know how long it would be before Tommy calmed down enough to eat.

His thoughts went back to Mariah's inevitable departure. He winced and shied away from that fact. Why was it so painful? They'd both known from the beginning that their marriage was only a temporary device to give Aaron custody of Tommy. That's the way they'd both wanted it. Wasn't it?

He shook his head. Not in denial, but in an effort to dislodge the whole subject. It would be months yet before he had to confront that issue, so why was he worrying about it now? When the time came he'd hire a full-time nanny and wish Mariah a happy and eventful life as he kissed her goodbye and sent her on her way.

The jab of pain that jolted him was so sharp that he dropped the top of the coffeemaker he'd just finished scooping coffee into. Damn it to hell. What was the matter with him? This had been his idea and it was a good one. He didn't want to get involved with any woman on a full-time basis. Mariah didn't want to make any commitments, either. She'd been pretty specific about that, so why was he having second thoughts?

A short time later Mariah brought Tommy downstairs, dressed and ready for his breakfast. He still clung to her, but as long as she stayed in sight he didn't cry.

She insisted that Aaron go to the office as he'd planned, and he didn't put up too much opposition. He'd been away a long time, and he needed to get started on the mountain of work that had piled up for him.

When he arrived at the building where his firm's accounting offices were located, he bought a copy of the Salt Lake City *Tribune*, one of the city's two newspapers, from the vendor in the lobby. As he waited for the elevator he glanced at the headlines and made a mental note to call and restart his home delivery as soon as he got to his office.

By ten o'clock Mariah had Tommy back in bed and was busy settling into her new temporary home. How she wished it were permanent! If Aaron was given total custody of his nephew would he still sell the house and move into a smaller one? Or would he give up his dream of bachelor digs and stay here?

It tore at her heart to think of him selling this beautiful place. It was even more painful to think of him living here in the future without her!

The ring of the telephone interrupted her thoughts as she was checking the cupboards and pantry for food supplies. Quickly she picked it up, before it could waken Tommy.

It was Aaron. "Hi, honey. Just calling to see if you're all right? Have they been bothering you?"

Mariah frowned. "Everything's fine here, Aaron. Who did you think would be bothering me?"

"I'm sorry," he apologized, "I'd forgotten that you don't have a copy of the paper. There's a small article in one of the inside pages about our arrival here yesterday. A lot of purple prose about how romantic it is that the angel who saved Tommy's life also brought us together as soul mates, or some such nonsense. I was afraid the reporters might be bothering you."

Mariah wasn't surprised at the story, not after their encounter with the reporter yesterday. But she was hurt.

Maybe it was purple prose, but did Aaron have to be so totally unmoved by it. It sounded pretty romantic to her.

"No," she assured him. "I haven't seen the paper, nor have I had any phone calls. Maybe we're old news."

"I hope so, too," he said wryly. "But maybe they just haven't managed to get my unlisted home number yet. If any of them do get through to you, just tell them you have no comment and hang up."

"I'll let the answering machine take all calls from now on, and you can decide which ones you want to return when you get home," she offered.

"Thanks, love," he said. "By the way, I'll probably be late getting home for dinner. I'm really swamped down here. I'm having trouble getting any work done. Everyone wants to hear about my new wife."

The following three weeks were busy and exciting ones. After a few days Tommy got used to his new home. Mariah saw to it that it was as childproof as possible so that he could crawl around on the carpeted floors instead of being cooped up in the playpen all the time.

Most importantly, they were not unduly bothered by reporters. Aaron had calls at the office the first few days, but when it became clear that he wasn't going to answer questions they stopped bothering him. It seemed to him they'd already wrung all they could get out of that story, anyway.

It became evident that Mariah would need some way to get around the city while Aaron was at work, so he gave her her Christmas present early. A brand-new red Oldsmobile!

It was gorgeous and expensive, and she loved it. She never missed a chance to tell him how much and thank him, but it made her feel uneasy and more than a little bit bought. Aaron had assured her it was hers to do with as she pleased, but did that mean she was free to drive it back to New York when she left?

They never talked about the fact that she'd be leaving when the custody battle was settled. For some reason they both shied away from it, so Mariah didn't know what he had in mind, but she had the uncomfortable feeling that she was more of a mistress than a wife.

The partners in the accounting office hosted a cocktail party for the newlyweds at one of the luxury hotels, and it seemed to Mariah they must have invited half the population of Salt Lake City. She had bought a new red chiffon dress in honor of the Christmas season, and Aaron looked dashing in the black suit he'd been married in.

Everyone commented on what a good-looking couple they were, and she could tell from the expression on Aaron's face that he was proud of her. Much to her delight he even told her so any number of times.

It had been a wonderfully exciting evening, and even Tommy cooperated by not waking up and discovering that Mariah was gone and he had a baby-sitter. When they got home their lovemaking had been truly awesome.

Now, on this Wednesday evening just five days before Christmas, Aaron and Mariah had put up and decorated a seven-foot tree with brightly colored, twinkling lights, and a large variety of sparkling ornaments. Christmas music from the expensive stereo system wafted through the rooms, and Tommy stood safely ensconced in his playpen, his little eyes round with wonder as he squealed in delight at the blinking red, green and gold bulbs that seemed to set the tree ablaze.

Aaron looked at him and laughed. "That kid is going to start walking any day now. I can't believe he's pulling himself up on his feet already. He's grown and changed so much just in the past six weeks."

"Yes, he certainly has," Mariah said absently from where she sat on the floor rummaging through the box the ornaments had been stored in. "Don't you have...?" Her hand touched a piece of tissue paper wrapped around something hard. She picked it up and unwrapped it. "Oh, this must be the decoration for the top," she said, and held up a hollow ceramic Santa Claus with a pack of toys slung over his back.

He took the Santa from her hand. "Yes, it is, but I have something you might like better," he said and left the room to return shortly with a red-and-gold foil-wrapped box.

She looked up at him and he handed it to her. "For me?"

He nodded. "Open it." There was a twinkle in his eye and excitement in his voice.

She carefully removed the beautiful wrappings that covered a white gift box. What had he bought her now? She hoped it wasn't another extravagant gift that she would feel uneasy about accepting.

Removing the lid she dug into the protective foam popcorn and brought up an exquisite porcelain angel. It took her a moment to catch her breath. "Oh, Aaron," was about all she could manage to say as he hunkered down beside her.

"I was in Temple Square yesterday on business, and as I walked past the jewelry store I glanced in the window and there was that angel. It caught my attention immediately and I knew it was meant for you. Isn't she lovely?"

Mariah took a deep breath. "She's magnificent. I've never seen a finer figurine."

She slowly turned it in her hands. The angel was about ten inches high and radiant in white except for her face and hair, which were tinted in delicate pastels. There was no halo, but a wreath of faintly colored flowers crowned her slightly tilted head, and her wings were high and graceful.

Mariah raised her head and reached up to kiss him. "Thank you, darling." Her voice was husky. "I'll treasure it always."

She insisted on putting the angel on the top of the tree herself. She wanted to be sure it was securely fastened so it wouldn't fall and break. Aaron held the stepladder for her while she worked.

She was up and down the ladder several times checking to make sure her placement was perfect before she finally decided that it was. She had just descended to the floor for the last time when the telephone rang.

"I'll get it," Aaron said, and hurried to pick it up in the kitchen.

Mariah began to clean up the mess they'd made and put away the storage boxes. Aaron's excited voice rang through the house. "Mariah, come here. It's Nate. He has something to tell us."

She ran to the kitchen and heard Aaron say, "Here's Mariah. Tell her what you told me." He put down the phone and turned on the speaker so they could both listen.

She didn't waste any time on chitchat. "Nate, what's happened?"

Nate laughed at the other end of the line. "Good news. I've been out of the office all day, and when I got back I found a registered letter from the appellate court."

She gasped, "Already! What did it say?"

Nate chuckled gleefully. "It said the court has reversed Judge Gibson's ruling and given Aaron permanent custody of Tommy."

Chapter Fourteen

Mariah squealed and reached for Aaron, who swept her into his arms and hugged her. She hugged back and he swung her around in circles as they both laughed exuberantly.

"Hey, you guys," Nate called happily over the speaker phone. "Are you still with me? Calm down and talk to me."

"I just can't believe it," she shouted toward the phone. "I thought it was supposed to be months before we got a ruling. I can't conceive of it happening so fast."

"I can't believe it myself," Nate said, "but for some reason they went right to work on your appeal. They didn't offer an explanation and I'm sure not going to ask for one."

"Oh, God, no!" Aaron exclaimed as he stopped twirling Mariah and just held her close against him. "Just tell them 'thank you! thank you! thank you!' Do we have to come back there for anything?''

"No," Nate assured him. "There will be some papers to sign and so forth, but that can be handled by fax or mail. I would suggest that you petition for adoption as soon as possible. That's the only way you can be sure he'll never be taken away from you. For now relax, and have a merry Christmas. Santa just brought you a baby boy. Enjoy!"

"We will!" they chorused in unison. "And we can never thank you enough," Aaron said. "I don't believe for a minute that this was as easy as you'd like us to think. I know you appeared before the court, and your argument must have been great."

"Thanks for the kind words," Nate answered, "but you had a classic case for appeal. Judge Gibson's ruling was way off base. I suspect this will be the last time a ruling of his is appealed. Sorry you had to be the ones to have that dubious honor, but steps are being taken to ensure his retirement shortly after the first of the year."

They talked for a few more minutes, then hung up and called Mariah's parents in Apple Junction to tell them the good news in a four-way conversation. "Oh, Aaron, I'm so happy for you," Jessica said, her voice bubbling with excitement. "What a wonderful Christmas present!"

"Yes, it is," he agreed, "and we couldn't be happier."

"I only wish you could be here with us," Mariah said. "This will be the first Christmas that we haven't all been together."

Even though she was wildly happy, she had to swallow back the lump that clogged her throat at the thought of being so far away from her family during the holidays.

"Yes, it will," Cliff answered. "Your mom and I miss you painfully, but we always knew we'd have to face the fact of losing you someday."

"Oh, but you haven't lost me..." she started to protest. Then it hit her like a jab in the stomach so powerful that it took her breath away. Of course they hadn't lost her. Now that the appeal was settled and Aaron had permanent custody of Tommy her marriage to him was to all intents and purposes null and void!

He didn't need a wife anymore. He didn't need her. She was free to leave as soon as she could get her things together and book a flight back to New York!

She was not only free to do so, but she was expected to go. Aaron had made that clear in their prenuptial agreement. Their marriage was a temporary business arrangement undertaken in the best interests of the child. Now that he had custody of his nephew, their union would be terminated as soon as possible!

"Mariah, what's the matter?" Aaron's anxious voice seemed to come at her from a long distance, and her mother's, too. "Mariah, are you there? Aaron, what's wrong?"

Mariah blinked and shook her head to clear it. Aaron stood beside her, looking worried, and Jessica continued to call her name over the phone.

"Sweetheart, are you sick?" Aaron asked anxiously, and she knew she could use that alibi without having to lie. She definitely was sick!

"I... Yes, I'm afraid I am. It must be something I ate. Excuse me." She turned and hurried to the nearest bathroom.

She saturated a washcloth with cold water, then leaned over the sink and buried her face in it. Her stomach rolled and tumbled as she repeated the procedure, but this time she wrung the water out of the wet cloth and sat down on the closed lid of the commode and held it to her face.

After a few deep breaths she was able to force back the nausea, and when Aaron knocked on the door and asked if she was all right she told him she'd be out in a minute.

How could she have been so careless as to allow herself to fall hopelessly in love with both Aaron and Tommy! She'd known that could happen, but she'd gone right ahead and let it happen anyway.

Or did she "let" it? Hadn't it been more a case of not being able to keep it from happening? Especially after she and Aaron started sleeping together. That was the biggest mistake she'd made. She'd known it would be when she'd seduced him, but she'd gone right ahead and done it anyway. Now she was going to pay for it, big-time!

Again he knocked on the door and called to her. This time she dried her face, forced a semblance of a smile, then opened the locked door and walked into his waiting arms.

"Honey, what happened? Do you want me to take you to the hospital emergency room? Why didn't you tell me you weren't feeling well earlier?"

She leaned into his embrace and let his arms engulf her. Sure, it was a stupid thing to do, but it was too late to worry about that now. The damage had already been done.

"The nausea just hit me all of a sudden," she said truthfully. "It's probably just a touch of intestinal flu. Are Mom and Dad still on the phone?"

His arms around her tightened. "No. I told them I'd call them back when I found out what was wrong with you. Right now I'm going to put you to bed." He picked her up and headed for the stairway.

She wiggled halfheartedly. "I have to put Tommy to bed first."

He started up the steps. "I can do that, too. Remember, you taught me how?"

Oh, yes, she remembered. She'd been so busy teaching him how to take care of the baby without her help that now he could get along nicely without her. She'd made herself expendable.

Upstairs he helped her undress and then tucked her into their big comfortable bed. "Try to sleep," he said as he leaned down and kissed her, "but if you get sick again call me, promise?"

She nodded, but knew she'd be all right now that the first shock was over. She let him continue to think she was ill because she needed time to prepare to play the role of the happy helpmate who had successfully completed her part in the charade they'd devised so that Aaron could keep his orphaned nephew.

Mariah couldn't let Aaron know how desperately she wanted to be his wife, always and forever. She'd come to know him so well in the short time they'd been together. He was gentle, and kind, and thoughtful, and he'd never deliberately hurt her. Not even if it meant sacrificing his own hopes and plans.

He had done everything he could to keep her from being hurt. He'd insisted that she be a participant in preparing the prenuptial agreement, and had gone over it with her in minute detail before he let her sign it.

But she was certain that if she told him she'd fallen in love with him and didn't want to dissolve their marriage, he would let her stay on as his wife. Even though he'd made it plain that he didn't want that commitment. Even though he preferred the bachelor life-style.

Aaron had felt guilty right from the beginning about her involvement in his deception. He'd offered to let her back out numerous times before they put the plan into action, but she'd refused.

She'd counted on having plenty of time for Aaron to get used to having her around, taking care of Tommy and the house. Taking care of him. She knew he enjoyed their lovemaking as much as she did. He was a passionate man and a skilled and sensitive lover. She'd banked on her ability to arouse and then satisfy him to make her irresistible to him.

She knew sexual compatibility didn't necessarily signify a deep and abiding love. She wished it did. But happy marriages had been built on less, and she loved Aaron enough to gamble that, given time, he'd fall in love with her, too.

But she hadn't had months, she'd had only twenty-three days. She'd only just learned her way around his house and the city in which he lived. She hadn't even started trying to find the way to his heart!

Mariah had agreed to the limitations of his proposal of marriage, and she was honor-bound to abide by that agreement. She had no choice but to offer him his freedom.

Mariah was still awake when Aaron climbed into bed beside her several hours later. She turned to him and he took her in his arms. "You're supposed to be asleep," he murmured as his lips caressed her face and neck. "Are you feeling better?"

"Much better," she whispered as her tongue explored his ear. "I've been waiting for you."

She'd finally come to a decision that she'd tell him about tomorrow, but tonight she was going to forget everything but the fact that she and her husband had a passion for each other that was both lustful and erotic. She intended to spend the night making sure he'd always remember that, and her.

He cuddled her against his nude body. "I seem to remember putting a nightgown on you," he said shakily as his hands began to roam slowly over her nakedness.

Her fingers stroked his back. "I seem to remember taking it off." She bit him gently on the shoulder. "Just saving you a little time and effort."

"Taking off your clothes is never an effort," he assured her huskily. "It's pure pleasure, but I thought you wouldn't want to... I mean, you're sick. We can let one night go by without..."

"Don't you want to make love with me?" Her lips trembled, but she didn't dare sob or let the tears that welled in her eyes fall.

He pushed her into his groin, and shivered as she moved against him. "Do you really need to ask?"

Her relief was instantaneous. She should never have doubted him. The one thing, just about the only thing she was sure of in their relationship, was his physical response to her.

The night was filled with magic as they achieved heights they never reached before, a feat Mariah would have said was impossible had she been asked. When Tommy woke the next morning she found it difficult to crawl out of bed and walk. Her muscles ached, but her libido was sated.

She had ample proof of Aaron's need for her in bed, although that wouldn't change their future. It would only make parting more difficult.

Mariah spent the day putting finishing touches on the house and wrapping packages. Christmas, and Tommy's first birthday, were just four days away. It was unlikely she'd be able to get a seat on any airline until next week, and she did so want to spend the holiday with Aaron and the baby.

* * *

Aaron was in a jolly mood as he hurried home after another hectic day at the office. He was still trying to catch up on the backlog of work his prolonged absence had caused, plus keeping up with the current workload, but nothing could dim his exuberance over finally gaining custody of Eileen's little son. *His* little son now. He intended to take his lawyer's advice and file for adoption as soon as possible.

When he walked into the house Mariah's greeting was a little subdued, but it warmed up quickly when he took her in his arms and kissed her. His wife's kisses were pure joy, and he could never get enough of them.

"Hey, it looks like Santa has already been here," he said as he glanced at the gaily wrapped packages under the tree.

"It does, doesn't it?" she answered. "But I can't help feeling that Tommy has been cheated out of a proper birthday. It sort of gets lost in all the Christmas hoopla."

She sounded so serious, and she wasn't smiling. "It may seem that way to him when he gets a little older," Aaron said, "but I don't think we'll let that happen. We'll see that he gets a birthday celebration every year."

He grinned at her, but she didn't return it. Instead she looked startled, as if he'd said something out of character. Before he could comment, she told him dinner was ready and would be on the table in five minutes, then headed for the kitchen.

After they'd eaten Aaron cleared off the table and put the dirty dishes in the dishwasher while Mariah put Tommy to bed. He'd just turned on the dishwasher when he heard her come back downstairs. He met her in the hallway.

"You've done a beautiful job of decorating," he commented as he gazed at the green-and-red holly and the gold satin ribbon and bows that trailed down the banister. "I don't remember this house ever looking so festive before. My parents never put up seasonal decorations, and after they were gone Eileen and I didn't bother with it, either."

She did smile at him then. "I'm glad you like it," she said softly, but then her expression changed again. "We need to talk, Aaron. Shall we go into the living room?"

Something was wrong. He'd sensed it earlier, but wouldn't let himself believe it. Everything was going so well for them. What could possibly be upsetting her?

"Of course, honey," he said and took her arm. "What's the matter?"

"Nothing's the matter, but we do have to make plans." He tried to steer her toward the sofa, but she sidestepped to one of the lounge chairs. He took the other one and fretted. What plans? This wasn't like her at all, and he had the uncomfortable feeling that he wasn't going to care for what she had to say.

He noticed that she seemed to be casting around for the right way to begin. "I'd...that is, if you don't mind, I'd like to stay on until after Christmas. I mean, I probably couldn't get a reservation before then, anyway...."

A pressure was building inside him to interrupt, make her stop, change the subject, but he still didn't know what the subject was.

"What do you mean, 'stay until after Christmas'? Where are you going...?"

Then it registered. The prenuptial agreement! That devilish contract he'd insisted on that said their marriage would last only as long as the custody of his nephew was being decided by the courts. She was telling him that she'd like to spend Christmas here, but then she was leaving him to file for divorce!

Somehow, in his elation over gaining custody of Tommy he'd managed to overlook the fact that his victory in the court freed both him and Mariah of the bonds of marriage. Mariah was only living up to the terms of the escape clause he'd insisted on when he'd proposed to her, so why did he feel like she'd just dealt him a mortal blow?

He could neither move or speak, but he could hear as she answered his half-formed question. "I . . . I'll go back to Apple Junction and spend the rest of the holidays with my family. I'll have to tell them the truth now about why we ran off and got married. They . . . they'll be upset, but they won't tell anybody. Also, Dad can no longer be held in dereliction of duty for not reporting our little deception to the judge should the whole story come out, since he didn't know anything about it until after the fact."

Aaron finally found his voice. "But you can't leave yet. I . . . I have to have time to find a nanny."

He was grasping at straws, but maybe her sense of responsibility to Tommy would keep her with them until he could deal with the thought of losing her.

She shook her head sadly. "I know. We should have been interviewing for the job, but we had no idea the court would act so quickly. It shouldn't be that difficult to find a well-qualified sitter, though. Salt Lake City is a very church- and family-oriented community. We'll get started on it right away."

She'd obviously been thinking about this. She was fielding all his objections, whereas he was still in shock and barely able to think. "But Tommy will miss you," he said, clutching at any reasonable excuse to keep her with him.

"And I'll miss him." Her voice was laced with tears. "But if I stay longer it will just make the parting worse, not better."

Aaron was getting desperate. Why was she being so stubborn? Couldn't she see he didn't want her to go? "All right, damn it," he snapped impatiently, "if you want me to say it I will. *I'll* miss you."

Oh hell, it sounded like he was mad at her, when in reality he was furious at himself for being so blind to his own emotions.

"Sure you will," she said coolly. "I'll miss you, too. The sex has been great, but we both knew it would only be temporary. You don't need me anymore, and I have a life of my own to get back to."

Like hell he didn't need her! How could he have been so pigheaded, stubborn and blind? He needed her more than he'd ever needed anybody or anything, and not just for sex or baby-sitting.

He loved her with a deep and compelling love that he'd been too damned stubborn to admit, and now it was too late. If he'd been more honest with himself, and with her, he might have been able to make her love him, too. Instead he'd been too busy denying his feelings to sort out what it was he really wanted.

Now he had no choice but to let her go. It would be despicable of him to burden her with his declaration of love at this late date. She was so sweet and compassionate that she might even give in to his pleas and agree to continue their present arrangement for a while, but he didn't want her just for a while. He wanted her forever, and he'd botched any chance of gaining that. He was honor-bound to keep his part of the asinine scheme he'd talked her into agreeing to.

"I'm sorry," he apologized, trying to keep his voice from shaking. "Of course you're eager to go back to your life in New York. I've already taken up far too much of your time—"

"I-it's not that I'm eager..." she stammered. "That is, I've enjoyed living here, but—"

"Mariah, please. You don't owe me an explanation," he assured her. She looked as if she was about to cry, and he couldn't stand the thought of her feeling guilty because she wanted out of their arrangement as soon as possible. She'd been so generous. He couldn't ask her to stay on. She'd already honored her part of their agreement.

"You're free to leave immediately if that's what you want," he continued, "but I doubt you'll be able to get a reservation on a flight so close to Christmas. Why don't you wait until the day after? Not many people travel at that time."

That wasn't what Mariah wanted to hear. She'd hoped he'd ask her to stay and make their marriage a real one, but obviously that's not what he wanted.

"I'd like that," she said, and tried to sound happy when her heart was breaking. "I really want to be here for Tommy's first birthday and Christmas."

Aaron winced. She couldn't make her feelings much plainer than that. She wanted to spend as much time as possible with the baby, but leaving him didn't bother her at all. Well, he wasn't going to let her see how painful this conversation was for him.

He pasted a smile on his face. "Great. Then it's settled. We'll spend Christmas together, and I'll make arrangements for you to catch a flight back home on Tuesday." He was still trying to pull himself together when she landed her bombshell.

"There...there's one more thing, Aaron," she said, unable or unwilling to meet his gaze. "Since there's no longer any reason for us to present ourselves as the happy and loving newlyweds, I think it would be better for both of us if we didn't...I mean, if we no longer...shared a bed. If you have no objection, I'll move my things to the room across the hall from the nursery for the rest of the time I'm here.''

If her words had been physical blows to the heart they couldn't have caused any more damage. Aaron felt shattered to the depth of his soul.

He wanted to beg her, plead with her to tear up that marriage contract and be his wife in every sense of the word. He ached to tell her how much he adored her, wanted her, needed her. How desolate and lonely he'd be without her, but he couldn't. It would be emotional blackmail, and he loved her too deeply to resort to that. He didn't want her to feel sorry for him. If she couldn't love him in return then he wanted her to leave, free of guilt or remorse.

The most important thing to him now was her happiness, and she'd made it plain that her well-being was not dependent on him.

He took a deep breath and nodded curtly. "I have no objection," he said gruffly. "Sleep wherever you like."

Chapter Fifteen

Mariah awoke on the morning of Christmas Eve to her self-imposed exile, all alone in her cold, solitary bed. Actually, "awoke" was something of a misnomer because sleep had come to her only in fits and starts since she'd moved out of Aaron's big, warm bed and into his lonely guest room three nights ago.

A glance out the window revealed dark clouds heavy with snow, and bare tree branches encased in frozen sleet. She huddled more deeply under the thick satin quilt and prayed for just one hour of sound unbroken sleep until Tommy woke up, but she knew it was an exercise in futility.

The past two days had been pure hell. She'd been naive enough to hope that she and Aaron could be friends even though they were no longer lovers, but it hadn't happened. She wasn't sure whose fault it was. Probably hers. She'd handled the whole thing badly.

Not that he was angry with her or anything. Actually, he'd been very polite and solicitous. So had she, for that matter. But it only widened the chasm between them. Now they were like courteous strangers living in the same house. Unfortunately that hadn't reduced the sexual tension between them, although they both pretended it had miraculously disappeared. But sexual attraction was fun and games, not everlasting love. At least for Aaron it wasn't.

Thank goodness there was only today and tomorrow left. Aaron had managed to get her a flight out on Tuesday, the day after Christmas. She'd been put on standby at first, but then they called yesterday to say they'd had a cancellation, so she had an assured seat.

She might be able to keep a tight rein on her self-control until then, but any longer and she'd break down and beg Aaron to let her stay, even if only as Tommy's nanny. The problem was that he wouldn't agree to that, even if she offered. He'd already found and hired a well-qualified nanny who was due to start work Monday morning.

A cry from Tommy's room alerted her that he was awake, and she tumbled out of bed. She'd have nothing to do but sleep once she got back to Apple Junction. She was going to spend every precious minute with her son while she was still here.

It terrified her to realize that she'd began to think of him as her *son!* Hers and Aaron's!

Since today was Sunday, Aaron didn't go to the office, although he'd spent all day Saturday there. He'd said he was catching up on his work, but she knew he was as uncomfortable with the cool detachment between them as she was. There were times lately when she actually found herself hiding from him in her bedroom or the nursery so she wouldn't have to pretend to be happy about going home to New York and her freedom.

Mariah was loading the breakfast dishes in the dishwasher when the phone rang. Since she was in the kitchen and closest to it, she answered it. It was the airline. "Mrs. Kerr, we have a cancellation on our one o'clock flight to Albany, New York, and we have you listed on standby. Are you still interested?"

The question startled her. "I don't understand. I was contacted yesterday about a vacancy on Tuesday, and am already booked on that flight. I understood my name would be taken off the standby list."

"Oh, dear," the woman's voice on the other end sounded harried. "Apparently there's been a mix-up. Let me check into it and get back to you."

Mariah said "All right" and hung up. A few minutes later the phone rang again.

"Mrs. Kerr, I'm so sorry, but apparently the computer was down for a short time yesterday, and your reservation seems to have gotten lost. The seat on the Tuesday flight has been booked to someone else."

Mariah was stunned. Airlines didn't make mistakes like that. Did they? "But how is that possible? The ticket has been paid for. My husband charged it to his credit card. I was supposed to pick it up at the airport before takeoff."

"Oh, dear. Well, in that case we'll see that you have the seat you reserved, but is there any chance you could change your plans and leave this afternoon instead? We'll make up to you for the inconvenience by refunding half of your fare and issuing you a travel voucher for a future flight."

"I'm sorry, but I couldn't...." At that point Mariah's mind caught up with her mouth and she hesitated.

Why not leave this afternoon? The tension between Aaron and herself seemed to escalate every hour. He wanted her gone, and she knew that her self-control, possibly even her sanity, depended on her getting away from him and Tommy as soon as possible.

"Can . . . that is, can I have a few minutes to think about it?" she asked. "I'll call you back within ten minutes."

The woman agreed, and Mariah hung up, then went in search of Aaron. She found him sitting at his desk in the office, but he wasn't doing anything other than staring off into space.

"Aaron, are you busy? I need to talk to you."

He looked up, then stood. "I'm never too busy to talk to you," he said softly and motioned her to sit in the chair on the other side of the desk.

When she was seated he sat down again. "Now, what can I do for you?"

"It's not something I want you to do," she assured him. "I just need your opinion. That phone call was from the airline. There's been a mix-up about my reservation for Tuesday, and they've offered me a discount on this fare plus a travel voucher for anywhere I want to go in the future if I'll agree to leave on the one o'clock flight this afternoon instead of Tuesday."

He looked startled. "This afternoon!" he practically shouted. "You mean today?"

She nodded. "Yes. I've been packing off and on since yesterday, so I can easily be ready by then, and you'd get half the price of the ticket refunded—"

"I don't want the money!" He lowered his voice, but it was still gruff. "You haven't even told your parents yet that you're coming. How do you know they can meet you in Burlington on such short notice?"

It surprised her that he was so agitated. She'd thought he'd be glad to be rid of her. "I don't know if they can, but if they can't I'll just rent a car and drive from Burlington to Apple Junction. It's not all that far."

"It's midwinter, Mariah," he said with exasperation, "and Jess and Cliff have commented in letters and on the phone about how much snow and ice they've had in those mountains lately. I don't want you driving in that kind of weather."

That last sentence sounded like an order, and Mariah didn't take orders well. Certainly not from a husband who didn't want to be married to her.

"I've been driving through snow and ice in those mountains since I got my driver's license when I was sixteen," she said through clenched teeth. "And I'll keep on doing it until I either move away from them or get too old to drive. All I need from you is assurance that you can get along all right taking care of Tommy until the nanny comes on Monday."

She didn't know why he was so angry, but he seemed to be making an effort to calm down as he ran his hands over his face and sighed. "I thought you wanted to spend Christmas here with Tommy and me." He sounded almost plaintive.

She blinked back the tears that pressed behind her eyes, and made an effort to keep her voice from trembling. "I did. I do, but Tommy's too young to know that it's Christmas and his birthday, so he won't miss me any more than he will if I wait until Tuesday."

A small sob escaped her precarious control, but she quickly suppressed it. "On the other hand, I'm going to miss him very much." *I'll miss you, too, but you don't want to hear that.* "I think the sooner I leave the better it will be for me."

Aaron's fists clenched and unclenched on the desk. For a minute he looked as if he wanted to argue further, but when he spoke his voice was husky but calm. "All right, Mariah. If you want to take the flight this afternoon, by all means do so. Tommy and I will miss you, but, thanks to all your coaching on the art of caring for a baby, we'll get along fine until the nanny takes over. Is there anything I can do to help you get ready?''

Three hours later Aaron loaded Mariah's luggage and Tommy's stroller into the trunk, strapped the baby in his car seat in the back, and checked to be sure Mariah's seat belt was fastened, then started the car and headed for the airport. He regretted every mile of the drive, but since Mariah was so eager to leave him that she'd catch the first available flight out instead of staying over Christmas as she'd originally planned, he wasn't going to argue with her.

Had he done something to upset her? He'd tried so hard not to. In fact he'd been tiptoeing on eggshells around her these past three days trying not to let her suspect how wretched he felt about her going away. If she knew the torment he was going through at the prospect of losing her, she'd feel guilty and sorry for him. He didn't want that, but he suspected that sometimes he'd tried a little too hard to hide it and came off as cold and uncaring.

He turned to look at her and tried for a smile that felt stiff and unnatural. "You did call your parents, didn't you? Will they be able to meet you tonight in Burlington?''

She seemed to be having trouble with her smile, too. "Yes, I talked to them, but I didn't ask them to meet me—''

"Mariah, I told you I don't want you driving in the snow after dark—''

She frowned but didn't seem to take offense as she had before. "I'm not going to drive. I'll register at a hotel and Dad and Mom will meet me there in the morning and take me home.''

Take her home. But her home was here in Salt Lake City with him! Why was he letting her leave?

The answer to that was that he had no right to ask her to stay. She was the one who'd made all the sacrifices in this marriage of convenience, and he wasn't going to ask her to accommodate him any further. She missed her family, and her independent life-style.

No, if this marriage was to survive, it had to be because she wanted it to, and so far she'd given no sign that she did.

"Did you tell Jess and Cliff why you were coming home on such short notice?" he asked.

"No, I didn't want to break it to them on the phone. I just said I'd tell them about it when I get there."

Aaron felt doubly sad. He was not only losing his wife, but also the big, close-knit family he'd married into. They'd welcomed him so warmly even though he'd cheated them out of giving their daughter a proper wedding, and he'd grown to love them dearly.

"Do you have plans for your future?" he asked. "Will you be looking for work after the holidays?"

"Yes, my savings won't last forever, but I won't be able to stay in Apple Junction."

That startled him. "Why not?"

She looked surprised. "But surely you know why. We can't let the townspeople know that I've left you and am filing for divorce within days after the appellate court's decision that gave you custody of Tommy. The legal community in Apple Junction would know that we'd only gotten married to circumvent the family court's ruling. They could still take Tommy away from you, and I won't let that happen."

Aaron groaned. He'd been so heartsick at Mariah's announcement that she wanted out of their marriage that he hadn't been thinking straight. She was right, of course. It wouldn't do to let the people of Apple Junction know they were no longer living together.

"Oh, sweetheart," he said remorsefully, "I never meant for you to have to leave your home and family on my account. Damn, all I've ever done is mess up your life. Why don't you stay here in Salt Lake City? You could get a job and rent an apartment—"

He was warming up to the subject when she cut him off. "No, Aaron, I don't think that's a good idea. One of the women I worked with in Albany went to Florida when she was laid off and got a job there. She really likes it and has been after me to come down. She says her company is hiring in several different categories. I'm seriously considering it."

He bit his lip to keep from making a sarcastic retort. There didn't seem to be any way he could keep Mariah from slipping away from him. At least he wanted them to part friends. Good friends, who would keep in touch. He couldn't bear it if he thought he'd never see or hear from her again.

The airport was jammed. Parking was nonexistent, and when they finally did find a place it was a long hike to the terminal. Thank God, they'd brought the stroller to push Tommy in.

By the time they got Mariah's luggage checked, picked up her ticket, and found the right gate it was only a few minutes before the call came to start boarding the plane. Mariah was glad there hadn't been a long wait. She'd never have survived it. Her heart was broken, her nerves were screaming, and any second now she was going to start crying.

As the passengers began to line up, she hunkered down beside the stroller and hugged Tommy. He looked like one

of Santa's elves all bundled up in his red snowsuit, and the
only bare skin she could kiss was his chubby little face and
his hands.

"Goodbye my little darling," she murmured in his ear.
"I love you so very much. Please remember that when..."

A sob shook her and tears ran down her cheeks. She
didn't have the stamina for prolonged goodbyes. She had
to get on that plane, *right now*. She couldn't keep Aaron
from seeing her distress, but maybe she could convince him
it was only the baby she was crying for.

Forcing herself to release Tommy, she stood and put out
her hand to Aaron, hoping for a quick handshake and a
hasty, *it's-been-good-to-know-you-keep-in-touch* type of
parting.

It didn't happen. Before she could say a word he gathered her in his arms and her resistance melted as she snuggled against him. "Don't cry, sweetheart," he said raggedly
as he rubbed his cheek against her wet one. "I can't stand
it if you cry. You don't have to leave...."

His voice broke, and for a moment he just held her as she
sobbed. "There's no hurry about getting a divorce, is
there?" he continued. "You can stay here with me and look
for a job. I have a big house, and I promise I wouldn't... I
wouldn't expect sex...."

That only made her cry all the harder. She was being
grossly unfair carrying on like this. A woman's tears were
a powerful weapon when it came to getting what she wanted
from a man, and Aaron was no exception. He'd already
admitted that he couldn't stand to see her cry, but she'd
gone right ahead and done it anyway. Not that she'd been
able to stop herself, but even so...

It took all the control she could muster to straighten up
and pull away from him. Wiping her eyes with the back of
her hands, she even managed to find her voice. "That's

sweet of you, Aaron, but I'll be all right. It's just that I've become attached to... to the baby. But, like I said before, the longer I stay, the harder it will be to leave him."

She saw the anguish that clouded his beautiful blue eyes, but before she could speak again he agreed with her. "Yes, I suppose it would be. You will call me when you get to Apple Junction, won't you? I'll worry until I know you're safe."

How like him. She sniffled and again wiped at her eyes. "Yes, of course I will."

She wanted to be in his arms again. To hug him, kiss him, tell him how much she was going to miss him, but she didn't dare. If she did, she'd blurt out the whole truth. Instead she touched his shoulder and forced a tiny smile. "Goodbye, Aaron, and thank you for everything. I'll call you tomorrow."

She turned and headed for the ramp without giving him a chance to reply.

Tears still streamed down her face as she handed her ticket to the flight attendant and squeezed into the crowd of holiday travelers making their way down the ramp and into the plane. It was almost impossible to move through the aisles congested with passengers standing to put carry-on luggage in overhead storage, or looking for and getting into their seats.

She was desperately trying to read the seat numbers through the moisture that blurred her eyes when she heard it. Above the rumble of conversations and the noise of luggage being stored, a soft, melodic voice spoke firm and clear.

"Go back, Mariah."

She jumped with surprise, and turned around to see who had spoken to her. She didn't know many people in Salt

Lake City, and nobody but Aaron knew she was taking this flight.

The person behind her in the narrow aisle was a big man with a booming voice who was complaining to another passenger that she was sitting in his seat. It certainly wasn't that voice she'd heard.

As her gaze swept over the line of people behind him she realized that the attendants were about to close the door.

"Go back, Mariah."

This time the voice seemed to come from all around her, like a stereo system, but no one else in the plane either looked up or showed any sign they'd heard it.

An overwhelming compulsion seized her, and without thought or hesitation she called out, "No, wait!"

She started pushing her way up the aisle and waving her hand for attention. "Please don't shut the door! I need to get off!"

She fought her way to the door. "I won't be going with you," she said as she rushed past the startled attendant and ran back up the ramp to the waiting room.

Aaron and Tommy were nowhere in sight, but she knew they couldn't have gone far. She continued running toward the exit and spotted Aaron pushing Tommy in the stroller just before they got to the door.

"Aaron! Aaron, wait!" she shouted, not sure he could hear her above the noises of the airport terminal.

He stopped for a moment, and she shouted again. "Aaron, wait for me!"

He turned around, his expression a mixture of surprise and disbelief. Then he raised his arms and held them out as she ran into them.

He hugged her to him as she babbled almost incoherently. "I love you. Oh, darling, I love you so much. I want to stay married to you. Please don't make me leave. I'll agree to any terms you want—''

His mouth covered hers, cutting off her desperate pleas with an eagerness that matched her own. She melted against him and forgot that anyone else existed except the two of them. It was a kiss of melding souls that went far beyond passion or physical pleasure.

It wasn't until someone bumped into them with a luggage cart that they were jolted back to earth. "Let's get out of here," Aaron muttered, as he kept one arm around Mariah and pushed Tommy's stroller with the other.

Neither of them spoke on the drive back to the house, but it was a silence of anticipation, not tension. Mariah snuggled against the back of the seat and put her hand on his thigh. He smiled at her, then covered the hand with his own and held it there.

As they pulled into the driveway, Mariah was never so happy to see a house, a home, as she was to see Aaron's. Was he going to let her live here with him as his wife, or was he just prolonging the divorce as a courtesy to her? Either way, she wasn't going to leave again until he kicked her out.

He shut off the motor, then picked up her hand and brushed the palm with his lips, sending tingles all the way up her arm.

She rubbed her cheek against his shoulder and murmured, "Are you going to let me stay?"

He lowered his head and nuzzled her hair. "I'll not only let you stay, my darling, I'm going to insist that you do. I'll never let you get away from me again, but let's put Tommy down for his nap before we talk."

Mariah insisted on carrying Tommy inside and putting him to bed, two things she'd never expected to do again. It was sheer heaven, and if she hadn't been so eager to get

back downstairs she'd have had a hard time tearing herself
away from the child.

She found Aaron in the living room, standing in front of
the window looking out at the snow-covered landscape. He
turned when she approached and once more held out his
arms to her.

"Tell me again why you want to stay with me," he murmured as he held her close and reined kisses on her up-
turned face.

She closed her eyes and reveled in the sensation. "Because I love you. Because I want to be your wife forever.
Because life without you is too painful to contemplate."

"And Tommy?" She heard the uncertainty in his tone.
"Are you staying with me because you can't bear to be
parted from the baby?"

She opened her eyes and saw the torment in his. Did he
think she was only professing love for him because he and
Tommy came together as a package and she couldn't leave
Tommy?

"That, too," she admitted, "I love that little boy, but
he's not the reason I got off the plane. I got off because I'd
rather live with you as a mistress after we're divorced than
as a wife with any other man."

He stiffened. "What do you mean, 'after we're divorced'?"

She drew back. "Did you think I wouldn't give you your
freedom? I agreed to a temporary marriage and I'll keep my
word. I won't file for divorce, but neither will I contest it
when you do."

He opened his mouth to speak, but she hurried on. "I've
grown up a lot since we've been together. I've learned that
people don't always get exactly what they want out of life.
Most times they have to make compromises, and that's
what I'm doing now. All I ask is that you let me live here

with you until you grow tired of me or meet somebody else.''

His expression softened, and he gently tightened his arms around her and tilted her head until her face rested against the side of his throat. "Oh, sweetheart, I've been such an idiot. I rambled on about how I treasured my freedom, how I had no intentions of getting married and raising a family, and all the time I was so wildly in love with you that the very thought of losing you was agony."

Both shock and excitement tore through her, and she raised her head, but he settled it back on his shoulder. "No, let me finish, love. Even then I wouldn't admit it. I made excuses for keeping you with me. I needed you to care for Tommy, I needed you to help me fight for his custody, I needed you to be my partner in a marriage of convenience. All contrived camouflage to keep from facing the inescapable fact that I needed you to love and take care of *me*. Not Tommy, *me!*''

She stroked the back of his head, and nibbled his neck. He shivered and held her closer as he continued. "Tommy is young enough to learn to live without you eventually, but I was too stubborn to see that I couldn't. That my life would be cold and empty without you in it. Then, when the custody issue was settled and you announced that you were going back to New York and filing for divorce, there were no more excuses for me to hide behind. I finally was forced to admit that I loved you and you were as necessary to me as the air I breathe. But by then it was too late. I'd insisted on that ridiculous prenuptial agreement and I was stuck with it.''

This time Mariah did raise her head. "Are you telling me you thought I wanted to leave you? To dissolve our marriage?'' Dear Lord, how could they have both been so mistaken?

"That's exactly what I'm saying," he admitted as his hands roamed over her back. "You'd said all along that you were only agreeing to the marriage because it was best for Tommy. Even a few minutes ago when you said goodbye before boarding the plane you said it was him you were upset about leaving, not me."

"I lied," she said starkly, then moved against him as his hand settled on her buttocks. "I've lied to you consistently about my feelings because I knew you didn't love me."

He gasped and pushed her harder against his groin. "Ah, but I did love you, sweetheart. I do love you. I think I fell in love with you the first time I walked into the hospital room and saw you soothing my terrified little nephew. I know now that I was in love with you when I married you, and I'll never stop loving you."

His other hand moved up and between them to cup her breast. "Would you like me to prove it?" he murmured raggedly and blew in her ear.

It had been so long since he'd touched her intimately, and she'd missed him so much that she was already trembling. "Oh, yes, please do," she whispered seductively as he picked her up and headed for the stairway.

The sun was setting when Mariah finally came down to earth enough to open her eyes. She and Aaron were cuddled up together in their big king-size bed and she silently swore that she'd never again sleep anywhere else in this house without him beside her.

She raised her head to look at him and saw that he was awake. He raised his hand and gently stroked a lock of disheveled hair out of her eyes. "I like to watch you sleep," he said tenderly. "You look like an angel, so peaceful and innocent."

That reminded her. She hadn't yet told him about her experience on the plane. "Speaking of angels," she said as she cuddled against him, "something happened on the plane today that I want to tell you about. But you have to promise not to mention it to anybody, ever."

He frowned. "I promise."

"Well, it's like this," she began, and told him about the voice that directed her to go back to him, a voice that was so compelling that she obeyed it without question, in spite of the fact that she thought he didn't want her.

"The voice was melodic but at the same time it was loud and distinct," she concluded. "I heard it clearly above the noise, but nobody else did. If they had, there would have been pandemonium on that plane with people rushing to get off."

Aaron was thoughtful for a moment, then he smiled and held her close. "I guess it's time you quit fighting that angel of yours and started taking her seriously," he murmured.

"She's not my angel, she's Tommy's," Mariah corrected. "Besides, I don't believe in angels."

"Neither do I," he said, "but I think we'd better start believing in this one. She not only saved Tommy's life, she brought you and me together although we lived two-thirds of the continent apart and would never have met if you hadn't seen the woman in white on the road that night."

"That's true," Mariah said thoughtfully, "and I did see her, Aaron. There's no doubt in my mind about it."

"I know you did, sweetheart," he assured her, "and you heard her tell you to go back after you got on the plane. She must have known the agony I was feeling at losing you and taken pity on me."

"No, it was me who was in agony," Mariah insists, "and she showed me what a mistaken and self-destructive thing second-guessing the one you love can be."

She turned her head slightly and kissed his bare chest. "Do you really think she might be a guardian angel? Our guardian angel? Yours, mine and Tommy's?"

Aaron stroked his fingers through her hair. "If you accept the premise of angels, then you have to believe that anything is possible for them. Let me put it this way, I'm an accountant. I work with figures all day every day, and it's an accepted supposition in mathematics that if you set up the proper equation you can prove anything."

Mariah frowned. "Then why hasn't someone set up the equation to prove the existence of angels? Doesn't that mean they don't exist?"

Aaron smiled. "I don't have all the answers, my darling, but mathematics is pure logic while angels defy comprehension. They have to be accepted on faith. If you believe your lady in white was an angel, then no proof is needed. If you don't believe she was, then no proof is possible."

Mariah snuggled closer. "I saw her, and if she hadn't appeared at that spot, at that time, Tommy would have died. We can't prove she's an angel, but she'll always live in our hearts and in our minds. I suspect we've been richly blessed." Mariah's voice held a touch of wonder.

"I suspect we have been, too," Aaron agreed, and kissed her.

*　*　*　*　*

COMING NEXT MONTH

#1003 JUST MARRIED—Debbie Macomber
Celebration 1000!
Retired soldier of fortune Zane Ackerman's hard heart had been waiting for someone to melt it. Lesley Walker fit the bill so perfectly, he asked her to marry him. But when he needed to right one final wrong, would he have to choose between his past and a future of wedded bliss?

#1004 NEW YEAR'S DADDY—Lisa Jackson
Holiday Elopement/Celebration 1000!
Ronni Walsh had no plans to fall in love again, but that didn't mean her four-year-old daughter, Amy, couldn't ask Santa for a new daddy. And although the sexy single dad next door, Travis Keegan, had sworn off romantic entanglements, Amy was sure she'd found the perfect candidate....

#1005 MORGAN'S MARRIAGE—Lindsay McKenna
Morgan's Mercenaries: Love and Danger/Celebration 1000!
After a dramatic rescue, amnesia robbed Morgan Trayhern of any recollection of his loved ones. But Laura Trayhern was determined to help bring her husband's memory back—and hoped they could renew the vows of love they'd once made to each other.

#1006 CODY'S FIANCÉE—Gina Ferris Wilkins
The Family Way/Celebration 1000!
Needing to prove she'd been a good guardian to her little brother, Dana Preston had no choice but to turn to Cody Carson for help. But what started as a marriage of convenience turned into something neither one bargained for—especially when their pretend emotions of love began to feel all too real....

#1007 NATURAL BORN DADDY—Sherryl Woods
And Baby Makes Three/Celebration 1000!
Getting Kelly Flint to say yes to his proposal of marriage was the easy part for Jordan Adams. Winning the reluctant bride's heart would be a lot tougher. But Jordan was determined to show her he was perfect husband material—and a natural-born daddy!

#1008 THE BODYGUARD & MS. JONES—Susan Mallery
Celebration 1000!
Mike Blackburne's life as a bodyguard had put him in exciting, dangerous situations. Single mom Cindy Jones was raising two kids and had never left the suburbs. The only thing they agreed on was that they were totally wrong for each other—and were falling completely and totally in love....

MILLION DOLLAR SWEEPSTAKES (III)

It's our 1000th Special Edition and we're celebrating!

Join us these coming months for some wonderful stories in a special celebration of our 1000th book with some of your favorite authors!

Diana Palmer
Debbie Macomber
Phyllis Halldorson

Nora Roberts
Christine Flynn
Lisa Jackson

Plus miniseries by:

Lindsay McKenna, Marie Ferrarella, Sherryl Woods and Gina Ferris Wilkins.

And many more books by special writers!

And as a special bonus, all Silhouette Special Edition titles published during Celebration 1000! will have _**double**_ Pages & Privileges proofs of purchase!

Silhouette Special Edition...heartwarming stories packed with emotion, just for you! You'll fall in love with our next 1000 special stories!

1000BK-R

INTRODUCING...

A collection of award-winning books by award-winning authors! From Harlequin and Silhouette.

Falling Angel
by Anne Stuart

WINNER OF THE RITA AWARD
FOR BEST ROMANCE!

Falling Angel by Anne Stuart is a RITA Award winner, voted Best Romance. A truly wonderful story, *Falling Angel* will transport you into a world of hidden identities, second chances and the magic of falling in love.

"Ms. Stuart's talent shines like the brightest of stars, making it very obvious that her ultimate destiny is to be the next romance author at the top of the best-seller charts."
—*Affaire de Coeur*

A heartwarming story for the holidays. You won't want to miss award-winning *Falling Angel*, available this January wherever Harlequin and Silhouette books are sold.

Silhouette

SPECIAL EDITION™

Holiday Elopements

New Year's Resolution: Don't fall in love!

Little Amy Walsh wanted a daddy. And she had picked out single dad Travis Keegan as the perfect match for her widowed mom, Veronica—two people who wanted no part of romance in the coming year. But that was *before* Amy's relentless matchmaking efforts....

Don't miss
NEW YEAR'S DADDY
by Lisa Jackson
(SE #1004, January)

It's a HOLIDAY ELOPEMENT—the season of loving gets an added boost with a wedding. Catch the holiday spirit and the bouquet! Only from Silhouette Special Edition!

Silhouette

SPECIAL EDITION™®

AND BABY MAKES THREE

The latest Silhouette Special Edition miniseries by

SHERRYL WOODS

continues in January with

NATURAL BORN DADDY (Special Edition #1007)

Jordan Adams was tired of being the most sought-after bachelor in the area. But his quick-fix proposal of a marriage of convenience to long-time pal Kelly Flint was not working out as he'd hoped. And being a daddy was *not* part of the plan.

Don't miss next compelling story in this series:

THE COWBOY AND HIS BABY
(Special Edition #1009), coming in February 1996

Silhouette
SPECIAL EDITION™

CELEBRATION 1000

Nora Roberts

THE PRIDE OF JARED MACKADE

(December 1995)

The MacKade Brothers are back! This month,
Jared MacKade's pride is on the line when he
sets his heart on a woman with a past.

If you liked THE RETURN OF RAFE MACKADE (Silhouette
Intimate Moments #631), you'll love Jared's story. Be on
the lookout for the next book in the series, THE HEART OF
DEVIN MACKADE (Silhouette Intimate Moments #697)
in March 1996—with the last MacKade brother's story,
THE FALL OF SHANE MACKADE, coming in April 1996
from Silhouette Special Edition.

 These sexy, trouble-loving men
will be heading out to you in
alternating books from Silhouette
Intimate Moments and Silhouette Special Edition.

NR-MACK2

You're About to Become a *Privileged Woman*

Reap the rewards of fabulous free gifts and benefits with proofs-of-purchase from Silhouette and Harlequin books

Pages & Privileges™

It's our way of thanking you for buying our books at your favorite retail stores.

Harlequin and Silhouette— the most privileged readers in the world!

For more information about Harlequin and Silhouette's PAGES & PRIVILEGES program call the Pages & Privileges Benefits Desk: 1-503-794-2499

Silhouette®

SSE-PP80